MURDER IN PARIS

Andrea Hicks

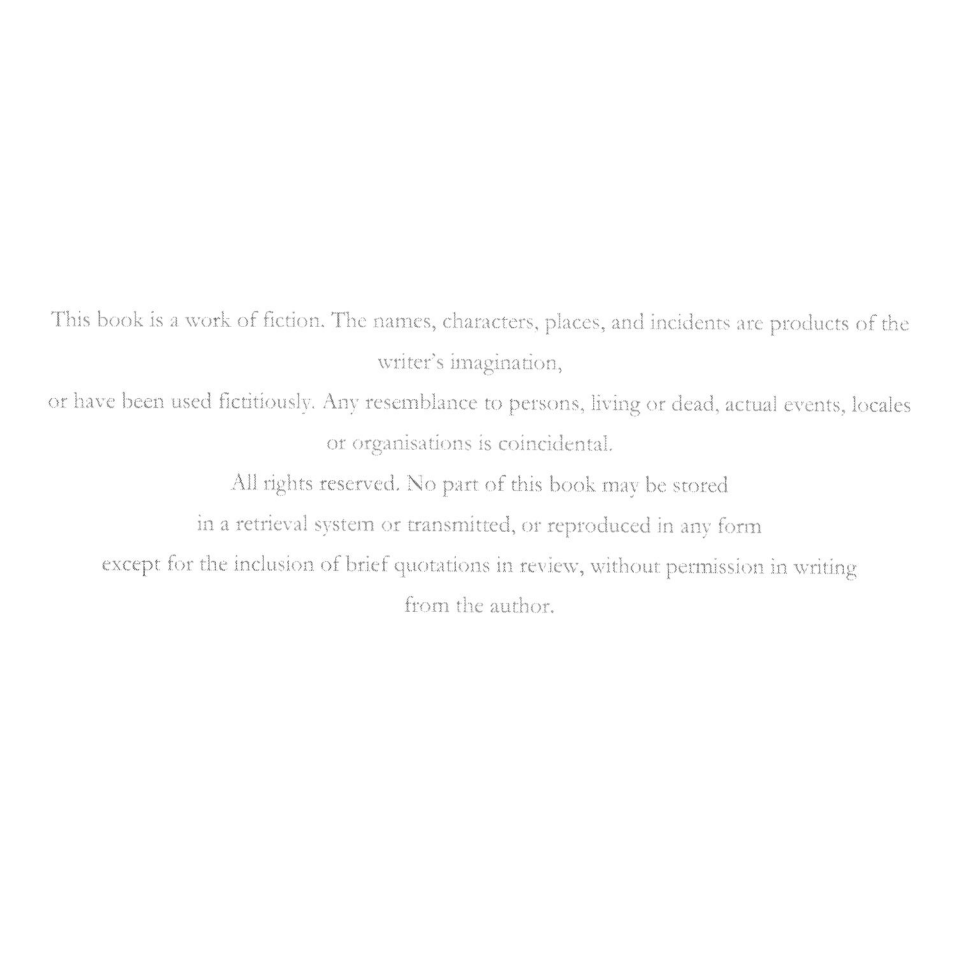

This book is a work of fiction. The names, characters, places, and incidents are products of the writer's imagination,
or have been used fictitiously. Any resemblance to persons, living or dead, actual events, locales
or organisations is coincidental.

All rights reserved. No part of this book may be stored
in a retrieval system or transmitted, or reproduced in any form
except for the inclusion of brief quotations in review, without permission in writing
from the author.

CHAPTERS

Prologue	1
Chapter 1	3
Chapter 2	9
Chapter 3	14
Chapter 4	20
Chapter 5	22
Chapter 6	26
Chapter 7	33
Chapter 8	42
Chapter 9	52
Chapter 10	56
Chapter 11	70
Chapter 12	76
Chapter 13	83
Chapter 14	88
Chapter 15	101
Chapter 16	108
Chapter 17	116
Chapter 18	126
Chapter 19	132
Chapter 20	142
Chapter 21	163
Chapter 22	173
Chapter 23	179
Chapter 24	191
Chapter 25	193
Chapter 26	204
Chapter 27	208
Chapter 28	224
Chapter 29	234
Chapter 30	248
Chapter 31	253
Chapter 32	256
Chapter 33	263
Chapter 34	274
Chapter 35	282
A Note from the Author	288

For my amazing family......always!

PROLOGUE

'I don't know why we just can't go on the boat,' Cecily grumbled to Knolly as she dried wine glasses from dinner with a tea towel and slammed them down onto the kitchen table. 'Boats 'ave water to keep 'em afloat. God knows what 'olds up one of them aeroplane things. I mean, they've got wings aven't they, but they don't even flap. Even birds 'ave to flap their wings to keep them up in the air.'

'You'll break them glasses if you keep banging 'em on the table like that.' Knolly turned to Cecily, wiping washing-up suds from her hands. 'If you're that worried tell Lady Camille you don't want to go, that you're frightened of being up in the air with nothin' to 'old you all up.'

Cecily looked glum. 'Would you go in one?'

Knolly pulled a face, knotting her eyebrows together. 'No, I would not. Birds fly, people walk. If God 'ad wanted us to fly he'd 'ave given us wings wouldn't 'e. Nope,' she said, pulling out the plug in the butlers' sink. 'I don't even want to get in the car with Lady Camille but she insists I do when we go to that market in Finchley. Ooh, I 'ate it I really do. And she goes so fast down them roads. We nearly mowed down a load 'a chickens last week what ran out in front of the car. She just laughed and said, 'Roast chicken for dinner tonight, Knolly'. I just 'eld on for dear life with me shopping bag in front of me.' She shook her head. 'Youngsters today. They're all as mad as March 'ares.'

Cecily laid her tea towel down and sat at the table, her head in her hands. 'Oh, Knolly,' she sighed. 'What am I going ter do?'

Knolly pulled out a chair and sat at the table with her. 'Well, ducky, the way I see it is like this. You've got two choices. You either go...or you don't.'

Cecily raised her head and gazed at her. 'Oh, Knolly!'

Chapter 1

'Is my trunk ready to go in the taxicab, Phillips?' Camille asked her footman as they stood in the hall. Camille was ready to leave and was impatient to get to the airport in good time. 'Lady Ottilie's is on the second floor landing. Can you manage it, or shall I ask the driver to help?'

'I can manage it, Lady Divine. Still got some life in the old body yet,' he puffed. Camille's lips twitched into a half-smile. Phillips was determined not to give up just because he was nearing retirement age and she admired him for it. Knolly and Ottilie joined Camille in the hall, Knolly looking worried, wiping her eyes on her apron.

Camille frowned at her cook, then widened her eyes at her daughter questioningly. 'Is everything alright, Knolly?'

'It's Cecily, Madam. She's bin sick.'

'Sick? Oh no. Is she unwell?'

'No..., not unwell exactly.' Knolly wrung her hands. 'She's worried about the hairoplane.'

Ottilie giggled. 'It's not a hairoplane, Knolly. It's an aeroplane, and it's terribly exciting don't you think?'

Knolly bit her lip. 'I don't think Cecily sees it that way. She's proper frightened that she is. That girl's bin worrying about it for weeks.'

Camille tutted. 'Oh, dear. I wish I'd known about it. I would have put her mind at rest. There is no need for her to come if she doesn't wish to. The poor girl. I thought she would be as excited as Ottilie and Amandine to be going to Paris.'

'I am excited,' said a little voice from the kitchen vestibule, 'but I am frightened too.'

Ottilie ran out into the vestibule. 'Oh, Cecily, please don't be upset. I've never been on aeroplane either. We can hold hands. You, me, and Amandine. And Mama will be there to make sure we're alright. You will, won't you, Mama?'

'Of course I will,' replied Camille. 'I haven't flown before either, and I must say I had a slight frisson of nervousness this morning, but all will be well. I can't wait to arrive in Paris and see Madam Tatou again. I'm sure you will all love her.'

She looked into the vestibule where Cecily was standing with Amandine. Cecily was wearing her coat, her hat rather skewwhiff where she had been unwell and it had left her dishevelled, her face flushed red. 'Cecily, my dear. There is no need for you to come if you really would prefer not to. The reason I chose the aeroplane and not the boat is because it is much faster, much cleaner, and will be quite the experience.'

Cecily took a deep breath. 'No, Madam, I can't let you go alone. I go everywhere with you don't I? I'll...I'll just have to be braver than I've ever been before, and pray that the aeroplane's wings are strong enough to keep us all in the air until we get to Paris.'

'I'm so glad you're coming with us, Cecily,' said Ottilie. 'It wouldn't be the same without you.' Cecily made a small smile. 'And Amandine would be lost without you, wouldn't you, Amandine? Tu veux que Cecily vienne avec nous n'est-ce pas, Amandine?'

'Oui. Oh, Miss Cecily. You must come. You are my friend,' cried Amandine.

Cecily's face broke into a smile, transforming her face from one drawn with concern to one of delight. 'Then yes, of course I'll come.' She turned to Camille looking contrite. 'I'm so sorry, Madam, for makin' such a bloomin' fuss I mean.'

'Let's forget it, Cecily. We're going on holiday to the city of romance. It's so beautiful there. Why don't you buy a book about Paris at the airport. You can read it on the flight, which is only about an hour and a half, and by the time we've had a snack and a drink it'll be time to get off the aeroplane.'

'Yes, Madam,' said Cecily, bobbing a quick curtsey. 'That's a very good idea. Do they sell alcohol at the airport?'

Camille laughed. 'I'm sure they do. We'll have a brandy to settle our nerves.'

By lunchtime the aeroplane had landed at Le Bourget Airport in Paris. Camille glanced across to Cecily who had looked out of the window through the flight, exclaiming at how small everything looked when they were up in the air, at how smooth the flight was when she thought they would be buffeted by the wind, and how comfortable and professional it all seemed.

'It was alright, weren't it, Madam?' she said smiling. 'In fact I think I quite enjoyed it. I feel a bit silly now to be honest, and it didn't take very long did it?'

'I think we all did extremely well as this was our first flight. What do you think, girls?' she asked, looking across the aisle to where the girls were sitting. 'Ça vous a plu, Amandine ?

'Oh, Madame Camille,' sighed Amandine. 'C'etait magnifique.'

'Mama, it was wonderful,' cried Ottilie. 'All those clouds. They looked like the meringues Knolly makes.' Camille and Cecily both laughed.

'Well, now we can go to the centre of Paris and perhaps have some. They have marvellous boulangeries and patisseries on the Champs Elysee, in fact, I think we'll be spoilt for choice.'

They gathered their bags and left the aeroplane which had landed at Le Bourget with hardly a bump. As they walked across the rather windswept tarmac Cecily shook her head.

'I feel a bit silly now, Madam,' she said to Camille. 'It was truly quite fascinatin' to see the world so small as we flew across the sky. All them 'ouses looked as though you could pick 'em up between yer finger and thumb they was so tiny. And then the sea. It sparkled like one of your dresses when the sun was on it. So beautiful. I can't say I was too keen when we went up and up and up into the air, but once we was there it was…well…fascinatin'.'

'So you weren't frightened, Cecily?' asked Camille, smiling.

'Not to speak of, and now I can tell everyone I've been in an aeroplane. I don't know no one who's done that. I feel quite proud of meself.'

'And so you should,' said Camille, chuckling.

'Where will we go first, Madam?'

'To the hotel I think. We'll get settled in and then go for some lunch somewhere typically French. Amandine seems very excited doesn't she? I hope she won't be disappointed.'

Cecily frowned. 'What do you mean, Madam, disappointed?'

'I'm concerned she thinks I've brought her to her home city because we have found her parents. Cecily, when the opposite is true.'

'Oh,' answered Cecily, looking glum.

They made their way into the airport building with Ottilie and Amandine following. As they got through the entrance they were shown to a desk where their passports were examined, one for Camille and Ottilie, one for Amandine, and one for Cecily.

'Why do we need passports, Madam?' asked Cecily. 'Don't they trust us?'

'It's to make sure they know who is coming into and out of the country. It's nothing to concern yourself with. Everyone has one. Would you like to keep yours?' She held the papers up for Cecily to see.

'Could I?' Cecily answered, her face a picture of happiness. 'I can tell people I've got a passport. Wonder what me Ma and Pa would make of it, to know I've got a passport. It's a bit special ain't it?'

'It's a first for all of us. And yes, it is special.' She turned to find the girls. 'Ottilie, Amandine, come along now.' The girls had been watching an aeroplane take off and they ran across to Camille and Cecily. 'Mama,' cried Ottilie. 'It's so exciting. I'd love to fly an aeroplane.'

'Come on you two,' said Camille. 'Let's get a taxicab to take us to the hotel. You'll see some of the sights on the way. Then we'll have some lunch and go to see Madam Tatou. She lives in the 7th Arrondissement of Paris which has proved to be fortunate. It is where Amandine's parents' apartment is. Hopefully, we'll be able to shed some light on what happened when Amandine went to England, and why her parents have not put out a missing persons enquiry for her.'

'Is that why we're here, Mama, to find Amandine's parents?'

'It's one of the reasons,' she nodded and made a small smile, 'the main reason. Until we know what has happened to them, we cannot make any decisions for Amandine's future. It's fortunate that the authorities, with Chief Inspector Owen's advice to them and his trust in me that allowed us to give Amandine a home, at least in the short term.'

'And what happens if we can't find them, Madam?' asked Cecily, who had more reason than most to hope that Amandine would make the return trip to London with them. She had become close to Amandine, even though she was unable to converse with her in her own language. Amandine had a deep affection for Cecily, viewing her almost as a mother figure. She felt safe with her, and Cecily had blossomed under Amandine's affection for her, giving her confidence and a boost to her self-worth. I am lovable, she had thought to herself one evening when she had put the ten-year-old to bed, who had kissed Cecily on the cheek before going to sleep. Amandine said, 'Je vous aime, Cecily', which Cecily knew meant, 'I love you'. She had asked Ottilie what the phrase meant in English and when Ottilie had told her Cecily had been thrilled. One day I might have children of me own, she'd thought, and then I can be a real mother to them.

Although she knew it was wrong, Cecily had fostered a tiny hope that Amandine would stay with them, that Lady Camille would be given permission to look after Amandine.

'It's not right,' she'd said to herself, 'but I can't help but 'ope for it.'

Chapter 2

Once they had familiarised themselves with their suite and sampled some of the wonderful things that had been left for them in their room by the concierge, Camille decided there was no time like the present and they should visit Madam Tatou forthwith.

'I told her we would be with her at some time today,' said Camille. 'And I don't want to disappoint her. She is a wonderful person. I know you will adore her.'

'Am I to come too, Madam,' asked Cecily, hoping with all her heart Camille would say yes. She was eager to see inside one of the beautiful apartments they had seen on their journey from the Champs Elysée to the hotel.

Camille chuckled. 'Of course, Cecily. I want you to enjoy yourself as much as the girls and I. You would make a wonderful Parisienne.'

'Would I?' said Cecily, looking into the distance. 'A Parisienne,' she whispered to herself. 'Who'd 'ave thought it.' Ottilie and Amandine giggled as they slipped on their jackets and Camille shook her head at them, smiling.

'Are we ready?' she said brightly. 'I have promised Madame Tatou dinner, and she has promised to take us to her favourite restaurant where she says the food is sublime. Something for us to look forward to.'

'Ooh, Mama,' cried Ottilie. 'It's so exciting. I can hardly believe we're here in Paris, the capital of romance. That's what the girls said at school when I told them I was coming here. They said the boys are all very good-looking and that I'm bound to fall in love.'

'I think you might be just a little too young for that, darling. When you're older, perhaps. Now, let's go. I've asked the concierge to order a taxicab for us.' She sighed and smiled. 'I'm so looking forward to seeing Madame Tatou again. It has been so long, far too long.'

Hardly a word was said as they sat in the taxicab, their noses almost glued to the windows as the streets of Paris went by. They couldn't take their eyes from the trees on the pavements, now enrobed in beautiful pink and white blossom, the people, as fashionable as expected in the 7th Arrondissement, which was the place where those who could afford it lived.

The apartments were beautiful, the white stucco frontages gleaming in the pale sunlight. At the front of each apartment was a balcony edged with newly painted black wrought iron, the balconies burgeoning with tubs of spring flowers, some of which trailed down to the windows of the apartment beneath them. They drove through the Rue Cler where the fromageries and boulangeries sold their delightful wares. Amandine gasped as they went past.

'My Maman, she would buy our bread there every day,' she said in French, pointing at a small bakery in the centre of the row of shops.

'Do you live near here?' asked Camille, excited that they were at last learning something about her French ward.

'We lived in the Rue de Varennes,' said Amandine in a small voice. 'In an apartment, Madam Camille. My bedroom was beautiful, decorated in all the colours I love. Maman is an artist you see. She has exhibited at the Musée D'Orsay and in some of the other galleries in Paris. There are many, of course.'

'Does your Maman still live at the Rue de Varennes?' asked Camille as lightly as she could. She was aware that too much questioning may frighten Amandine, so thought it best to encourage her with an almost disinterested voice.

'Yes...well,' Amandine faltered. 'Maman went away.'

'Went away, darling?' asked Camille, frowning. 'Where did she go?'

Amandine turned from the window and looked down at her hands her expression distraught. 'Elle mourut.'

Ottilie gasped and Camille quickly shook her head at her. 'Darling, are you sure? Are you thinking it because you have not seen her for a long time.'

'Papa told me. He said she was dead to him, and we have not seen her. Papa has not mentioned Maman in a long time, even when Le President asked him about her.'

Camille frowned. 'Le President, Amandine. Whatever do you mean?'

'My Papa works at The Elysee Palace with the president. He is a friend of Maman and Papa, my godfather too. He is great fun, but can be strict. He asked Papa about Maman then stopped asking him when Papa said she is dead to him.'

'Dead to him?' Camille turned away from Amandine, thinking the poor girl had had quite enough questioning for one day. Dead, or dead to *him*, she thought. There is an enormous difference. She glanced at Amandine again who had resumed looking out of the window. Camille could feel two pairs of eyes watching her.

'That could mean two very different things,' she said to Cecily and Ottilie.

'But, Mama,' whispered Ottilie. 'Amandine said...'

'I know, Ottilie. I know what she said, but...' Camille wasn't sure how to explain it to her daughter. 'When we get back to the hotel, I will enlighten you. Now is not the right time.'

Ottilie nodded and gave a small smile. 'Yes, Mama.'

'Does it mean dead, Madam?' asked Cecily quietly. 'It sounded like the word we use for mortuary.' She looked anguished. 'I wish I understood more.'

'You are right, Cecily, it does sound like it, but the context…it wasn't quite right. When we return to the hotel I will explain. I know you feel at a disadvantage because you don't understand the French language, but I'm quite sure you will learn a little of it while you are here. In fact, it's quite difficult not to.'

The taxicab turned into the Rue Saint-Dominique and Camille felt herself relax. This was the square where Madame Tatou's apartment was, and she couldn't wait to see her old friend again. She hoped Madame Tatou would recognise her. It had been some years since they had seen each other and Camille was quite sure they had both changed a great deal.

There was the Fontaine de Mars and the restaurant of the same name, complete with its pink and white awnings, and the vast statuary standing in the middle of the square. They got out of the taxicab, and while Camille paid the driver the girls and Cecily went over to the fountain. Cecily turned as Camille approached, her face slightly flushed.

'They don't seem to be wearing much, Madam,' she said, sotto voce. 'Glad it's not me standin' up there.'

Camille laughed and Ottilie giggled. 'The fountain has been standing in this square for many years,' said Camille.

'Reckon they must be feeling a bit cold by now, then.' Cecily leaned in a bit closer for a better look, and Ottilie smiled at Camille.

'Which apartment is Madame Tatou's, Mama?' asked Ottilie.

Camille turned and pointed to an apartment above the Fontaine de Mars restaurant. 'Just there,' she said, 'the one with the greenery hanging down from the balcony. Madame Tatou always loved her plants. She spent many a happy hour on the balcony, watering and talking to them.'

'She talks to her plants? That's a bit odd, isn't it? Does she not have a husband?'

Camille nodded. 'She did, but he died many years ago. She loved him so much she said and could not ever consider remarrying. She has been alone ever since, apart from her staff, but she was never unhappy and certainly never lonely. She has many friends who have the same interests, the opera, the museums, the ballet. She has promised to take us.' She smiled at her daughter. 'Would you like that?'

'Oh, Mama, I would love it.'

Chapter 3

They found the entrance to the staircase that led up to the first floor of the building and Madame Tatou's apartment. When they reached the landing Camille led them to the apartment which was halfway down.

'Oh,' she cried, stopping suddenly.

'What is it, Madam?' asked Cecily, going to Camille's side.

'The door to the apartment is open.' Camille leant into the vestibule inside the door. 'Madame must have forgotten to close it. She is getting on in years. It could happen to anyone I suppose.'

Camille stepped inside and listened. All was quiet inside the apartment. The only sound she could hear were voices from the restaurant below.

'Madame Tatou,' she called. 'Madame Tatou, c'est Camille.'

'Does she speak English, Madam?' Cecily asked.

Camille nodded. 'She does, and very well.' She shook her head and sighed. 'We'll just have to go in. It's very rude to enter an apartment without an invitation but...it's strange she is not answering when I call. I hope nothing untoward has happened to her. There is a spiral staircase in the apartment, and I often thought it would become more difficult for Madame Tatou to negotiate the older she became.'

Camille stepped into the main hall of the apartment and the others followed, wide-eyed. The apartment was indeed beautifully decorated, the walls painted in a watery green. In the salon the furniture was vast; huge settees in teal velvet were gathered around a central wooden coffee table. There were huge portraits on the walls, and above their heads were stunning crystal chandeliers that sent out prisms of light as the sun shining through the open balcony doors hit the many facets of the crystal droplets.

'Oh, Madam,' gasped Cecily. 'It's so beautiful.'

'It is,' said Camille, 'but where is Madame Tatou?'

Camille led them towards another vestibule, then stepped into a vast kitchen that housed an old range and many cupboards. Madame Tatou was sitting on the floor in front of one of the cupboards, her hands covering her mouth, her eyes shimmering with tears.

'Madame,' Camille cried, running across the shiny tiled, black and white chequered floor. She lowered herself to her haunches and put an arm around Madame Tatou's shoulders. 'Did you fall, Madame? Have you hurt yourself?' Madame Tatou pointed to the cupboard which went from floor to ceiling. The cupboard door was open. Camille glanced in and gasped with shock.

Inside the cupboard was a woman. She was sitting on the cupboard floor, her knees pulled up to her chest, her hands clenched in front of her as if in prayer. She wore a plain black dress and a white apron with ruffles which was soaked with blood that dripped from a wound in the woman's neck. The blood had gathered on the floor of the cupboard and had begun to overflow copiously onto the pristine kitchen floor. She was dead, of that Camille was in no doubt. Her skin had attained an appearance she had sadly seen before; the skin yellowing like parchment, a grey pallor to the lips, and the limbs stiffening with rigor.

Camille turned her head. 'Cecily!' she cried. 'Take the girls downstairs. To the restaurant, the Fontaine de Mars.'

'Madam, are you alright?' Cecily said through the door, holding the girls back with her arm.

'It's best you don't come into the kitchen. I'll join you in the restaurant. Order some coffee and cakes. I'll pay when I join you.'

'It's alright, Madam. I can pay.'

Camille heard Cecily chivvying the girls out of the apartment. She waited for the door to close, then turned her attention to Madame Tatou.'

'Madame,' Camille whispered, hugging her friend to her. 'Let me take you into the salon. There's nothing you can do for this poor girl now.'

'I'm not sure I can move, Camille. I am in shock. My limbs have all but given up on me.'

'I'll help you, darling.'

Camille stood and placed her hands under Madame Tatou's elbows and lifted her from the floor, not a difficult task. Madame Tatou was tiny, like a little bird. Camille helped her into the salon and gently allowed her to sink onto one of the settees. The elderly woman was almost catatonic with shock. Tears ran copiously down her paper-thin cheeks which Camille noticed were lined, although her complexion had been well looked after. French women, she thought. They look after their skin like one would take care of a child. It was clear to Camille that Madame Tatou had rarely allowed the sun to shine on her face, or permit it to tan, even lightly. Camille sat next to her and clasped her hands which were tightly knotted in her lap.

'Madame?' she said softly. 'Honoré?'

Honoré Tatou glanced up at Camille and made a small smile. 'How much you have changed, my dear,' she said squeezing Camille's hands. 'No longer a gauche girl, but a beautiful, confident woman. I have been looking forward to your visit for so long.'

'And I, Honoré,' replied Camille, 'but this was not what I was expecting to find.' Camille went across to the console table and poured two brandies, then returned to Honoré's side. 'Drink this, darling. I think you need it.' Honoré threw back the brandy and sighed, closing her eyes that were still wet with tears.

'Who is she?' asked Camille softly.

'My maid.'

'Was there a break in, a burglar...who did this?'

'I don't know,' whispered Honoré. 'I don't know. I got up late, much later than I meant to. Marthe always calls me at seven with coffee. She allows me to wake slowly while I drink it. She makes breakfast for us both, just croissants, jam, honey...' she glanced at Camille. 'You know the kind of thing...then I rise, and we have breakfast before I have my bath. It's the same every morning, but this morning...there was no Marthe, no coffee,' she shook her head, 'no sound of her singing. I wondered what could have happened, whether she had been taken ill, so I got out of bed. I thought she'd gone out which would have been unusual, but...' Honoré shrugged, 'not impossible. I made coffee in the kitchen. I had my bath, got dressed.' She frowned. 'I was looking for a cloth to wipe up a spill I had made on the kitchen floor. I opened the cupboard door to where we keep the cleaning equipment, brooms, mops...' Honoré burst into tears. 'And there she was. Marthe. Blood falling from a gash in her neck and running down her apron. I sank to the floor; my legs wouldn't hold me. I didn't know what to do. I thought I was going mad. Why would someone do this? How did they get into the apartment?'

'The door was open, Honoré.'

Honoré stared at Camille in surprise 'It was?'

Camille nodded. 'Do you think she opened the door to someone?'

'I think it's likely. But why would they kill her? Marthe has worked for me for five years. We have been together all that time.'

'Does she live in?'

'No. She has a small apartment in the North-East of Paris, in the 19th Arrondissement. She has a room though, in my apartment. She stays sometimes when the weather is bad, but on her days off she goes home. She said she need a home, her own home, but she could not afford an apartment in the 7th Arrondissement.' Honoré shrugged. 'I think she was happy with the arrangement. She would get the Metro from her apartment to mine when she returned from her days off.'

'She stayed with you last night?'

'No, she wanted to go home. She said she had some things to take care of. I did not pry. She is a grown woman with a private life.' Honoré swallowed hard. 'I mean, was.'

'How old was she?'

Honoré blew out a breath. 'Maybe nearly thirty, something like that.'

'So young. Family?'

'No,' Honoré shook her head. I think her parents still lived in Paris, but she didn't speak of them much.'

Camille nodded.' Darling, we must telephone the police.'

Honoré made a sound like a sob. 'Oh, dear. Oh, dear.' She turned to Camille. 'Will you help me, Camille? I don't think I can do this alone.'

'Of course I'll help, Honoré. You're not alone. I'm just so glad that our visit coincided with your needing us. How would you have managed if you had been alone?'

'I'm not sure I could have? There will be questions, won't there?'

'I'm afraid so. There will be an investigation. I'm not sure you will be allowed to stay in your apartment. It is the scene of a murder.'

'A murder!' Honoré covered her face with her hands. When she placed them back on her lap her eyes were clouded over with sadness. 'I liked her so much.' She glanced at Camille. 'We became friends. She was like a companion to me. Now she's gone.'

'You have a telephone, Honoré?'

Honoré nodded and sighed. Camille knew she would be reluctant to call the police, but it was a necessity. She also wanted to encourage her friend to stay with them at the hotel. 'It's in the hall on the Davenport,' Honoré answered.

'Will you be alright for a few minutes while I call the police?'

Honoré nodded again. 'Yes, of course. Do what you must do.'

Camille discovered the telephone on a small, beautiful Davenport in an alcove in the hall. She managed, with difficulty, to explain to the police what had happened. They arrived within the hour.

Chapter 4

Inspecteur de police Apollinaire removed his shoes before entering the apartment and instructed the gendarmes who accompanied him to do the same.

He introduced himself in a quiet, rather contemplative tone which instantly put Camille at her ease. He and the gendarmes went immediately to the kitchen where Camille could hear them conversing in low voices. She sat close by Honoré, to give the woman some comfort and to reassure her she was not alone. While they waited for the Inspecteur de police to return to the salon she spent the time trying to work out how old Honoré was. She decided she was about sixty-seven, or perhaps a little more. To Camille's surprise she did not look so different, the main difference being her hair which was now completely grey and worn in a smart chignon fastened with a barrette. Camille remembered Honoré as always dressing in a typically Parisienne way; smart, with a nod to fashion, elegant, even striking. Yes, Honoré was a typical Parisienne.

'Madame Tatou.' Inspecteur Apollinaire joined Camille and Honoré in the salon. He indicated the settee opposite. 'May I sit, Madame?' he asked her in French.

'Of course, Inspecteur.'

'I will keep this short for today. I imagine you are suffering from a great deal of shock.'

'Yes.'

'A doctor perhaps?' Honoré shook her head, frowning.

'But...you will be required to undergo some further questioning.'

'I understand.' Camille felt Honoré clutch her hand even tighter.

'She was your maid, Madame?'

'She was.'

'Her name?'

'Marthe Benoit.'

'You are certain it was her name, Madame?'

Honoré looked startled. 'I... I.. .well, yes. I always knew her by that name.'

'You paid her in cash I take it?'

'I did.'

'So you have no official record of her.'

Camille frowned. 'Did she need one, Monsieur Inspecteur?'

'He gave a small smile. 'No, but it makes the investigation easier if there are official records for payment. We can find out a great deal from them.'

'You think her name was false.'

He shrugged. 'Not necessarily.' He smiled again. 'And you are, Madame?'

'I'm Lady Camille Divine. I arrived in Paris today to visit with Madame Tatou. I discovered her sitting in front of the cupboard, in shock you understand, at what had happened to her maid. I thought it best to call you.'

He gave another enigmatic smile. 'You did the correct thing, Lady Divine.'

Chapter 5

Camille and Honoré joined the others in the Fontaine de Mars restaurant. Camille continued to hold Honoré's hand and kept glancing at her with concern. Her friend was pale, her features closed as though she wasn't quite sure of where she was. Camille led her to a chair where Cecily and the girls were sitting and encouraged her to sit. She looked like a small bird which had been buffeted by a storm. Her hair was not as pristine as it had been where she had been running her fingers through it in dismay. Camille was sure that had Honoré been a bird she would have put her head under her wing and wished herself away to somewhere else, and that what had happened that morning had not happened at all.

'We saw the police go into the entrance, Madam,' Cecily whispered to Camille. She frowned at Honoré. 'You friend don't look too good. Do you think she'll be alright?'

Camille shrugged. 'She's had a great shock...and so have I to be honest. When I brought you to Paris this was not what I was expecting at all. It's all quite dreadful.'

'Who do yer think dunnit?'

'That's anyone's guess, Cecily. Truly, I can't imagine why anyone would go into a stranger's apartment and slaughter their maid. It doesn't make sense. We've assumed that this was why the door to the apartment was left open...the killer simply did away with the maid then left.'

'Unless it weren't a stranger.'

Camille frowned and glanced at Cecily. 'What do you mean, Cecily?'

Cecily inclined her head to one side. 'Well, maybe it weren't a stranger. Maybe it were someone Madame Tatou knew, or the maid knew.'

Camille nodded. 'Well, yes, you could be right. I think we both assumed it was just an opportunist attack, a crazed stranger who had made their way into the apartment.'

'But why would he...or she, pick on that apartment. It ain't the first one yer come to is it, when yer go up the stairs and go across the landing. It's the second. If the killer wanted to make a quick getaway, they would have gone to the first. It would have been quicker I would 'ave thought.' Camille nodded, thinking how much insight her maid...and dear friend...had.

'I'll get some coffee, Madam,' continued Cecily, 'for you and Madame Tatou.'

'Thank you, Cecily. That would be wonderful.'

'And a croissant each?'

'No, no, I'm not sure either of us want to eat, particularly after what we both saw today.'

'Was it awful, Madam?'

'The most awful I've ever seen. Something not to be repeated I would say.'

Cecily bit her lip, then rose from her chair and went to the counter. She turned towards the girls. 'Miss Ottilie, would you like something else?' Ottilie asked.

'Oh, oui s'il vous plaît. Un sorbet serait délicieux,' cried Amandine to which Camille smiled with affection.

'Some sorbet, please, Cecily, for Amandine,' Ottilie translated excitedly. 'I'll have one too.'

'Which flavours, Miss Ottilie?'

'Quelle saveur voudriez-vous?' Ottilie asked Amandine.

'Er, citron s'il te plait.'

'Lemon, please, Cecily, and I'll have the same.'

Cecily order both the coffee and sorbets and returned to the table.

'What will we do when we leave here, Madam,' she asked Camille. 'Have the police said what you should do?'

'They suggested that Madame Tatou return to our hotel with us. She is not allowed back into her apartment which is causing her a great deal of anxiety. She loves her apartment. It is where she and her husband made their home when they were married and I think she will find it difficult to cope. We will have to be extremely gentle with her. She is not a young woman as you can see.'

'The hotel has a doctor, Madam. I saw it on a gold-lettered board as we went into the foyer. Perhaps it would be a good idea for her to be attended by him. He might give her something for the shock.'

The waiter delivered their order and Camille nodded. She sipped her hot coffee carefully and encouraged Honoré Tatou to see the hotel doctor, although the older woman was reluctant. Camille made the decision for her.

'I think it would be a very good idea. Could you organise it while I take Madame Tatou to our suite please? There is a small bedroom leading off the main salon next to my bedroom. I think she will stay there. I couldn't possibly leave her alone, I would worry continually, particularly at night.'

'So she is to join us for the rest of our stay, Madam?'

Camille shrugged. 'At least until the police have finished with the apartment. It's closed off for the investigation. One wonders how long it will take for the police to decide it's habitable again.' She shook her head and sighed. 'What will happen when they decide to release it back to Honoré I simply don't know. She may not want to continue living there. The memories of what she saw might be too disturbing for her.'

'But where will she go, Madam?' Cecily asked Camille, sotto voce.

Camille shook her head with consternation and played with the tiny chocolate on the saucer. 'I don't know, Cecily, but I will stay and help her. She has no family, no children or siblings. I will contact her friends. Perhaps one of them will suggest something for her. They may even ask her to stay with them in their own apartment for the time being, otherwise, I can see my short visit to Paris may very well turn into a much longer one.'

Chapter 6

They left the restaurant and paraded down the Rue Saint Dominique after leaving Fontaine de Mars. Camille looked back sadly to the square, remembering all the happy times she had spent there with Honoré Tatou when her parents had been exploring other parts of the city. She wondered if she would ever feel the same way about it again. Certainly, Honoré may well have had her memories coloured with sadness, more so, for it was her home, the one she had shared with her beloved husband.

They hailed a cab on the corner of the Rue Saint-Dominique and the Boulevard Saint Germain, which took them back to the hotel. On the return journey Camille realised that the visit to Paris she had planned for the girls and for herself and Cecily would have a different outcome. She had already made a list of all the places she had wanted them to experience, like the Eiffel Tower, and the Musée D'Orsay, but she wondered how this could be achieved. The City of Lights held much fascination for Camille and she was sure the girls would be simply entranced by it, particularly as she had secretly organised a trip around Paris in a horse-drawn carriage, which would take them over the cobblestones beside the Seine. There was a horticultural exhibition in Grand Palais which she thought Ottilie would like, and the Place de L'Opera which she thought they would all love, but she questioned whether these delights would take place. Honoré Tatou could not be left alone, and then of course there was the investigation. They would no doubt be questioned at length about the murder, particularly Honoré who was the first to find the body. An investigation into a murder could take weeks and she had certainly not planned to stay in Paris for so long. Unless she could rally Honoré's friends to help her, she would no doubt need to lengthen her stay.

The cab pulled up outside Le Narcisse Blanc Hotel and they disembarked.

'This is where you're staying, my dear?' Honoré asked Camille as she looked up at the elegant facade. 'This is a beautiful, rather expensive hotel, Camille, one of the best in Paris.'

'I know, Honoré. I wanted the girls to experience the very best Paris could offer, and this is it. It is a fabulous hotel, the suites are delightful, and there is room in our suite for another to stay with us. I will let the concierge know you are to stay for a few days. We can have room service of course if you cannot face the restaurant. You will feel safe here I'm sure.'

'But how will I afford it?' she frowned. 'I have a tiny income. I don't even own the apartment although I have lived there for many years as you know. This is beyond me I'm afraid.'

'But not beyond me, darling. Please don't worry about it. It will be taken care of. I don't want you to worry about a thing.' Camille put her arm around Honoré's shoulders as they entered the hotel foyer. 'You will feel safe here, I know, and when the Inspecteur comes calling we will deal with it together.'

'Are you sure, Camille,' Honoré said, her voice tired.

'I'm sure, Honoré.'

They made their way to the suite where Camille booked room service for dinner that evening for herself and Honoré. Camille encouraged Honoré to lie down for the rest of the afternoon, promising to wake her before dinner. The girls went into their room to change, full of excited chatter which included wondering what French boys were like.

'You can take the girls to the restaurant, Cecily. I'm sure they would much rather explore the hotel than be stuck in our suite.'

'And what about you, Madam?' Cecily asked her. 'This is not what you were expecting is it?'

'Quite the opposite, Cecily, I assure you. But I must explain to you what I discovered about Amandine when we were in the taxicab after we had left the airport.' Camille proceeded to tell Cecily what she had found out which left Cecily reeling.

'The President?'

'Yes.'

'Of France?'

'Indeed.'

Cecily frowned and narrowed her eyes. 'So why have there been no searches for 'er, Madam? It sounds like she comes from an important family. Why would they not have gone to the police and reported 'er absence? They could have had 'er back by now. She would 'ave been with her Mama and Papa and they would have been together again...as a family.'

Camille sat on the chaise and lit a cigarette she pulled from her bag. 'Who knows. But...when I asked Amandine about her mother, she said she was dead.'

'So 'er mother died and what...' Cecily shook her head, 'she ran away...with her brother's help by the sounds of it.'

'I think not.'

Cecily pulled a chair from the small dining table and sat on it. 'You think she didn't run away, Madam?'

'I am beginning to believe she was encouraged to go on an adventure with her brother from a male household.'

'A male household because her mother was dead and Amandine was the only girl.'

'I rather think her mother is not dead.'

'But Amandine said she was. Oh, Madam, I'm getting proper confused.'

'Amandine's father did not say she was dead per se. He said Amandine's mother was dead...to him.'

'But what does that mean?'

'It means she has been ejected from the family for reasons we do not know.'

'Ooh, Madam, you think an affair with another man.'

Camille drew on her cigarette. 'Perhaps. We will not know until it has been investigated. Her father must be questioned, and at least now we know where we might find him.'

'And where would that be, Madam?'

'The Elysée Palace.'

'And how will we get to question the President, Madam? Will we be allowed in?'

Camille stubbed out her cigarette and chuckled. 'I very much doubt it, but Chief Inspector Owen will carry more weight don't you think?'

Cecily nodded. 'I do, Madam,' she said smiling. 'And I always feel safe when 'e's around.'

'I think you mean he inspires you with confidence, Cecily. Am I right?'

'I think so, Madam,' answered Cecily, screwing up her face. 'It sounds about right.'

With Honoré resting in her bedroom and the girls in the hotel restaurant with Cecily, Camille decided it would be a good idea to telephone Richard. She was aware he had arranged a few days fishing during a month-long sabbatical, so hoped he would be at home. It was imperative that she told him about what she had discovered about Amandine's parents and their connection to the President of France. She contacted the hotel operator and gave her his number with some apprehension, yet also looked forward to hearing his voice.

'Camille?'

She was astonished for a few moments, then smiled. 'Richard. How on earth…'

'Did I know it was you?'

'Well, yes.'

'I don't get many telephone calls as I've mentioned before, and I've instructed Scotland Yard not to contact me. I'm on holiday and want to make the most of it. It could only be you.'

'Are you enjoying your rest?'

'Not much.'

Camille frowned. 'Oh, whyever not?'

'There's nothing to do.'

She laughed. 'Isn't that the point, Richard. You're meant to rest.'

'It's rather boring.'

'I think I can help you with that. I have some news for you regarding Amandine.'

'It must be important. You're in Paris aren't you? The operator sounded French.'

'We are in Paris. We only arrived today, but already our plans have been required to change but I'll tell you all about that when you get here.'

'Get there!'

'But of course. The information I have for you is regarding Amandine. Her parents are associates of the President of France, which is perhaps why you and the French police could not locate them.'

'Lachappelle is not her real name?'

'I wondered about that.' She told Richard about the conversation she had had with Amandine in the cab, and what her father had said about her mother.

'But why did they not contact the police?'

'Exactly. All I could come up with was that her mother did not know that Amandine was missing. If her mother had been aware of the fact her brother had taken her on an "adventure" as she called it, I cannot imagine any mother countenancing it. No mother would.'

'So…her mother is no longer with the family?'

'It would seem not.'

'An affaire de Coeur?'

'Possibly. We know it happens.'

'Indeed.' Camille imagined Richard scratching his chin and running his fingers through his dark hair which made her stomach roll with attraction. She wondered whether he would agree to join them in Paris.

'Do you think I should join you in Paris?'

She smiled to herself. 'I rather think you should. Cecily thinks so.'

Richard chuckled. 'Does she?'

'She feels safer when you're with us. I really don't think you should disappoint her, and besides that, you will have the authority to speak with the President's office which I definitely will not.'

She heard Richard humph. 'You're a Lady of the Realm, Camille. Why would they turn you away?'

'Because I'm a woman, Richard. The rules in France are the same as they are in Britain. If not more so. It's a man's world as we know.'

'Should I fly?'

'Of course, Richard. It's quite scintillating. Even Cecily said so.'

'She said, scintillating.'

Camille heard the frown in his voice and chuckled. 'Not quite.'

Chapter 7

The following day, after breakfast which Camille and Honoré took in the suite, they dressed for the weather and took a morning walk in the park in the Rue de Babylone.

'I love it here,' breathed Honoré. 'Albert and I used to come here all the time. It is so restful, and the walk under the grapevine arch is simply lovely.'

'It is certainly very beautiful,' said Camille. She turned to see the girls who were walking behind them. They were dragging their feet, particularly Ottilie, and she knew that walking in a park was rather tame for her. Her eyes went to Amandine who seemed particularly quiet that morning.

'Have you been here before, Amandine?' Camille asked her.

'Oui, Madame, many times,' she answered, 'with my mother. She liked it here. She said it helped her to get away from the noise of life.'

Camille raised her eyebrows at such a young person speaking in such a profound way. 'The noise of life? Was her life particularly noisy?'

'Indeed, Madame, when she had to host.'

Camille wasn't sure if she should ask her the question on her lips, but knew she would get nowhere to discover the whereabouts of Amandine's parents if she did not.

'And what was it she hosted, darling.'

'Le President of course. And his entourage. Sometimes they would come to the apartment and Maman would make dinner and they would drink to the early hours.' She frowned. 'I think Maman did not like those occasions, but she did it for Papa, to ensure his place in the entourage.'

'And did it?'

'Non.'

Honoré glanced up at Camille. Her head came to Camille's shoulder and Camille thought how small she was.

'What do you make of that?' she whispered to Camille. 'What could be going on there?'

'I'm not sure, Honoré. I have a friend arriving this evening who I'm hoping will find out.'

Honoré smiled for the first time since the previous day. 'A man?' she asked.

Camille laughed. 'Well, yes indeed, a man. How did you know?'

Honoré grabbed Camille's arm. 'I know when a woman is in love, Camille. You have changed in ways a woman in love changes. Before dinner you were sad, worried obviously, because of what had happened, but after dinner your eyes were sparkling, and I noticed you were browsing your wardrobe and your shoes. You were choosing something to wear to meet him, n'est pas? Is it your husband, the Lord Divine? He cannot bear to be apart from you?'

Camille chuckled. 'No, Honoré, not my husband. We are estranged I'm afraid. He found another and asked me to leave our home. Ottilie lived with him for a while, but I persuaded him to allow her to come to me for half the time when she isn't at her school in Hampshire.'

'So who is this man?'

'He is a policeman.'

Honoré's eyes widened. 'A policeman?' She shook her head. 'Is he of your class?'

Camille shrugged. 'Do you know, I really don't know. I've never asked him about his background. Perhaps I should.'

'Of course you should. It is imperative is it not, that we know the background of the man we wish to be with.' Her eyes misted over. 'I knew everything about Albert before we married, and what I discovered made me love him even more. You must discover the true man before you take this affaire any further.'

'It's not an affair exactly, Honoré. I'm still married to Harry until the divorce is approved. It's taking quite a time. My friend and I...we don't spend much time together, only when we're thrown together during an investigation.'

'An investigation! My dear girl. What have you been up to?'

'You'd be surprised, Honoré. Very surprised indeed.'

They went back to the hotel where Inspecteur Apollinaire had left a message for Camille requesting she accompany Honoré to the le commissariat de police on the Rue Fabert.

'We must go,' said Camille. 'They might want to tell you that they are to release your apartment, Honoré.' She glanced at her friend. 'Do you want to return there?'

'Of course, Camille. It is my home. I am never frightened there even after what happened. Albert is still there. I must go to him. He will be looking for me.'

Camille nodded and beckoned Cecily to her.

'Will you take the girls to the Eiffel Tower, please, Cecily. You and they need an outing and I'm afraid I'm going to be tied up with the police for some time. Amandine will know how to get there I'm sure, it is just a few streets away from here. If the meeting with the police is over quickly I will join you there. We can have lunch in one of the restaurants in one of the quaint streets nearby. There are many beautiful restaurants to choose from, but if you feel lost take a cab and ask them to return you to the Narcisse Blanc. They will know where it is. Everyone in Paris knows where it is.' She reached into her bag and pulled out a bundle of Francs, then handed them to Cecily. 'This should be enough...and Cecily,' Cecily nodded, 'please take good care of my girls. They're precious to me, as are you.'

Cecily looked concerned. 'But, Madam, what about you?'

'I'll be alright. Chief Inspector Owen is coming to Paris this evening. I would imagine he is on the airplane already. He knows the hotel in which we are staying and he knows about Amandine. All will be well.'

'I 'ope so, Madam. I truly 'ope so.'

Camille and Honoré sat in the foyer of the commissariat de police. They had taken a taxicab to the Rue de Fabert. Honoré felt she had walked far enough, and although Camille felt she would have preferred to go on foot and take in some of the sights she bowed to Honoré's needs. Honoré looked more tired than Camille had ever seen and a flash of guilt went through her. She should have visited her friend more often she knew, but her life had been so busy there never seemed to be time. An excuse, Camille scolded herself as they sat in the back of a taxicab. So easy to find excuses for everything. When she thought back, she realised she had not seen Honoré for nearly ten years and in that time her friend had changed.

Of course she has, she thought to herself, the years have gone by and we have all changed, but...well, even with what had happened the day before, Honoré seemed very different; clearly missing Albert, tired of life perhaps? A surge of fear went through Camille. To be tired of life meant only one thing.

Inspecteur Apollinaire joined them in the foyer and greeted them with a small bow. Camille had been impressed with him when he had questioned her and Honoré in the apartment, his quiet, undemanding manner had comforted her and she was convinced they were in good hands.

'Would you come this way into my office?' he asked with a smile. 'I have requested some coffee. I hope it is okay.' Both Camille and Honoré nodded. Camille had sat in Richard's office at Scotland Yard many times but she knew this was a new experience for Honoré. She squeezed her arm and smiled at her friend to reassure her.

Apollinaire indicated for them to sit in the chairs he had placed in front of his desk. He sat opposite them, leaning on his forearms as he began to question them.

'Lady Divine, Madame Tatou. I have called you in to the commissariat because I have some news with regard to the deceased.' Camille swallowed and she glanced at Honoré. 'Marthe Benoir was in fact the daughter of one of the most dangerous criminals in all of Paris. She did not live in the 19th Arrondissement, but in the 7th on the Rue Saint Dominique.' He stopped speaking to await their reactions. Honoré was paler than before and Camille clutched her hand.

'Did you truly not know, darling?' Camille asked Honoré.

Honoré shook her head. 'I promise you, Camille, Inspecteur, I did not know. She said she lived in the 19th Arrondissement because she could not afford an apartment anywhere else. The 7th as you know has always been one of the most expensive parts of Paris; in truth I can hardly afford to live there myself, but Albert and I...' she looked sad, 'I could not bear to give it up when he passed. I feel him there, in the air, in the walls, everywhere. If I leave the apartment behind, the one I have known for most of my life, I leave him behind too. No,' she shook her head. 'I could not bear it.'

Inspecteur Apollinaire nodded and sat back in his chair. 'We think it is possible she was murdered by a rival gang, another bunch of thieves and murderers who want something they have. It is usually the reason. We just cannot decide what it is they want.'

'Her parents, they are both alive?' asked Camille.

Inspecteur Apollinaire nodded. 'Yes, she is well-known in all the aristocratic salons in Paris, but be under no illusions, Lady Divine, her mother is just as capable of involving herself in criminal activities. The whole family...they are rotten to the core.'

'Was Marthe Benoir her real name?' asked Honoré.

'No. Her real name is...was Janine Heroux.'

Honoré gasped. 'Heroux! But they are...they are the most criminal family. Of course I do not know them, but one reads the newspapers. They are imprisoned regularly, usually one of the sons it would seem, but everyone knows their father buys them out. They have friends in high places. They seem to be capable of anything.' She shook her head in dismay. 'But not Marthe...surely not Marthe.'

At that moment, a gendarme knocked on the door and entered with a tray of coffee for which Camille was thankful. Yet again it seemed that a single action led to a more complicated set of circumstances. She simply had not expected it to happen when she was in Paris. She took her coffee from the tray and sipped it gratefully. It doesn't matter where a person lives, she thought. There is always crime, always people who want more than they deserve.

'They are certainly capable of anything,' answered Apollinaire, taking his coffee from the tray, and a handful of biscuits with which to help it go down. He noticed Camille observing him, then glanced down at his stomach. He shrugged and she smiled. 'They have no boundaries, and no conscience it would seem.'

'Have you spoken to Janine's family?' asked Camille, aware even the most criminal family would be bereft at losing one of their own.

'My gendarmes have gone to their apartment this morning. Of course, we cannot demand they come to the commissariat...they have committed no crime,' he chuckled, 'as far as we know of course. We need to ascertain if there is an ongoing grievance with one of the other criminal families in the city. It could very likely be more than one. These families operate in very similar circumstances but often there is intense animosity between them and they will happily kill each other.'

'And you think this is what happened to Janine?'

'It's possible, Lady Divine.' He shrugged. 'Anything is possible.'

Honoré had been very quiet. Camille glanced at her as tears rolled down her friend's face. 'She was so good to me, such a nice girl. We had known each other for years. I thought I knew her. It is so hard to believe that she was not who she said she was. I am heartbroken.'

'But she was who she said she was to you, darling,' said Camille, reaching out for Honoré's hands which were clasped tightly in her lap. She turned to Apollinaire. 'Although one wonders why she was working as a maid.'

'To create normality,' he answered. 'To anyone observing she would simply leave her apartment each morning to go to work. No one would question it. It is what hundreds, if not thousands, of Parisiennes do every day of the week, although for her it would have been somewhat different. Members of these families are used to taking different routes to where they are going. They will not take chances. There must be no repetition of how they get to where they're going, because if anyone has targeted them, they will know how to get to them.'

'So are you saying that someone discovered where Janine was working; that she was working for Madame Tatou as her maid?'

'Again, Lady Divine, it is possible. Janine would have known how all of this works. She would have been extremely careful about her routes to Madame Tatou's apartment. Who she called a friend. There would have been no acquaintances. An acquaintance could be a member of another criminal family and that is something the Heroux family would not allow. With every new person who enters their circle comes risk.'

He turned to Honoré. 'Madame, I'm sorry, I know you are distraught, but I must ask you. Did many people call on you at your apartment?'

'Very few,' answered Honoré. 'I have friends of course, but we usually meet at a restaurant or the ballet. We rarely visit each other's homes.'

'Did anyone ever call on your maid? Did any post arrive for her at your apartment.'

Honoré bit her lip in thought and shook her head. 'No one, Inspecteur. None of which I was aware. If any post had come for her I would not have known. Marthe dealt with the post and only gave me the ones I needed to attend to. She was a wonderful maid, a companion to me. She was very caring...I can hardly believe...'

'Don't distress yourself, Honoré,' said Camille. She glanced at Apollinaire. 'When will the apartment be available for Madame Tatou to return?'

'Not yet, Lady Camille. The forensics team are there today. If they discover anything I will know immediately. They will examine everything very carefully and will miss nothing. I have my own theories about what actually happened at the apartment, but I will wait for their report.'

'The apartment,' cried Honoré. 'It will be left the same?'

'Oh, yes, Madame. We do not wish to cause you any further stress than you have already suffered.' He looked surprised. 'You wish to return there?'

Honoré nodded. 'I will end my days there, Inspecteur Apollinaire. It is my home.'

'Very well, Madame.'

'Lady Divine. How long had you planned to stay in Paris?'

'A few days only, Inspecteur, but things have changed somewhat. I will remain as long as Madame Tatou needs me, and as long as you require my assistance.'

'I would prefer it if you did not leave Paris just yet, Madame. You were the second person to find Janine Heroux's body. I'm afraid because of that alone you are implicated in the investigation. I will try to make it as painless as possible.'

'Merci. For that I would be grateful, Inspecteur Apollinaire.'

Chapter 8

At length Camille and Honoré left the commissariat. They strolled down the Rue de Fabert with Honoré linking her arm through Camille's.

'I promised the girls I would meet them at the Eiffel Tower, Honoré,' said Camille, 'then go for lunch somewhere. I'd love it if you would come with us.'

'Would I not be a burden, Camille? Those two girls. They want some fun, do they not? It's the reason they came to Paris surely.'

'My reason for my trip to Paris was twofold, Honoré. First was to see my friend whom I have not seen in too many years. The other was to discover Amandine's parents and perhaps reunite her with them. Things have turned out rather differently from how I expected our trip to be, but I would love it if you would join us. Do you not need some fun too?'

Honoré chuckled and shrugged her shoulders. As they walked Camille proceeded to tell her Amandine's story and what had happened in Brighton.

'Amandine seems to be very happy with you, my dear,' said Honoré. 'How long has it been?'

'Six months, maybe a little more. I went to Brighton at Christmas to decide what I would do with the boathouse that Harry has given me in our divorce agreement. I went back to London with a new ward.'

'And your policeman friend?'

'He is joining us because I discovered some information regarding Amandine's parents. I tried to encourage her to tell me about them many times, but she was reluctant to speak about them. Coming to Paris seemed to unlock something for her and in the taxicab to the hotel she began to unfold her memories. She said her mother was dead.'

'Something tells me that you don't think so.'

'I'm not sure. Richard will make it known he is here to the French police and work with them. He has already been in touch with an Inspecteur Durand. They know about Amandine. Hopefully, we'll discover who she really is.'

Honoré sighed and shook her head sadly. 'So many secrets, so many lies. I don't understand any of it.'

'You're disappointed about Marthe, aren't you?'

'Yes, of course. She is not who she said she was.'

'But was always loyal to you, even though she used another name. Perhaps she was not given a choice.'

Honoré glanced up at Camille with sad eyes. 'Perhaps not.'

They continued to walk the Rue Saint Dominique. Camille offered Honoré a taxicab but she refused.

'I can walk that far, my dear,' she said. 'And the weather.' She raised her hand to the sky. 'So beautiful is it not. Who would care to miss it?'

When they reached Le Jardin de la Tour Eiffel, Camille was relieved. Madame Tatou's walk was laboured; they had had to stop a few times so she could catch her breath, yet she seemed invigorated by the fresh air and the beautiful sunshine. Le Jardin de la Tour Eiffel was a wonderful sight;

Camille remembered the vast swathes of green, and running in and out of the trees with her parents chasing her. Such happy memories from another life. Tears gathered at her eyelashes and she swallowed hard. How she missed those days.

They stopped for a short while, finding a wooden bench so Honoré could rest.

'Where will you meet them?' she asked.

'They will be at the Eiffel Tower,' Camille replied, looking at her watch.

'Why don't you go and find them. I'll sit here and wait for you. Look, the tower is just there. I can rest and then we can go for lunch.'

Camille frowned. 'Are you sure, Honoré. I don't want to leave you.'

Honoré threw back her head and laughed. 'Darling, this is my home city. I have wandered the streets of Paris and this park all my life. Do you think I can't look after myself?'

Camille smiled. 'I know you are more than able, but...well things have been rather strange recently haven't they? Even I feel unsettled, as though the ground is moving under my feet.'

Honoré nodded. 'Yes, yes, I know what you mean, but you will only be a short while. And I'm ready for a delicious lunch. Some of the restaurants here are fabulous. I will take you to the very best.'

Camille squeezed her hand and rose from the bench. 'I'll be back as soon as I can.'

She walked across the park to the Avenue Gustav Eiffel then made her way to the Eiffel Tower. As she had expected, there were many visitors milling about underneath the four legs of the tower that stood as steadfastly as they always had. She wondered how she would ever find Cecily and the girls. She stood for a moment, searching the faces of people in the crowd, thinking that it would be an impossible task to find them, but suddenly a voice rang out, one she recognised.

'Mama! Mama.' Camille glanced over to where the voice had come from, and there was Ottilie, running towards her, her cheeks a rosy pink, her hair flying out behind her. 'Mama, we wondered where you had got to.' She flung her arms around Camille's waist and hugged her tightly, almost bowling Camille over. Camille laughed and hugged Ottilie closely, relieved they were together again at last. Ottilie took a step back. 'Isn't it wonderful, Mama?' she cried. 'I never dreamt it would be like this. Amandine said she has been here many times.'

'Where are the others?' Just as the question had been spoken she glanced up to see Cecily and Amandine walking towards her, huge smiles on their faces. Cecily looked overwhelmed.

'What do you think, Cecily?' Camille asked her.

'I can't believe it, Madam. When you showed me them pictures of the tower, I never believed it would be so big. It's huge. And all the people talking different languages. It's amazin'.'

Camille smiled at Cecily. She always took immense pleasure in Cecily's amazement at new things. She was a wonderful companion and always showed such great enthusiasm for everything they had experienced together.

'I agree, Cecily, it is amazing.' She looked down at Cecily's hand. 'I see you bought one of the cards with a potted history of the building of the tower.'

'Yes, Madam. It was designed by Gustave Eiffel with two engineers, Emile Nouguier and Maurice Koechlin.' She giggled. 'Don't fink I said them names right. Then they got an architect to work on 'ow it were ter look,' she glanced at her card, 'Stephen Sauvestre. It's 300 metres 'igh, which means it's a thousand feet in English. No wonder it's so big, Madam. When I was standing underneath and looked up to the top I thought I was about to fall over. It gave me such a funny feeling in my 'ead.'

Both Camille and Ottilie laughed out loud at Cecily's description of the way the tower made her feel.

'I remember feeling like that the first time I saw the tower, Cecily,' said Camille. 'Did it make you queasy?'

'Just a bit, Madam.'

'Where's Madame Tatou?' asked Ottilie. 'Did she not want to come?'

'She's waiting for us in Le Jardin de la Tour Eiffel. I left her sitting on one of the park benches, enjoying the silence and the beautiful weather, but it's probably too hot for her now. The sun is high in the sky. We'll go to the park and she can join us for lunch which she was very much looking forward to.'

Camille, Cecily, and the girls retraced Camille's steps down the Avenue Gustave Eiffel towards the park.

'Is she better, Madam?' asked Cecily. 'She looked like she'd been rushed at and missed yesterday.'

Camille glanced at Cecily and smiled, thinking how funny her sayings were, little anecdotes she had not come across in her own life. 'Yes, Cecily, thank you for asking. I do believe she feels a little better. Inspecteur Apollinaire told us this morning they will release her apartment back into her hands as soon as possible.'

'She wants to go back even after what 'appened there, Madam? I'm surprised.'

'It's her home, Cecily. She has lived there many years, and her husband, Albert lived there with her. She said she could not bear to be parted from it. Parting from the apartment meant being parted from Albert.'

Cecily sniffed. 'That's very sad, Madam.'

'Yes, Cecily. It is.'

At length they reached the Le Jardin de la Tour Eiffel. Ottilie and Amandine began to run through the trees just as Camille had when she was a child. Her eyes softened and yet again tears gathered, but she shook her head and told herself not to be so silly. She shielded her eyes with her hand as she walked, looking for the bench where she had left Honoré. Looking into the distance she searched for Honoré's bright pink duster coat but could not place it. Camille turned, thinking that perhaps she had walked in the wrong direction, but she was certain she was not mistaken. There was the bench where she had left Honoré, but there was no Madame Tatou.

Camille began to run. In front of her was the bench she was sure was where Honoré was sitting. She heard footsteps behind her and she turned with a smile, thinking her friend had wandered through the trees while she waited. It was not Honoré. The smile fell from her face when she realised it was Cecily.

'Where is she, Madam? Is this where you left 'er?'

'Yes, yes, I'm sure it is. Can you see her, Cecily.'

'What was she wearing, Madam?'

'Her pink duster coat, the one she wore to the park this morning.'

'You couldn't miss that.'

'No. Oh, dear. I wonder where she is.'

Cecily went to the other side of the bench and bent down to pick something up. 'Is this not her 'andkerchief, Madam? It's embroidered, look, with birds. I thought it was so pretty when I saw her with it. It is 'ers, isn't it?'

Camille took it from Cecily. 'Yes, it's hers. I bought them for her years ago, some with birds, some with flowers. I would recognise them anywhere.'

'P'raps she's gone back to the 'otel. She might 'ave got tired waiting for us. She knows 'er way round, don't she, what with 'er bein' a Parisienne.'

Camille nodded. 'Yes, you're probably right, Cecily. I was so sure she would wait. She offered to take us to the restaurants near the tower.' She shook her head. 'I'm not sure what to do.'

'I think we should do what you said we would do. Yer never know, she might 'ave got fed up waiting and decided to follow. She's probably sitting in one of the cafés right now, Madam, and you'll 'ave got all upset for nothing.'

'That's a clever idea. We'll go back to the Eiffel Tower. The girls will be hungry and I'm sure you could eat something. We'll look in all the restaurants and cafés. I'm sure we'll find her in one of them.'

Cecily rounded up the girls and they retraced their steps once again along the Avenue Gustave Eiffel, Cecily holding Amandine's hand as she skipped along, and Ottilie with one arm linked though her mother's.

The sky was as blue as Camille had ever seen it. The sun's rays dappled through the trees in the park and Ottilie and Amandine ran in front, jumping in and out of the dappled shadows. When they got to the tower Ottilie linked up with Camille again.

'Where's Madame Tatou, Mama?'

'I think she may have gone back to Le Narcisse Blanc. She was feeling rather tired which was why she didn't join us at the Eiffel Tower.'

'But I heard you say to Cecily that you would look in the restaurants and cafés to look for her. Why would you do that if you knew where she was?'

Camille looked down at her daughter. How astute you are, she thought. 'I was expecting Madame Tatou to be waiting for us in the park. Cecily suggested she might have got tired of waiting and followed me.'

'And if she's not in the restaurants, or at the hotel?'

Camille pressed her lips hard together. The thought had occurred to her of course, that Honoré might not be in either place, although she could not come up with a reason why she would not. 'I'm sure she'll be in one of those places. She's a grown woman who makes her own decisions, Ottilie. She has lived on her own for years, looked after herself for a long time. I'm sure she's alright.' She smiled confidently at her daughter but was aware her confidence was only skin deep.

Madame Tatou was not to be found in any of the restaurants or cafés near the tower. Camille knew she must keep calm and allow the girls to enjoy their time in Paris without any worries, so didn't mention how concerned she was.

They found a lovely outdoor café with round tables and striped parasols. It was sheltered from the hot sun and a gentle breeze made the frills on the parasols flutter.

'Oh, Mama, it's so sweet.' She turned her face to Camille. 'May we eat here?'

'Yes, darling, of course. It's rather beautiful isn't it, very French. Choose a table and I'll go inside and find some menus.' A few minutes later they were sitting at the table Ottilie and Amandine had chosen perusing the menus.

'Would you like me to translate, Cecily?' Ottilie asked her.

'If you wouldn't mind, Miss Ottilie,' replied Cecily. 'It all looks like gobbledy-gook to me.'

Camille chose grilled tuna steaks a la Nicoise, and Cecily decided to have the same because she didn't recognise anything on the menu. 'What's tuna?' asked Cecily.

'It's fish,' replied Ottilie. 'You'll love it.'

Cecily looked sceptical. 'I might not like it.'

'Oh, you will, Cecily,' cried Ottilie. 'You must try new things otherwise how will you know whether you'll like them or not. And you're in Paris. You should try French things.'

The girls were determined to have something sweet so chose Chocolate Mousse followed by pastries. As they chattered away, willing the waiter to hurry with their Chocolate Mousse, Cecily turned to Camille.

'You're very quiet, Madam. You're worried aren't you?'

Camille blew out a puff of breath. 'This isn't like her, Cecily. Something's happened, my instincts are shouting loud and clear.'

'But what, Madam? She was in no danger was she? In the park. It looked quite empty. Everyone was at the tower.'

'If she's not at the hotel I will call Inspecteur Apollinaire.'

'Do you think she might have gone back to her apartment? You said how fond of it she is. P'raps she just couldn't stand to be away from it any longer.'

'I hope you're right, Cecily. Actually, I'm praying you're right.'

Madame Tatou was not at the hotel when they returned. Camille had insisted on getting a taxicab to hasten their return, and when they got into the foyer she asked the concierge if he had seen her.

'Non, Madame. I have been at my desk all morning and she has not passed me.'

'Is there another way in, an entrance at the back or side of the hotel?'

'None that would be accessible to guests unless it was requested. I'm sorry, Madame. Is there anything I can do.'

Camille smiled her thanks and shook her head. The four of them went up to the suite.

'Madame Tatou's not here, Mama,' said Ottilie. 'She must be at the apartment.'

'Yes...I'm sure that's where she is. Why don't you take Cecily to the hotel café and have some iced cordial. It's so hot today.'

'Are you coming down?'

'I have something to do, Ottilie, but I'll join you shortly, I promise.'

When Cecily had shut the door to the suite after glancing at Camille and shaking her head in dismay, Camille picked up the telephone earpiece and asked the hotel operator to connect her to the commissariat in the Rue de Fabert. She prayed she hadn't left it too long before contacting Inspecteur Apollinaire. There was something not at all right and Camille was determined to find out what it was.

Chapter 9

'Could she have gone to her apartment?' asked Richard. He had arrived at the hotel just before dinner, and he and Camille were sitting in the restaurant sipping brandy with their coffee after eating.

'Inspecteur Apollinaire sent a gendarme to search the apartment but she wasn't there. I know she wanted to return to her home but…the apartment had been closed off with tapes, and there was powder all over the surfaces which the police had promised to remove before she moved back in. She knew this; the Inspecteur had also asked her to be patient and that they would clear the apartment as soon as possible. Honoré is a sensible woman. She would have waited until it was the right time to move back in.'

'So you think she has been abducted?'

'What else can I think? She's nowhere to be found. We searched the park and the restaurants and cafés near the Eiffel Tower. We looked on every street as we travelled in the taxicab and not a sign.'

'Was she…had she…? Richard wasn't sure how to finish the sentence without being offensive.

Camille put her coffee cup down on the saucer and made a small smile. 'I know what you're trying to say, Richard. You want to know if she was in her right mind.'

'Was she?'

'I would say absolutely she was.' Camille shook her head. 'She has lived by herself for years. She has many friends, goes to the opera and ballet. Eats out regularly. There is nothing to suggest that she would have wandered off because she didn't know where she was.'

'So I take it you have spoken to Inspecteur Apollinaire regarding Madame Tatou's disappearance.'

'I have.'

'And what is his take on matters? I made it one of the first things to do when I arrived in Paris this afternoon to inform him of my presence. It is always polite to let the commissariat know when a Chief Inspector from another country is visiting, particularly as I'm looking into Amandine Lachappelle's family.'

'He asked the same questions as you have…about Honoré's ability to look after herself and whether she had ever wandered off in the past. Of course, I could not tell him for certain. It must be ten years since we last saw each other so I cannot confidently say that she has never done so.' Camille sipped her coffee and sighed. 'She isn't elderly as one would describe it, Richard. She is just in her sixties and fully aware of life going on around her. Yes, she has changed, we all have, but before this afternoon I would not have worried.'

'How old were you when you last saw her?'

'Nearly twenty.' Richard nodded and tossed back his brandy. 'Does Inspecteur Apollinaire know about Amandine?'

'He does. He is aware that officially I'm off duty, but I'm still a member of His Majesty's police force so can look into her parents' disappearance. That's if they have disappeared.'

Camille frowned. 'You don't think so.'

Richard inclined his head and looked thoughtful. Camille watched him closely and thought how attractive he was. He was a fit man, clearly took care over his appearance and looked much younger than he was. A little spark blossomed inside her, she knew not from where, making her wish they could be closer, that the kiss they had enjoyed in Brighton and at Christmas could go further…that perhaps they could be a couple. She wondered if he felt the same, hoped he did, but of course nothing could happen between them until her divorce was rubber-stamped and she and Harry were free from each other. She suddenly realised Richard had been speaking to her throughout her reverie.

'I think there is more to it than that. From what you have told me Amandine's parentage is complicated, the situation with her family not direct.' He frowned and lit a cigarette, offering one to Camille which she accepted. 'There is a hidden agenda here, something not quite right.' He lit Camille's cigarette for her and she thanked him.

'Yes, I thought the same. The fact that no one has reported Amandine missing is ludicrous. Why would they not? She's a child and surely they would have missed her, but I have a feeling it is linked to her mother.'

Richard raised his eyebrows. 'Really.'

'Her father said, "she is dead to me". I thought the same once about Harry, because in my new world I felt that he was…dead. Our marriage was dead. He was no longer in my life. He had slept with another woman, and in our bed. I would have happily killed both of them.' She chuckled at Richard's expression, 'Well of course that's how I felt. I was hurting…it was painful. And I was in shock. I didn't want anything to happen to them really. The thought of hurting them as they had hurt me got me through a very difficult time.'

'Amandine thinks her mother is dead because that is what her father said to her.'

'So what do we need to do.'

'I feel an investigation just around the corner.' Camille laughed. 'I don't know why I'm laughing. I'm so worried about Honoré.' She paused then stubbed out her cigarette. 'She's been taken hasn't she, even though she has no connection to Janine Heroux apart from the fact Janine was her maid. Now we must find out why.'

Chapter 10

When Camille returned to her suite both Ottilie and Amandine were fast asleep, and Cecily had taken a book to her room. Hearing Camille in the salon she peeped out of her room to see Camille throw herself onto the chaise and blow out a heavy sigh.

'Madam?'

'Hello, Cecily.'

Cecily placed her book on her dressing table and joined Camille in the salon. 'Is there anything I can get you, Madam?'

She smiled at Cecily and patted the seat next to her on the chaise. Cecily joined her, placing her hands between her knees in her default position. 'Only if you can find Honoré for me.'

Cecily nodded. 'I was thinking about that.'

'Were you?'

'I s'pose you were thinkin' that Madam Tatou lived a quiet life.'

'Well, yes. She told me about her life, her friends, and where she went for entertainment.'

Cecily nodded again then frowned. 'But that's what she said, Madam, not what you've seen.'

Camille changed her position on the chaise to face Cecily. 'What are you saying?'

'I 'ad a grandmother once. She lived with us in our court in St Giles. Gone now though. I found 'er in 'er bed, dead as doornail. I'd been out working, for a pittance I might say, and no one thought to check on 'er. Stone cold she was. It was me Ma's mum. God, they were so much alike it was 'ard to separate 'em. Sometimes I could 'ardly tell the difference when one or the other of 'em 'ad their back to me, that was until I looked at the feet and then I knew. My grannie always wore old slippers with a pompom on the front. The uppers were nearly off the bottoms of 'em, but would she get rid of 'em? No she would not. And she liked a pig's trotter too; when we could get one.

'The thing is she always used to say to me, believe nuffink of what you 'ear, and only 'arf of what you see.'

Camille pursed her lips. 'Your point being?'

'Don't you think it's funny that all this 'as 'appened since you came 'ere?'

'Is it?'

'From the sounds of it, Madame Tatou led a quiet, solitary life. She wouldn't leave 'er apartment because of 'er 'usband, Albert, that they'd lived there together and she didn't want ter leave 'is memory which I think is understandable, she loved 'im. But she said, and I'm sorry, Madam, but I was ear wiggin' and I knew shouldn't a bin, but I thought it was all a bit odd. She said that the 7th Arrondeezeemont, or whatever they're called was an expensive place to live. P'raps even the most expensive place to live. So 'ow does she pay for it? 'Ow does she pay for the rent on the flat...apartment?'

Camille looked startled. 'Er...er, she said she had an income.'

'I know she did, I 'eard 'er. But what kind of income, Madam?'

'I don't know. I didn't think of it.' Camille shrugged her shoulders and frowned, wishing she had been more astute. 'But surely you don't think she is doing something she shouldn't be? Something criminal. I could never believe it of her.'

'No, well, I mean, not necessarily, but maybe...her friends? Do yer know who they are?'

'I don't, and I won't until I can get into the apartment. When I spoke to Inspecteur Apollinaire about Madame Tatou's disappearance he said that the gendarmes had looked in the apartment for clues to her disappearance, you know the kind of thing, a journal perhaps, or an address book, but had found nothing. That I *did* find odd. I know she had one, a notebook, because Albert had bought it for her. It was a beautiful thing in green chagrin embroidered with birds. It was why I bought her the handkerchiefs with birds embroidered on them. I tried to get them to match. I knew she liked birds and so did Albert. She told me his present of the notebook was the last thing he had given her before he died and it meant a great deal to her.'

Cecily looked distraught. 'I'm sorry, Madam.'

Camille placed her hand on Cecily's arm to reassure her. 'Oh, Cecily, please don't be sorry. I can always rely on you to think of the things I don't. It's why we're such a good team.' Cecily smiled, relieved she hadn't caused Camille any offence. 'I also think I should tell Chief Inspector Owen what Honoré said, and what you have made of it.'

'Do you 'ave a key, Madam? To the apartment?'

Camille nodded and inclined her head to her shoulder. 'Are you thinking what I think you're thinking, Cecily.'

'I don't know what you think I'm thinking, Madam.'

'I think you're thinking we should search the apartment, with or without Inspecteur Apollinaire's approval.'

'Yes, Madam, I *was* thinking that.'

'When should we go do you think?' she asked Cecily, her eyes sparkling.

'Well yer know what they say, Madam. There's no time like the present.'

'What about the girls? They can't be left by themselves.'

'They've got sitters 'ere, in the 'otel. I saw it in the 'otel book, y'know the one they give the guests when they arrive. It says you can pay for a qualified nurse to sit with children if parents want to go to the restaurant in the evenin'. I wondered if it was somethin' you would want to do. Not go to the restaurant, Madam. You got me for that. I mean, to do other things. The nurses are qualified an' everythin'.'

'Cecily, I didn't even look at the book. You are so very thorough.'

Cecily grinned. 'I 'ave to be, Madam. I work for you, don' I?'

Half an hour later Camille and Cecily were walking down the Boulevard de la Tour Maubourg. Camille was quite certain that had Inspecteur Apollinaire been aware of what she and Cecily planned he would have been less than impressed, but she also knew from past investigations that sometimes one had to do what one thought best. The police in London often dragged their feet when investigating a crime, and the police in Brighton had been beyond belief in their inefficiency. She was confident that the gendarmes in Paris would behave in a similar way.

''Ave you mentioned it ter Chief Inspector Owen what we intend to do, Madam?'

'I have not, Cecily. The point is I'm certain he will disapprove of us going there, so I decided the best thing would be if I did not ask the question he cannot answer in the negative.'

'He might not be pleased, Madam.'

Camille raised her eyebrows. 'Oh, I'm quite sure he won't, but he is not emotionally invested in Honoré's disappearance as I am. I am her friend of many years standing. I was the first on the scene when she was on the floor of her kitchen in utter shock, staring at the body of her maid. And I know her. He does not. I also think it is imperative that we find Honoré's notebook. I'm quite sure it is in the apartment. As usual the police do not cover themselves in glory when they are looking for something.' She glanced down at Cecily. 'You and I both are aware of that.'

'We are, Madam. It's like they've got the blinkers on. Or can't be bovvered. Both prob'ly. And they are men, and we all know they can be quite useless sometimes.'

Camille decided it would be best to walk to Rue Saint-Dominique. Taking a taxicab meant involving someone else on their route, and she had learnt from experience it was best to keep things simple. The fewer people who knew where they were going the safer.

'You're quite alright to walk, Cecily?'

'Yes, Madam. I've eaten too much since we've been 'ere. I can already feel it round me middle. It'll be good to walk it off. If we stay 'ere much longer I'll look like a cannon ball.'

'That won't ever happen,' chuckled Camille. 'You're not built like that.'

'Neither was me granny. She didn't eat much, we didn't have much to eat in St Giles, but she was as broad as a cart. I 'ope I don't take after 'er. Madam.'

At length they reached the Fontaine de Mars. Camille felt her stomach turn over. What they were about to do would go against the law in London, and probably even more of the laws in Paris, but it needed to be done. They had to find Honoré's notebook. Camille was sure it would give them an insight into her life.

'Are you ready, Cecily.'

'As I'll ever be, Madam.'

They made their way to the side entrance that led to the staircase up to the first floor where Madam Tatou's apartment was situated.

'I do hope no one sees us, said Camille. 'It will make life very awkward. Very awkward indeed.'

'What a noise they make in the restaurants, Madam. I've never 'eard anything like it. Sounds like a lot of 'ens fighting over their dinner.'

'It is the French way, Cecily. They love tasty food, good company, and an enjoyable time. Dinner is best eaten amongst friends and of course the wine will be flowing. I think it's rather a wonderful way to live. We are so formal in London. Everything must be just so.'

'It weren't formal in St Giles, Madam. Dinner 'ardly ever turned up and we didn't 'ave no friends. It would 'ave been nice though,' Cecily said wistfully.

'I'm glad the light is fading. It will give us some anonymity.'

'What if someone comes out of their apartment on the same landing?'

'We'll just say we're lost and leave the square as fast as we can.'

When they were finally on the landing Camille paused and listened.

'All I can hear is chatter from the restaurant downstairs. The landing seems quite peaceful and there's no light coming from Madame Tatou's apartment. I was concerned that the gendarmes might have returned.' She pulled the twine away from the front of the apartment and put the key in the front door, opening it carefully, trying not to make any sound.

'In you go, Cecily,' she whispered.

Cecily stepped over the twine and went into the small vestibule that led into the hall. 'Why does it feel so cold?' she asked sotto voce. 'It's been warm today. I would've thought it would have heated the apartment up.'

'If the curtains are closed,' Camille peeked into the salon before closing the front door behind her, 'which they are, it will keep the sun out. It is one of the things Honoré like about this particular apartment; it was cool in the summer and warm in winter. And it was. I remember it clearly.'

'Should we switch the lights on, Madam?'

Camille shook her head. 'I don't think so. I'll open the curtains a shade. It will give some natural light for us to search the rooms.' Camille went across to the long drapes and opened them a few inches.

'The problem is if we switch on the lights someone is bound to see them and report them to the police. You know how nosey people can be, and if they can involve themselves in some excitement they will.'

'Where should we look, Madam? Where's the most likely place she would have hidden her notebook do you think?'

Camille put her hands on her hips and glanced around the salon. 'Not in plain sight, not that I know why. She lived alone, but we all have our little foibles, don't we? And if it had been the police would have surely found it.'

'Unless she was concerned her maid might find it.'

Camille pulled a face. 'Mm, I can't imagine so. She viewed her as more of a companion than a maid, but we're all entitled to some privacy of course.'

'Yes, Madam, we are. It's why I'm so proud of my bedroom back at Duke Street. Never in all my days did I ever think I would 'ave a bedroom of me own. It's like a miracle to me, and I thank the Lord for it every day.'

Camille's heart lurched and she felt a surge of affection for Cecily. How lucky I am, she thought. I'm sure Honoré felt about Marthe the way I feel about Cecily. I couldn't bear to lose her. It would break my heart.

'Let's begin in the bedroom. Filling in her notebook with anecdotes or little snippets might have been the last thing she did before bedtime and going off to sleep. And it would have meant she was holding in her hands the very last thing Albert gave her as a gift. You know how she is about him.'

They went into the bedroom. The curtains were closed in there too.

'Just an inch or so,' said Camille, parting the curtains and peering out onto the square below. She turned and looked into the room, rubbing her hand across her cheek. 'Gosh, I feel rather guilty being in the bedroom without Madame Tatou's permission. It seems an awful invasion of privacy.'

'We're here for good reasons, Madam. We're not trying to pry. I'm sure she'll be grateful when she knows why we decided to come here. From what you've said her going off like this is very out of character for 'er. Of course you're worried. It's only natural ain't it. And we need to find out who 'er friends are. As soon as we've found 'er notebook we can return to the 'otel.'

Camille nodded and looked reassured. 'You're absolutely right, Cecily. We must find out who she has regular contact with and if she has decided to stay with any of them.' She sighed, 'but if she isn't with them, I'm afraid I don't know what the next step would be.'

'Chief Inspector Owen will know, Madam. Shall I look in the dresser drawers or would you rather I didn't touch anything?'

'No, Cecily, it's perfectly alright. It'll be much quicker with both of us looking. Yes, begin in the dresser and I'll search the wardrobe. There might be some boxes inside that I can look through.'

Cecily stepped gingerly across to the huge French chest of drawers sitting in the corner of the room. She felt as uncomfortable as Camille about looking through someone's belongings, but she knew it had to be done. She opened the top two drawers first; underwear, scarves, and gloves. Then the larger drawers underneath; sweaters, tops, and slim pants which the French seemed to be so fond of. No sign of a notebook or anything else that could have been considered private.

'There's nothing 'ere, Madam,' said Cecily softly. 'No notebooks or anything like that.'

'Nor here,' said Camille as she pushed a cardboard box back onto the top shelf in the wardrobe. 'I wasn't expecting it to be quite so hidden away but people have their own reasons for hiding things. Actually, as we said, why would she hide it? From whom would she have hidden it?'

'Those little bedside dressers, Madam. They look like that bamboo stuff, lots of gaps and that, but could there be a little drawer hidden somewhere.'

Camille took one side, Cecily the other. There were two drawers, one either side, slim, each with a crystal handle, but neither gave up the notebook. 'Nothing here,' said Camille.

'No, Madam,' sighed Cecily. 'Wherever it is it's well hidden.'

'Let's try the salon and the kitchen,' suggested Camille. 'Don't forget the police have searched the apartment. Really, they should have found it. One wonders why not.'

'So, that would mean it's still here, Madam.'

'Yes, I suppose so.'

They searched both the salon and the kitchen to no avail. Camille pulled an expression of frustration and Cecily shook her head.

'This ain't right, Madam. If the police din't find it, it must be 'ere. Somewhere.'

'Where would you hide your precious notebook?' Camille asked Cecily. 'And why?'

'Well, in me bedroom, but we've searched there. And why?' She shrugged. 'Cos there's something in it I don't want other people to see.'

'They are exactly my thoughts, Cecily.' They headed back to the bedroom. 'We've obviously missed something.'

The stood in the middle of the room. 'Right. We've looked in all the obvious places, now we must look in all the places which aren't immediately obvious.'

'We 'aven't searched the water closet, Madam.'

'Alright. You go there and I'll begin again in here.'

Cecily went into the water closet, searching through the towel cupboard which brought no success, then the mirrored cabinet on the wall.

'You might want to look at the medicines, Madam. In the cabinet. It might tell us something.'

Camille joined Cecily and looked into the cabinet. 'Oh, what's this?' She pulled a small, dark brown glass bottle from the shelf inside the cabinet. 'Dr Bach.'

'Who's that, Madam.'

'I've read about him. He makes potions from flowers.'

'Why?'

'I'm not sure. This one is Rock Rose, oh, and look, here's another Scleranthus, and another, Mimulus.'

Cecily frowned. 'What do they do?'

'Every potion treats something different.' Camille turned to Cecily and passed one of the small bottles to her. 'Perhaps if one is feeling anxious, or frightened of something, one would take a little of the potion on one's tongue and it will make one feel better.'

Cecily screwed up her face looking sceptical. 'Sounds like a load of old bunkum to me.'

Camille chuckled. 'You shouldn't discount something based merely on the fact you know nothing about it. This is a very new science. Perhaps if we find out what these potions are meant to remedy we'll discover what was ailing Madame Tatou. Put them in your bag, Cecily.'

Cecily's eyes widened even further. 'Isn't that stealing, Madam?'

'Yes, it is.'

Back in the bedroom they began their search again.

'There's nothing 'ere, Madam. Maybe she took it with 'er.'

'I'm sure she didn't. It would have been too bulky. I'm sure I would have seen it.'

Both Camille and Cecily stood in the middle of the room, wondering if there was anywhere that they had not examined.

'There *is* a place where we 'aven't looked, Madam.'

'Really. I feel as though I have searched every inch of the room.'

'You're right, Madam, we 'ave searched the room top and bottom, but not the bed.'

'The bed? Oh, yes, it's true, we have not searched the bed. Surely it couldn't be in there?'

'Or the wooden bit.'

'It's a sleigh bed, Cecily. It's called the frame.'

'We ain't searched the frame, neither.'

'Well come on then, let's do it now before I change my mind. It seems wholly unsavoury.'

They stripped the bed of sheets, pillows and cases, and the eiderdown and comforter. When the bed was bare Camille shook her head. 'Oh, damn, look what we've done. We must remake it. I can't believe I've just searched someone's bed. A bed is so personal.'

Cecily was only half-listening. She slid her hand down the side of the frame and pressed. With a click a small piece gradually glided out and inside the surround was a notebook.

'I've found it, Madam. Look, it was in the bed frame.'

'How?' exclaimed Camille.

'In this bit of wood which slid out the side of the top bit what curves back.' Camille went around to Cecily's side of the bed and took the notebook from its hiding place. 'It was 'idden for the purpose, weren't it, Madam. Madame Tatou did not want it ter be found did she?'

'It certainly looks like it.' She narrowed her eyes which then went to the unmade bed, the sheets and pillows scattered across the floor. 'We must make the bed, then go back to the hotel. I'm extremely curious as to what is written in here. She said she would use it for addresses and telephone information for those friends who could afford one. Why did it need to be hidden? I suddenly need to get out of here. I can't wait to get back to the girls.'

They left Madame Tatou's apartment ten minutes later after remaking the bed and closing the curtains. With one last look before they left, they gently closed the apartment door so as to make no noise, the sounds coming from the restaurant below muffling their footsteps, then made their way down the stairs, through the entryway and into the Fontaine de Mars square.

'We'll walk halfway down the Rue Saint-Dominique then get a taxicab back to the hotel,' said Camille. 'I'm eager to examine the notebook,' she patted her bag,' to discover why Honoré felt the need to hide it. I'm not surprised the gendarmes didn't find it.'

'They're not as efficient as we are, Madam. We've said it before 'aven't we, a few times?'

'We have, Cecily. And we're right.'

At length they reached the hotel. Camille wasn't content to wait for the lift so ran up the stairs to the second floor with Cecily close behind her. When they got to the suite Cecily was relieved to see that the girls were still asleep. The nurse rose from a chair in the salon as they entered it, pushing her knitting and needles into a bag, looking with surprise at Camille and Cecily's flushed cheeks.

'How was it, Nurse?' asked Camille.

'All is well, Madame. Not a sound.'

Camille thanked her and gave the nurse a healthy tip to which she smiled; her eyes sparkling. 'Merci, Madame,' she said, making a small curtsey. 'You are very generous.'

When she left the salon and Camille and Cecily were alone, Camille blew out a sigh.

'Oh, it's so good to be safely back in the hotel. I must say I didn't much enjoy our little outing.'

'Neither did I, Madam. D'int feel right some'ow.' She blew out her breath in a puff. 'P'raps we can 'ave some peace and quiet while we investigate that notebook.'

'Oh, yes, indeed.' She sunk down onto the chaise. 'And we'll have a brandy, too, Cognac please Cecily. We deserve it, don't you think.'

'I do, Madam.'

Cecily went across to the console and poured two brandies, then settled on the chaise next to Camille. Camille pulled the notebook from her bag, looked at it affectionately and placed it on her lap. She was just about to open it when a commotion in the corridor outside the suite startled her.

'I know Lady Divine's 'ere,' said a loud voice. 'You can't stop me from seeing my friend. I don't care if she don't know I'm 'ere. I've just booked a room in your 'otel and that makes me a guest, and you ain't stoppin' me. Let me pass.' There was a kerfuffle in the corridor, then something hit the other side of the door with a crash.

Camille got up and almost flew to the suite door, opening it with a flourish. Her mouth dropped open with shock before she could utter a word.

'Elsie!' she cried.

Chapter 11

Elsie was sitting on the floor in the corridor. Her hat had been pushed over one eye which made her look like a pirate, and her legs were splayed out in front of her. One of her shoes had come off and was over the other side of the corridor. The young room attendant who had been arguing with her looked acutely embarrassed. His face was bright red, and Elsie's was of a similar colour, but not for the same reason. Camille stared down on her, her lips pressed tightly together to prevent herself from laughing.

'Elsie, dear. What on earth are you doing down there?'

She bent to help Elsie up off the floor, the young room attendant reaching out to do the same, but Elsie shook off his hand, looking cross.

'No thank you,' she said, straightening her hat and smoothing down her coat. She glared at him. 'You've 'ad yer 'ands on me enough. You've made a right fool of me you 'ave. What the 'ells up wiv yer? Do I look like an axe murderer?'

'Elsie, I'm sure the attendant didn't think you were an axe murderer but he's not allowed to permit anyone to come up to the rooms until he has cleared it with the guests. It's the rule of the hotel.'

'That's all 'e 'ad to say wern'it. 'E should've said.'

'He did say, Ma,' said a little voice down the corridor. Camille stuck her head out of the suite to see Rose standing by herself in the corridor looking embarrassed. 'It's just that he was speaking French and you couldn't understand him.'

'You could a told me, Rose. I feel a proper idiot now.' She stared at Camille. 'Well, are you gonna ask me in or what?'

Camille held the door open. Elsie flounced in and parked herself on the chaise next to Cecily. Cecily got up and stood by the window her eyes going first to Elsie then to Camille wondering what would happen next. Rose followed Elsie into the suite and chose a chair next to the window where she looked out onto the street below. Camille gave the room attendant a tip and a quiet, 'desolee, Monsieur,' to which Elsie tutted. When Camille had closed the door, she went to stand in front of Elsie, her hands on her hips.

'You certainly know how to make an entrance, Elsie. I should think you've woken the whole of Paris.'

'I think the girls are awake, Madam,' said Cecily, biting her lip.

Rose instantly jumped out of her chair. 'Can I go and see them,' she implored them. Camille nodded smiling and the little girl went into the bedroom to squeals of delight from Ottilie and Amandine.'

'Well, she got a better welcome than I did, that's for sure.'

'Elsie, I'm quite shocked to see you. What are you doing here?'

'What am I doin' 'ere?'

'I think that's what I asked.'

'Well, that's rich that is. I thought we was friends, Camille.'

Camille sat next to Elsie on the chaise, grinning. 'And so we are.'

'No we ain't. You said you would tell me when you came to Paris.'

'I did tell you.'

'No...you said you was comin'. You didn't say when. It's only 'cause I met Knolly at the market that I found out that you was already 'ere.' She looked upset. 'I wanted ter bring, Rose, y'know, so she could speak French to real French people. And I wanted us to come together. I was disappointed that I was left out, that me and my Rose wasn't included on the trip.' She looked downcast. 'Oh, and by the way. I saw 'is nibs. 'E got an invitation, but I didn't.'

Camille glanced up at Cecily who returned the look with not a small amount of sorrow. Camille put her hand on one of Elsie's.

'I'm...I'm very sorry. I think maybe there was break down of communication between us. I accept that it's my fault, that I should have told you when we were coming to Paris and I should have invited you.'

'Yer did sort of invite me when was talking about it.' Camille nodded and did her best to look contrite. 'So...you're sorry?' Camille nodded again. 'And yer meant to invite me?'

'I most certainly did.'

Elsie puffed out a breath, her face breaking into a broad smile. 'That's alright then, ain't it, now you've said you're sorry.' Camille sniffed thinking that Elsie was definitely pushing her luck, then began to chuckle. She glanced at Cecily who was grinning.

'So, what's 'is nibs doin' 'ere then?'

'We discovered some information about Amandine.'

'Ooh. How did yer do that? I thought she weren't sayin' nothin' about her Ma and Pa.' Camille proceeded to tell Elsie the story Amandine had told her in the taxicab. 'So it sounds like they're still alive.'

'Indeed.'

'And the question is, why weren't they lookin' for 'er?'

'Which is why Chief Inspector Owen has come to Paris. He can speak to the right people which I cannot. I can't do anything without him.'

Elsie glanced at Cecily with a smirk on her face. 'We all know that don't we?' She winked at Cecily who stifled a giggle, thinking everything had changed since Elsie West had arrived. She had a tendency to turn everything on its head.

'He wasn't invited as part of our holiday, Elsie. Chief Inspector Owen is here in a professional capacity. He came because he needs to speak with Amandine's father. We have assumed that Lachappelle is not her real name which is why the French police could not find her parents, why there was no record of them living in the 7th Arrondissement as Amandine had told us.'

'Do they? Live in the 7th whats-its-name, whatever it's called?'

'We don't know. She mentioned the Elysée Palace, but,' Camille sighed, 'we have travelled the 7th Arrondissement and Amandine showed no particular recognition of any of the streets or squares. One could not forget such a place, not even a child.'

'So what now?'

'Richard only arrived this evening. Tomorrow he will go to the commissariat to speak with Inspecteur Apollinaire about Amandine. He is a man who has quite enough on his plate at the moment, I can assure you.'

'And then they'll go to the Elysée Palace?'

'Yes. They will have to go if they are to find out exactly who Amandine is and who her parents are.'

'Why can't you go? You're a Lady from England. Don't that get you anywhere 'ere?'

'I'm a woman, and not a French one to boot. I doubt that I would have got within a hundred feet of the President. They are very careful who they allow in the confines of the Elysée Palace. Had I been a French woman, I may have had more success. It's not dissimilar to the Houses of Parliament. I would need an invitation.'

Elsie shook her head. 'Will we ever get treated the same?'

Camille shrugged and sighed. 'Who knows, Elsie? We've made a little headway haven't we, but there is so much more to do.'

'Ain't that the truth. Anyway, I need to get my Rose to bed. She's 'ad a long day and some new fings 'appen to 'er. She'll say she's not tired like they all do, but you can bet your bottom dollar she is.'

'Did you fly?'

'I did, an' I didn't like it. Birds fly, not people.'

'Knolly said the same.'

'Knolly's right. Any'ow, we'll go on an aeroplane back 'ome, but don't know if I'd do it again.'

'That's a shame. We're going to New York next.'

Elsie smiled. 'Is that an invite, Lady Divine?'

'I suppose it is.'

'Why New York?'

'I'm curious, and I want Ottilie to see the world. Travel broadens the mind.'

'Looks like I'm goin' ter 'ave to broaden my purse then. Travel costs money.'

'It does, but it's worth it.'

'One more customer each for my girls a night would probably pay for it.' She wrinkled her nose. 'I reckon they can manage that.'

When Elsie had finally managed to pull Rose away from Ottilie and Amandine after promising the girls she'd take them to the ice cream parlour the next day and had gone to her own room, Camille and Cecily sank on the chaise and burst into laughter.

'Oh, Madam,' cried Cecily. 'Mrs West is so funny. I 'ope you don't mind me laughing.'

Camille wiped her eyes with a handkerchief. 'Not at all, Cecily. She's what we all needed isn't she? Yet again Elsie West has cheered me up no end. She is quite the card.'

"Er poor girls. Thing is, Madam, I think she means it.'

'Actually, Cecily, I know she does.'

Chapter 12

The following day Richard went to the hotel restaurant for an early breakfast before taking a cab to the Rue de Fabert and the commissariat to speak with Inspecteur Apollinaire. They had spoken on the telephone, but Richard knew it was always best, and more polite of course, bearing in mind he was an English police officer on French soil, to introduce himself personally if he wanted his help. Richard knew he had no authority in Paris. He had relied on the French police to make the necessary checks into Amandine's family, but clearly the name Lachappelle had thrown them. Richard was almost certain it was not her real name, or at least the family name, but as he sat in the back of the taxicab something occurred to him. Was it not possible that Lachappelle was her mother's name which was why Amandine had been so comfortable with it? She had always referred to herself as Amandine Lachappelle and had never given them cause to think she had any other.

He sighed to himself and took a cigarette case from his inside jacket pocket. It was a solid silver case left to him by his father, and a family heirloom. He stared at it then sighed again, closing his eyes, relaxing his shoulders almost simultaneously. Why am I thinking about Father again, he thought? On raising his face, he looked out of the windscreen to see the Eiffel Tower rising up in front of him.

'The City of Lights and Romance,' he whispered to himself. 'And yet again, I'm working.' He pulled a thin smile then retrieved a cigarette from the case, stuck it in between his lips and lit it, taking a long draw.

The motion of the taxicab sent him into a reverie, and he thought of Camille. How wonderful she had looked last night when she had accompanied him to dinner. Her shot silk dress was perfect for the most fashionable city in the world, and her eyes had shone all evening. She also seemed to hang on his every word which had boosted his ego somewhat. He gave a low chuckle. I'm a typical man, he thought. Always so concerned about our masculinity and how we're perceived by the opposite sex. In truth he wanted her to be attracted to him, but he wasn't sure he would ever be enough for her. If she ever discovered his background...he inhaled a breath. What would she think of him?

'Nous sommes arrivés, monsieur,' the driver called over his shoulder, breaking Richard's daydream. He got out of the taxicab and paid the driver.

'Merci,' the driver said, touching the brim of his hat. Richard turned and glanced up at the building, a red brick three-storey high structure which dominated the Rue de Fabert. Once inside he went to the front desk and introduced himself, asking for Inspecteur Apollinaire.

'He will be with you shortly, sir,' said the young gendarme at the desk. 'He is just finishing an interview. Can I get you coffee? You can wait over there.'

Richard nodded and thanked him and sat in the seats provided, expecting a long wait. The gendarme had just brought a tray of coffee when Inspecteur Apollinaire opened the front counter and invited him into his office, indicating for him to sit in the chair opposite his own.

'I see my gendarme has brought you coffee. That is good. That is good.' He sat at his desk and leant back in his chair. 'Now, Chief Inspector Owen, what can I do for you?'

Richard explained the circumstances surrounding Amandine, and the seeming disinterestedness of her family. He also described the events in the taxicab when Amandine had spoken of the President and the Elysée Palace.' Apollinaire had frowned at this point.

'Hmm.' He tutted and leant forward looking sceptical. 'Are you sure these are not just fantasies of a young girl, Monsieur? If someone at the palace had missed a child, do you not think they would have reported it?'

'Amandine told Lady Divine that her father said her mother was dead to him, which Amandine took to mean that she was dead. We think she isn't.'

'And the name Lachappelle?'

'It could be her mother's name. She is quite comfortable with it. When I spoke to the French police some months ago, they could not place the name. Surely they would have mentioned it if someone at the Elysée Palace owned it?'

'That is correct. I have the papers here, Chief Inspector, and when the case was reported and what was said. I understand she has been in residence with Lady Divine,' he frowned, 'whom I have had some dealings with very recently.'

'I know about the case, Inspecteur. Lady Divine explained what has happened.'

'You are familiar with Madame Tatou?'

Richard shook his head. 'I am not.'

'She is Lady Divine's friend I understand.'

'That is my understanding also.'

Apollinaire leant back in his chair again and folded his arms over his not inconsiderable stomach. 'So, we have a child who was taken to the port of Calais by her brother and subsequently abducted and taken to England without him, seemingly against her will. And we have an elderly woman, Honoré Tatou, who it would seem has also been abducted. Do you think it is connected, Chief Inspector? Is this what you are saying?'

'I do not think they are connected, Inspecteur Apollinaire.'

'A coincidence then?'

Richard eyed him with respect. Apollinaire was not a man to trifle with. 'I'm not a believer in coincidences, Inspecteur.'

'Nor me, Inspector Owen, but these cases have equal importance. I assume you wish for me to help you in the Amandine Lachappelle case.'

'As you know I have no authority here. I would like Amandine to be reunited with her parents. Paris is her home seemingly, and if she had not been reported missing there must be a reason for it. I have given it a great deal of thought and I feel that the answer lies with the relationship between her mother and father.'

'An affair perhaps?'

Richard nodded once. 'I think it is possible. If a man says his wife is dead to him then she could have committed some misdemeanour or other which divided the family. I don't think we'll discover what happened until we speak to someone at the Elysée Palace. Lady Divine is convinced Amandine is telling the truth because she spoke of the President as if he were an uncle to her, said he was her godfather, and described evenings when the President and others went to their apartment for dinner.' Richard paused to see what effect this would have on Apollinaire. The Inspecteur nodded. 'Surely it would take a very inventive mind for a child to create such a story?'

'She may well have,' he began to shuffle the papers on his desk together, 'children can be inventive at times, but do not fear, Chief Inspector, I will help you in your search. This morning I have an interview with someone who I believe is concerned with Madame Tatou's disappearance, but perhaps you would like to meet me at the Elysée Palace,' he pulled a face turning his mouth into an upside down crescent, 'shall we say after lunch, two-thirty if it suits you.'

'It does Inspecteur Apollinaire.' Richard held his hand out to Apollinaire who shook it with one firm shake of his hand and a smile.

'I'm sure we can get to the bottom of this particular conundrum with Amandine Lachappelle. I think the element of surprise is always best. I will not make an appointment, but…we'll see.'

Richard left the commissariat and turned left to walk down the Rue de Fabert. He replaced his hat and took the silver cigarette case from his inside jacket pocket, lifting out a cigarette. He stopped on the pavement and lit it, cupping the tip of the cigarette and the flame from the match against the light breeze.

He was relieved it wasn't as hot a day as those that had been recently reported. He wasn't fond of the heat and often wondered why people were so keen to go to hot countries for a holiday. He was much more content in the English countryside where one never knew what the weather would do. Rain or shine it was where he was most comfortable.

He followed the Rue de Fabert to the end, heeling his cigarette out on the pavement, then hailed a taxicab to take him back to the hotel. There was something on his mind, a dilemma he needed to think about before he could move forward. It was one of the reasons why he had requested a sabbatical from work, that and that he was tired...no, exhausted, because since his wife's death he had barely taken a day off. Helen had died at the end of 1918; had succumbed to the Spanish Influenza when they had been led to believe that the pandemic had been beaten, and so it had been, but she had been unlucky. She had caught it just before Christmas and had been swept away by it swiftly. This was the reason he always volunteered to work over Christmas, apart from the most recent, which he had spent with Camille, her daughter, and her staff.

He and Helen were not in love at the end; were not lovers. He was convinced she barely liked him, hardly ever showing him any affection. She always seemed annoyed and impatient when he returned home from the station. It had saddened him every day. He knew when he lost her that his love for her had also diminished. He felt he did not miss her as he should have, and threw himself into his work. He had applied himself with such diligence he had had no time for anything...or anyone...else. He usually told anyone who asked that work helped him accept her death more easily, but in truth it assisted him to assuage his guilt because he had not made her happy, and that towards the end she hadn't made him happy either. If she had not succumbed to the influenza, he wondered what would have happened between them, whether they would have simply limped on, or parted.

He shook his head, tears sparkling on his eyelashes. He had not once cried for Helen in the way he should have and it deepened the guilt he felt even further.

And then there was Camille.

He swallowed hard and wiped his eyes with the back of his hand, embarrassed at the emotion, and hardly noticing the delights of Paris the other side of the window. Do I love her, he thought to himself? Am I so incapable of real love I don't recognise it when it happens to me?

He inhaled and turned his attention to the sparkling Seine and the hordes of people strolling beside it on the pavement; chatting, laughing, their arms wrapped around each other. Motor cars sped past, some honking loudly, others more sedate, the inhabitants taking in the view at their leisure.

They had kissed. A long, lingering, wonderful kiss when he had joined her in Brighton. They had kissed again at Christmas. Her lips had told him that she felt the same about him as he felt about her. She was about to be divorced from Lord Henry Divine which would set her free and allow her to go forward with her life. Camille knew Richard as a Chief Inspector of Scotland Yard, a man who upheld the law and had brought some of the toughest criminals in London to book, but there was another side to him, one that he knew could end any chance of a relationship before it had even begun.

He hardened his jaw and closed his eyes. I must make a decision, he thought. I tell her the truth and risk her condemnation, or simply walk away.

Chapter 13

Elsie, Camille and Cecily sat with the girls in the hotel restaurant eating breakfast. They had had a lazy morning, Camille allowing the girls extra time in bed as was usual on any holiday from school. She remembered when she was a girl; globe-trotting with her parents. There never seemed to be any time to lay in bed and luxuriate in the warmth, perhaps with a good book or just daydreaming. Her Mama and Papa were doers and they would "do" something at every moment.

The trip to Paris was meant to have been a cultural, yet relaxed, holiday for Ottilie and Camille, but it had been anything but relaxed. First was the discovery of the murder, then subsequently the disappearance of Honoré Tatou which had shaken them to the core. Then of course was the bombshell that Amandine had dropped, albeit casually as though it was the most normal thing in the world, that she was a child of the Elysée Palace, that the President of France was a close friend of her parents, and saw him regularly.

Camille sipped her coffee, quietly taking in the scene around her; Elsie and Cecily talking animatedly about the investigation they had undertaken in London at the Selfridges store the previous Christmas, and Ottilie, Amandine, and Rose speaking to each other in French, giggling at something one or the other of them said, then glancing over their shoulders whenever any of the young waiters appeared. Camille smiled to herself. Ottilie was growing up. She would be fourteen on her next birthday and had suddenly shown an interest in young men. I'll have to watch her, she thought. Harry would throw a blue fit if she fell for someone he didn't approve of. She was quite sure he would never allow her to step out with a waiter, particularly if she met him while staying with her.

She looked up as Richard joined them in the restaurant, giving him a smile which turned into a frown when she saw his pale complexion.

'Did you not sleep well, Richard? Paris is like London you know. It never sleeps and it can be noisy. Living in Duke Street has inured us to noise.'

He returned her smile, then ordered some tea and a croissant. Breakfast felt as though it been a long time before.

'I'm afraid I didn't,' he replied. 'I usually sleep well, but for some reason…' he sipped his tea, 'it wasn't to be. I must admit I'm rather tired, however I went to the commissariat on the Rue de Fabert first thing and met with Inspecteur Apollinaire.'

'What did you make of him?'

He placed his cup on the saucer and nodded. 'Efficient, straight to the point. He is interviewing someone this morning regarding Honoré Tatou's disappearance,' he said sotto voce. 'He didn't say who.'

'It will be the Herouxs.'

'Who are they?'

'Honoré's maid was using a false name when she worked for her. Honoré knew her as Marthe Benoit, but her real name was Janine Heroux, the daughter of a family well known in Paris for their criminal activities.'

'Why did she lie?'

'Inspecteur Apollinaire said it was likely that her employment in Honoré's apartment was to give her some respectability, to make her look like an ordinary Parisienne leaving the apartment to go to work just like any other Parisienne, although she also lied about where she lived. She told Honoré that she lived in the 19th Arrondissement because she could not afford to live anywhere else.'

'That was because she did not want Madame Tatou to know about her other life?' He gazed into the distance.

'Indeed, although I don't think it would have made any difference to Honoré. She was very fond of Marthe, or Janine, whatever she wanted to be called. Honoré looked upon her as much more than a maid, more of a companion.'

Richard nodded and Camille narrowed her eyes at him. He seems rather low in mood, she thought. I wonder why.

'We're going to the Musée D'Orsay after lunch. Perhaps you would like to join us?' she said brightly. 'The girls are looking forward to it. I think you'll find it interesting.'

Richard shook his head. 'I'm meeting Inspecteur Apollinaire.' His eyes went to Amandine.

'Any news?'

'He has agreed to accompany me to the Elysée Palace,' he said as quietly as he could. 'I'm very curious as to what we will find there.'

'He has made an appointment? That was quick.'

Richard grinned. 'No appointment. Apparently the good Inspecteur likes the element of surprise. I couldn't help thinking he was rather looking forward to our visit.'

Camille leant back in her chair and crossed her arms. 'I know at least one person who will not look forward to your visit to the palace.'

'Oh.' Richard frowned. 'Who?'

'Cecily,' Camille mouthed.

She looked across to her maid and her heart lurched. Cecily treated Amandine like her own daughter, fussing around her, attending to her every need, making sure all was well in her world. Camille felt pulled in two directions, one where Amandine stayed at Duke Street with them and became an accepted part of the family; the other where Amandine was reunited with her parents. Amandine had not once said she missed her mother or father which Camille had found strange. She knew in her heart that if Ottilie had been in the same position she would have begged to be reunited with her parents; would have been utterly desolate at having been parted from Camille and Harry for so long.

'And if we find them?'

'I'm assuming legally, Amandine must be returned to them.'

'Unless they don't want her.'

Camille looked astonished. 'Why ever would that be?'

They were interrupted by a waiter bringing Richard's warm croissant to the table. He turned to Cecily and winked at her. The girls erupted.

'Ooh, Cecily, he winked at you,' exclaimed Ottilie. 'I think he must like you. Gosh, a Frenchman. Cecily, you must be thrilled.'

Camille tried not to laugh. Cecily had gone a very deep shade of red. 'Ottilie, you're embarrassing, Cecily.'

'But, Mama.' Camille widened her eyes at her daughter to admonish her and Ottilie looked down at her hands, but then began to talk to Rose and Amandine in French resulting in a fresh round of giggles.

Richard chuckled and Camille groaned. 'Oh, who would have girls? They are so difficult.'

'Particularly at Ottilie's age I would imagine. I understand it will get worse.'

Camille smiled and nodded. 'That's my understanding too, but you were saying there could be a possibility Amandine may not be required to return to France.'

'If the courts officially make her your ward...' he shrugged, 'she will return to London with you. Of course, it's something you would need to agree to.'

Camille nodded and glanced at Amandine. 'She must return to her parents, Richard. It's where she belongs don't you think?'

'I do, but it would appear there is a possibility they will see things very differently.'

Chapter 14

Inspecteur Apollinaire made his way to the Rue Saint-Dominique with a gendarme who had been chosen, to his dismay, to drive them both. As they drove through the streets of Paris, Apollinaire glanced to his left at the young gendarme who had said nothing. Apollinaire was more than aware the gendarme was probably dreading the interview with the Herouxs as much as he himself.

The Herouxs were tricky. Whenever a serious crime was committed in France's capital, the Herouxs were always in the spotlight and at the top of the list of suspects. The Heroux family was not the only family who aroused suspicion and interest. There were at least three other families which were on par with the Herouxs. The families famously hated one another, and were equally as capable of causing harm to one another, which was why Apollinaire assumed, as did his superiors, it was most likely a member of a rival family who had killed Janine Heroux.

'You look nervous, Gendarme Raulf. Why is that?'

Gendarme Raulf threw a glance at his boss and shrugged. 'This is a first for me, sir. The Heroux...they are almost celebrities in Paris. They are always in the newspapers, always invited to the most important events in the capital. Their women wear clothes from top designers. They're almost icons.'

'You envy them?'

The young gendarme frowned. 'No, sir. I do not. They must spend their whole lives looking over their shoulders. The Bechards and Vachons are always ready to use the most persuasive methods to get what they want from them and they will use any method regardless of how brutal. I could not imagine how that must feel.'

'You realise the Herouxs are the most brutal?'

'That does not make me feel better, sir.'

Rauf pulled up outside the impressive building which housed several large apartments. The building was rather unusual in that it was not rendered in the white stucco of so many of the apartments in Paris. The facade had been left in its unadorned form, red brick ornately fashioned, the huge windows sparkling like prisms. This was an area of pure luxury where the most celebrated of Paris had their pieds-a-terre.

Many of the apartments were used only at weekends when the owners would come into Paris from the country; to shop, to eat, and to avail themselves of all the entertainments Paris offered. This was not the case with the Herouxs. The Heroux family had made the apartment in the Rue Saint-Dominque their home; many of the gangster families lived in the capital ensuring their fingers were kept in their criminal pies, and their ears to the ground. If something was bubbling up, they wanted to know about it.

Inspecteur Apollinaire got out of the passenger side of the car and slammed it hard, pulling the waistband of his trousers up over his portly stomach. He then straightened his hat and buttoned his jacket. He was not a man given to fashion or designer clothes costing ridiculous amounts, and he was a stranger to Coco Chanel, although his wife would have very much liked to make the celebrated designers acquaintance. He'd eventually persuaded her, after a certain amount of debate, that a simple policeman's salary was not generous enough to line Coco's pockets. He was aware, however, that the Herouxs would indeed be dressed in such finery, even in the days of mourning, and Janine's funeral would no doubt be an occasion of great ceremony.

Inspecteur Apollinaire had been saddened at her death. She had been a victim of her birth. There had been no incidences he could recall where she had been involved in any of the family's criminal dealings, but the same could not be said for her brothers. Or her sister, Angelique.

Gendarme Raulf followed Inspecteur Apollinaire to the impressive front entrance of the building, and through the revolving doors which took them into a mirrored vestibule with a commissionaire seated behind an ornate desk. He rose from his seat when Apollinaire and Raulf entered.

'Monsieur. How may I help?'

'We are here to see Monsieur and Madame Heroux.'

'They know you're coming, sir?'

'They do.' Apollinaire held up his identity card.

'The lift will take you to the top floor. They have the penthouse apartment, Inspecteur.'

'Are there other apartments on the top floor?'

The commissionaire shook his head. 'No, sir. They own the floor.'

Apollinaire and Raulf made their way to a bank of lifts and stepped into one that opened as they approached. Apollinaire raised an eyebrow. 'Of course they do,' said Apollinaire. He shook his head in frustration and disbelief. 'Do you know anyone who owns the top floor of an apartment building, Rauf?'

'No, sir.'

Apollinaire sighed. 'Neither do I.'

The lift took them to a hall, beautifully decorated in classical style. In front of them was a large oak door which had a grille backed with glass and a sliding door at eyelevel. Apollinaire rang the bell. The sliding door was pushed to one side with a clunk and a pair of chestnut brown eyes were revealed.

'Yes?'

'I am Inspecteur Apollinaire and this is Gendarme Rauf. We are here to see Madame and Monsieur Heroux.'

The door was slid back into place and a number of locks were undone. 'This is the price they pay for being criminals,' Apollinaire said to Rauf sotto voce. 'They never feel safe and trust no one.' Rauf visibly swallowed and wiped his clammy hands down the side of his trousers.

A housekeeper opened the door. She was neatly dressed in a black dress which finished at the calf and had wrist length sleeves. She was clearly well-rewarded for keeping her silence regarding the family and their activities. Around her wrist was a sparkling bracelet of gold and diamonds, and on her other wrist was a watch which Apollinaire was sure would have cost his annual salary.

'You will find Madame and Monsieur in the drawing room, Inspecteur. You will understand how they are feeling. Janine was dear to them, to all of us.'

'Oui, Mademoiselle, of course.'

'Please, do not stay too long. Madame is particularly distraught.' Apollinaire nodded, thinking he would stay as long as was necessary to discover the truth.

The housekeeper led them into a beautifully appointed drawing room, expensive and no doubt designer decorated, where the family were sitting in silence apart from muffled sobs from Madame Heroux, and Angelique, who sat by one of the long windows looking out onto the street below, dabbing her cheeks with a handkerchief and sniffing loudly.

Apollinaire bowed to them as he entered the room and gave them his condolences. Monsieur Heroux indicated for him to sit on a chair that had obviously been placed appropriately in front of them all, as though he was under the spotlight. Apollinaire was aware of the tactics they used, but was determined not to be intimidated.

'I am sorry for the loss of your daughter, Madame, Monsieur. I will try to make our meeting as painless as possible, but clearly there is a requirement for us to discuss who may have been responsible.'

'I hope you will make every effort to catch the bastard who did this,' said Monsieur Heroux. 'Janine did not deserve this. She was an innocent.'

Apollinaire felt his breath catch in his throat that a man such as this who was the head of a family so criminal in its dealings that no one in Paris dare mention the name Heroux in public, could speak of innocence. Apollinaire nodded sagely and called upon his professionalism to pose his questions.

Heroux was dressed deceptively simply in a cashmere sweater over a fine cotton shirt. His trousers had pinpoint creases and he was unusually tanned for a Parisienne. This could only point to the travel to foreign climes he and his family enjoyed. Simple yet luxurious and expensive attire. Apollinaire glanced at Madame Heroux who sat on a settee, dressed simply in black. Her face was pale and free of cosmetics, a handkerchief to her lips and her eyes covered with sunglasses, presumably to cover the evidence of weeping. Her hair was blonde and caught up in an elegant chignon. On her ears were huge diamond earbobs that sparkled erroneously in such a sad tableau, and caught the eye with their lustre.

The three sons, all of whom had committed heinous crimes but had never been imprisoned for a full sentence, stood behind her, one with a hand on her shoulder. Madame Heroux released another sob and he rubbed his mother's shoulder distractedly.

'Maman,' he said quietly, staring into the distance. 'We must answer the Inspecteurs questions so he can find out who did this to our beloved Janine.'

'We know who did this,' she wailed. 'We know.'

Inspecteur Apollinaire turned his attention to Monsieur Heroux and lifted his chin.

'Do you know, Monsieur?'

Heroux sat on the settee next to his wife. He crossed his legs and took a cigarette from a crystal cigarette box, lit it with a match and leant back on the settee. He nonchalantly took a long draw on the cigarette and blew out a stream of smoke. Apollinaire thought how confident he was, one might say charming, yet he was a dangerous man.

'We think we know.'

'Who, Monsieur?'

'One of the Bechards. Or perhaps the Vachons. Even the La Cours would do something such as this.'

'Why?'

Rauf stood behind Apollinaire, his arms by his side. He did not know where to look and he was aware his breathing seemed too loud. He was impressed by Apollinaire who did not seem overawed by these people who would remove your hand in a heartbeat.

'I cannot tell you that, Inspecteur.'

Apollinaire nodded and pulled a face. 'Why not?'

Heroux took another draw on his cigarette before stubbing it out in a crystal ashtray. 'You are no doubt aware that the Herouxs, Bechards, Vachons, and La Cours are rival...businesses.'

Apollinaire spread his hands. 'That is of no concern to me, Monsieur Heroux. My job is to discover whoever killed your daughter.' He frowned. 'Surely you must agree with me that it is most important that I do so. They may make attempts on other members of your family.'

'You will provide protection of course,' said Madame Heroux.

An inclination of the head by Apollinaire clearly rattled her husband and his jaw visibly hardened. 'I'm not sure we can promise it, Madame, not until we have established there is a threat to your family.'

Madame Heroux reared up. She whipped off her sunglasses to reveal bloodshot eyes that were puffy with crying. 'You have not yet established a threat to my family! Are you playing a game, Monsieur. My daughter has been slaughtered and the person who did it walks free. We have told you who we think it is but you say you will not act upon it.' Her husband patted her down and she sank back on the settee, replacing her sunglasses and dabbing her lips with her handkerchief.

'Angelique.' He turned to his daughter who remained on the window seat overlooking the Rue Saint-Dominique. Fetch your mother a drink, s'il vous plaît, and one for me and your brothers. Brandy I think.' He turned back to Apollinaire. 'Inspecteur?'

Inspecteur Apollinaire shook his head. 'Thank you, no. I'm on duty.'

Monsieur Heroux chuckled. 'I can assure you not all your colleagues are so solicitous.' Apollinaire shrugged. Angelique slid off the window seat and went to a side table on which there were myriad bottles of every kind of alcohol. She chose one and poured five glasses of brandy which she handed, one each, to her mother, father, and three brothers. Her face was delicately pale, but it did not detract from her obvious beauty. Flaxen haired and blue eyed she closely resembled her mother.

'Your daughter, Angelique,' said Inspecteur Apollinaire. She is your youngest child?'

'She is,' nodded Monsieur Heroux, who took a long gulp of his brandy. 'A beautiful surprise as you can see. Davide is the eldest, then Julian, Janine, and Gilbert. Angelique is just nineteen.'

At the mention of Janine's name Madame Heroux began to sob again, and Monsieur Heroux asked his daughter to take her to the bedroom.

'She can tell you nothing, Inspecteur, at least nothing I can't tell you, and she is so distressed. I think it's better for her to spend some time in her room where she can sleep if needs be. She has not slept since we heard about Janine.'

'Of course, Monsieur,' said Apollinaire. 'Now will you tell me please, why you and your wife believe it to be one of the 'noted families' who killed your daughter?' Heroux began to shake his head and Apollinaire interjected. 'Monsieur, how do you expect me to help you if you do not tell me everything? I know what your business interests are. I imagine there isn't a person who resides in Paris who does not know the name Heroux and what it means. You must be honest with me otherwise I cannot help you.'

Heroux glanced at his sons who shrugged in unison. He looked back at Apollinaire and nodded.

'We had had some dealings with the Bechards last year. We are interested in antiquities and had planned a trip to Egypt.'

'On a tip off?'

Heroux closed his eyes and nodded. 'The Bechards got in the way. They'd had a similar idea when they heard how much profit could be made by trading antiquities by auction. They tried to muscle in on the venture. There was an altercation.' He paused. 'One of them had an accident.'

'A death, Monsieur?' Inspecteur Apollinaire frowned. 'I don't recall any Bechard deaths in Paris. I can assure you I would have heard about it.'

'Not a death, Inspecteur... an accident. One of the Bechard brothers was left...indisposed.'

'Caused by you?'

'Not me personally, or one of my sons.'

Apollinaire sighed. 'Of course not. One of your associates?'

'Oui, Monsieur.'

'And you think what happened to Janine was in retaliation.

Heroux widened his hands. 'It seems logical does it not. You know the Bechards as well as I, Inspecteur. They leave nothing unpunished. We've lost our beautiful Janine because of it.'

Inspecteur Apollinaire nodded and rose from his seat. 'Monsieur Heroux. Is there anything else you can tell me that might lead me to an arrest? Your sons perhaps?' He glanced across to Davide, Julian, and Gilbert but they simply shrugged and shook their heads. Of course you would say nothing even if you did know, thought Apollinaire. It is what you have been instructed to do by your father. These people. They will not forget their rules even when one of their own is murdered.

'Fair enough, but if you think of anything that might lead us to the perpetrator we would appreciate the information.'

Monsieur Heroux stood, a simple politeness. Apollinaire hoped he would not offer his hand as was natural between men.

'I will take my leave, Monsieur Heroux. Please convey my condolences to your wife. We will do everything we can to discover who it was who killed your daughter and why. But before I go, are you familiar with Madame Honoré Tatou?'

Heroux frowned. 'I know the name,' he shook his head, 'but I don't know why.'

'She is the woman who employed your daughter, Monsieur. It was her apartment where Janine was found. Did she come home the night before she died?'

'No, Inspecteur, she did not.'

'Were you expecting her?'

'She was a grown woman, Inspecteur. When she stayed away we assumed she was staying with her employer.'

Apollinaire nodded. 'Madame Tatou is missing, Monsieur. You said you thought the Bechards were responsible for your daughter's death. Is there any reason they would want to abduct an elderly woman?'

'None, Inspecteur. If she is elderly perhaps the shock of finding my daughter slaughtered in her apartment altered her mind and she wandered off. It happens.'

'Yes, I believe it does, but rather a coincidence don't you think? And Janine, she never mentioned her?'

'From time to time. My wife would know more. I think she was fond of her employer.'

'We will be requiring entry to you daughter's room, Monsieur. My men are on the way now. Ah, is it not them I can hear in the street below?'

Davide ran to the window and looked out. Below were two police cars. 'The police are here, Papa.'

Monsieur Heroux looked furious. 'We should have had more notification, Apollinaire. We are mourning. Could you not have given us more time?'

'Time is the thing we do not have, sir, not if we are to discover the perpetrator. They will be thorough but respectful I assure you.'

'They'd better be.'

Apollinaire made his way to the vestibule where the housekeeper was waiting to show him and Rauf out of the apartment. Just before he reached the front door he turned and spoke to Monsieur Heroux.

'I would be grateful if you and your family would stay in Paris, Monsieur Heroux. Do not leave for any reason, in fact, if what you say is true, it might be safer if you stayed in your apartment. And please, consider telling me who your associates are. They might also be in danger if the Bechards are willing to kill your daughter, an innocent who knew nothing.' Heroux stared at Inspecteur Apollinaire with hardened eyes for a long moment, then reluctantly nodded a single nod.

Inspecteur Apollinaire and Gendarme Rauf got into the car. The gendarme shivered then switched on the engine.

'Cold, Rauf?'

'No, sir, just...I don't know what the word is.'

'Alarmed?'

'On edge I think is more accurate, sir.'

He released the handbrake and they drove towards the Rue de Fabert.

'Do you think the Bechards killed Janine Heroux?'

'I don't know, sir. They seemed to have a motive. These families will kill anyone who gets in their way.'

'But Janine did not get in their way. She was, if we can believe one of the most influential criminals in Paris, an innocent.'

Rauf frowned. 'So you think it was someone else, sir?'

Apollinaire pursed his lips. 'I think it's entirely possible.' He turned to look at Rauf. 'So, my friend, why so alarmed by the Herouxs?'

'The only way I can explain it is,' he grimaced then frowned, 'they made me feel inferior, even though I'm a gendarme, an upholder of the law and proud of what I do. They have...such a way about them, such confidence, such belief in what they do is acceptable. How can they behave like it, knowing they do not live within the law and never have? My teeth were clenched the whole time and I became overly aware of my own breathing. I'm glad we're out of there.' He glanced at Inspecteur Apollinaire. 'Am I allowed to say I thought you did very well at the Heroux apartment, sir. You didn't allow them to intimidate you.'

'Did you feel intimidated, Rauf?'

'Yes, sir.'

Apollinaire chuckled. 'You won't always feel like that. You see, I don't care about them. I don't care what they have, their penthouse apartment, their cars, their clothes, their expensive holidays in St Tropez and Egypt. I don't care and I don't want what they have. A much-loved daughter of the family has just been stabbed to death, presumably because of the life they lead. They know it and I know it. And even if it wasn't one of the Bechards who killed Janine there will always be someone who wants them dead.' He paused to light a cigarette.

'My wife is at home. It's baking day and she will make bread and cakes, and pies that will see us through the week. Then she will do some mending and might meet a friend for afternoon tea. My son and daughter are at school where they will decide what they want for their futures. I will go home this evening and kiss my wife and eat too many of the pies and cakes, then help the kids with their homework.' He blew out a plume of smoke.

'You see, Rauf, simplicity. Keep it simple. Don't deliberately hurt anyone. Do not be afraid to defend the ones you love but live a simple, happy life. Those people back there do not know how to live. They cause trouble for others then whine when it happens to them, wondering why they have been so unjustly treated. It is not a good way to live, in fact it is a very bad way to live because it can only end in tears, as we have witnessed this morning.'

'I'll remember that, sir.'

Inspecteur Apollinaire gave a satisfied nod. 'Make sure you do.'

Chapter 15

Camille, Cecily and the girls returned to the suite to get ready for sightseeing.

'I feel rather guilty sightseeing when Madame Tatou is missing,' Camille said to Cecily with a sigh. 'I feel as if I should be doing something.'

'What can you do, Madam? I 'eard Chief Inspector Owen saying the French policeman was going to see the murdered woman's family this morning. P'raps 'e'll find something out from them.'

'Mm,' said Camille, going over to the long window and looking out onto a sun-drenched street. 'The problem is people like that aren't too keen to give up their secrets.'

'They might say something without thinking. Oh! The notebook! Madam! With everythin' that's 'appened, we didn't open it.'

'You're right, Cecily. I put it in here for safe keeping.' She opened a slim drawer in the drinks console and pulled out the beautifully decorated notebook.

'Isn't it lovely?' Camille chuckled. 'One wouldn't want to write in it for fear of sullying its pages.'

'She 'as written in it though, 'asn't she, Madam?'

Camille opened the notebook and flicked through the pages. 'Oh, yes she has, and extensively too.'

They sat on the chaise together and Camille opened the cover. Inside was a small drawing of a ladybird. 'Oh,' Camille cried, her hand covering her mouth. She could feel tears at her eyelashes and a wave of sorrow went through her. 'Ma coccinelle. Oh, how lovely.'

'What does it mean, Madam?'

'Albert used to call Honoré his little ladybird.' Camille swallowed hard. 'Life is so harsh sometimes isn't it? They adored one another.'

'Oh, Madam,' cried Cecily. 'What a lovely name. He must have loved 'er very much.'

'Yes. Yes, he did.'

Inside the notebook were writings of a day-to-day nature, rather like a diary, little snippets of what had happened on any particular day. Camille inhaled a deep breath.

'Not much to go on here. She mentions Marthe a few times, and the weather of course. Everyone talks about the weather.' She lifted the notebook and shook it. A piece of paper slipped out. It had been concealed in a small leaf in the back of the notebook. Folded in four, it looked like a letter.

'I wonder what this is,' said Camille. 'It looks rather private.'

'Will we read it, Madam?'

'I wish we didn't have to, but I feel we must. If it's just a letter from a friend then we'll fold it back into four and forget about it, but…considering that Honoré is missing I feel we must consider every avenue.' She unfolded the letter. 'Oh, dear,' she said frowning. 'This is not what I was expecting. No, indeed. I wasn't expecting it at all.'

'What is it, Madam?'

'I think it's what one would call…a love letter.'

'From Albert?'

'No.' She shook her head. 'No, it's not from Albert. Look at the paper. It's almost new. There's no date on it unfortunately. Do you want me to translate it for you?'

Cecily looked uncomfortable. 'I'm not sure, Madam.'

'I'd like to. You have an astute mind and I would like your opinion.' Cecily nodded and Camille began to read aloud.

'*My dearest Honoré,*

It was wonderful to meet you at the theatre last evening. I must say with hand on heart you looked as beautiful as ever. You have changed little, my darling, unlike myself. The years are not always so kind to others as they have been to you. I was so happy that you spoke with me. I wondered if you would.

When we parted last; it seems so long ago now, although just a few months have passed, it was with rancour. I know I expected too much of you and I have lived to regret it. I miss you, dearest Honoré. You are the only person who truly understood me and I failed to realise it until it was too late.

Perhaps one day you will find it in your heart to forgive me for what I said. I spoke with venom on my lips but love in my heart. I loved you then and I love you now. I will always.

Albert was a fortunate man. Your attendance to him during his illness shows your depth of courage and love, no less than I would expect from you, my dear. I was sorry to hear of his passing.

If we can be friends, Honoré, just friends and no more, it will be all I ask of you, this I promise. I would be honoured if you would have dinner with me, as friends, perhaps to talk over old times. I am still where I always was. You know the way.

With deepest love,

Guillaume

Cecily was transfixed. Her mouth had dropped open and Camille put a finger under her chin to close it.

'Oh, Madam. What a beautiful letter. I've never 'ad a letter like that, 'ave you? Well, I've never 'ad a letter full stop.' Cecily startled when she realised what she'd asked. 'Ooh, sorry, Madam. None of my business a course.'

'I've had my share, Cecily, but not quite like this one.'

'Um, was Madame Tatou seeing someone else when 'er 'usband was alive, Madam? I wouldn't want to pry but it sort of sounds like she was.'

Camille refolded the letter and slipped it into the back of the notebook. 'It does rather, although I can hardly believe it. She adored Albert, took care of him with so much love when he was ill. She was always with him, hardly left his side.' She shook her head. Yet again tears sparkled at her lashes which she brushed away with her fingers.

'Are you alright, Madam? Are you disappointed?'

'No, not disappointed. We don't know what happened in those times, and we don't know how old this letter is. Perhaps Honoré felt lonely and needed a shoulder to cry on. Perhaps this...Guillaume...got the wrong idea about her feelings for him. Maybe there were no feelings and he misread it all. He fell in love with her and wanted to take it further. It sounds very much to me as though she may have refused.'

'And that's why he's apologising, in the letter, because he said some rotten things to 'er. P'raps he reckoned she was stringin' 'im along when all she wanted was friendship.'

Camille nodded. 'That's excellent supposition, Cecily, but we might never know. When Honoré is found it's not the sort of thing one would want to ask. And if she is safe and well, I suppose it doesn't matter.'

'But what if this Guillaume abducted 'er? What if 'e saw 'er in the park when we was at the Eiffel Tower and persuaded to go somewhere with 'im under a...a pretence, play-acting kindness when really he was up to no good.'

'I think you've been reading too many novels, Cecily, but yes, yes there is every chance it happened. We must keep an open mind and I must tell Richard about what was in the letter before he meets Inspecteur Apollinaire at the Elysée Palace. He will want to inform him of the letter and what was in it. Any information to discover her is paramount.'

Cecily looked doubtful. 'But won't we 'ave to tell 'im where we got the letter from, Madam, that we went to Madame Tatou's apartment when we shouldn't 'ave and, well, sort of broke in?'

'We didn't break in, Cecily. I had a key.'

'Was you meant to 'ave a key, Madam?'

'No one said I shouldn't. In fact, no one asked me.'

'I'm not sure it will wash, Madam.'

Camille shrugged and sighed. 'Yes, I'll have to tell them. I cannot lie. It gets one nowhere and one is always found out.' She patted Cecily's hand. 'Don't worry, Cecily. I'll take full responsibility.'

Cecily grimaced. 'I'm glad to 'ear it, Madam.'

Camille decided they should have lunch at the hotel before going out into Paris that afternoon. She sent a message to Richard inviting him to join them, primarily to tell him about the letter, but also to discover if he felt better than he had the evening before. At breakfast there hadn't been time for a personal chat and she thought a relaxed lunch in the hotel's outdoor restaurant would be the perfect venue.

The weather was perfect for eating al fresco. Camille dressed carefully, choosing a pale blue dress with a sash tied at the hip, completing her outfit with matching shoes and bag. A straw hat to shield her from the sun looked utterly chic.

'You look lovely, Mama,' said Ottilie. 'Is Chief Inspector Owen coming to lunch too?'

'Yes, Ottilie. He sent a message to say he would meet us in the outdoor restaurant and has offered to pay for lunch.' Ottilie giggled and glanced at Amandine whose lips twitched into a small smile. 'And what was that giggle for, Ottilie?' Camille asked her, knowing full well what it was about.

'You always dress so carefully when you see the Chief Inspector, Mama. It's almost like he's your beau.'

'Well, he isn't,' she said firmly. She glanced into the mirror and straightened her hat. 'One should make an effort when one is being treated to lunch. Don't you think so?'

'Yes, Mama. Of course.'

Richard was waiting for them when they arrived and he stood to greet them. Ottilie giggled again and Camille glared at her.

'Thank you for joining us...Chief Inspector Owen...' she said, staring pointedly at Ottilie as a warning.

'My pleasure, Lady Divine,' he answered, his eyes taking in every inch of her.

He pulled a chair out for Camille, while Cecily and the girls sat at the table, the girls with grins on their faces.

'I wonder if your waiter is working today, Cecily?' Ottilie asked her. 'He made eyes at you last time.'

Cecily flushed pink. 'He's not my waiter, Miss Ottilie,' she replied. 'And I don't think I noticed 'im making eyes at me.'

'Oh, he did, didn't he, Mama?'

'I think perhaps you should concentrate on the menu, Ottilie, instead of tormenting Cecily, or perhaps you would rather stay in the hotel with a nurse this afternoon while Amandine, Cecily and I go sightseeing in Paris.' Ottilie went red and bit her lip. Richard glanced at Camille and grinned.

'Teenage girls,' sighed Camille. 'I don't remember being like that.' Richard smiled.

Cecily and the girls perused the menu while Camille spoke with Richard about what she and Cecily had found. She explained about the notebook and the letter hidden inside it.

'So...you went to the apartment and let yourself in.' He frowned then smiled. 'Camille,' he whispered. 'You should be more careful.'

'I need you to tell Inspecteur Apollinaire.'

'But I'll also have to tell him how you found it.'

'You needn't, Richard. Say you don't know. I'll tell him the next time I see him. What can he do?'

'Arrest you for interfering with a police investigation.'

Camille looked decidedly uncomfortable. 'Oh.'

Chapter 16

The Elysée Palace is situated on the Avenue Gabriel some twenty minutes from the Hotel Narcisse Blanc on the Boulevard de la Tour-Maubourg. Richard left Camille and the others in good time, deciding to walk instead of hailing a taxicab. He felt he could think better when he walked.

From the Boulevard de la Tour-Maubourg he turned right onto the Place de Finlande, then onto the Quai D'Orsay. He crossed the Seine on the Pont Alexandre III, pausing for a few moments to admire the utter beauty of the river and the city through which it travelled. He breathed in, allowing the light breeze to cool his face, grinning when he recognised the familiar aroma of river water. Even Paris, the City of Lights, could not pull a veil over it.

Looking at his watch he realised he'd stayed too long and so quickened his pace. He crossed the Avenue Champs Elysée onto Avenue Marigny until he arrived on the Avenue Gabriel. The sumptuous, 18th Century mansion, the Elysée Palace, rose up before him.

The palace, the official home of the President of France was constructed from sand-coloured stone in the French neo-classical style, and was set back from the street and fronted by a monumental gate with four gothic columns. Richard gasped when he saw it.

'Chief Inspector Owen,' cried a voice from behind him. 'You walked, Monsieur?'

Richard turned to find Inspecteur Apollinaire getting out of a police car. 'Yes, Inspecteur. I needed some air.'

'We would have brought you, Monsieur. You only needed to ask.'

'I enjoyed it, Inspecteur. It was quite bracing.'

'I should think so.' Apollinaire turned to the palace and lifted his hand. 'What are your thoughts, Chief Inspector. Impressive is it not?'

'Indeed it is. Quite stunning. I was amazed when I saw it.'

'Your first visit?'

'I have visited the south in the past. My wife had relatives there.'

'Ah, our beautiful countryside. Yes, I get down there when I can. Are you ready for the interview?'

'Certainly, but there was something I wanted to ask you before we go inside.'

'Of course, Inspector,' Apollinaire said frowning.

'Chief Inspecteur Durand.'

Apollinaire nodded. 'Retired some months ago. Through ill health I believe. Why do you ask?'

'He was the person I spoke to when first investigating Amandine Lachappelle. I thought he was still on the case.'

Apollinaire shook his head. 'No, Monsieur. Durand retired,' he shrugged, 'maybe six months ago.'

'Just after I spoke to him.'

'So it would seem.'

Richard nodded and Apollinaire went to the main gate and rang the bell.

A small door cut into the door of an office in one of the gothic columns opened with a gritty noise. Two rheumy eyes, ringed by age lines and half-covered with sagging eyelids, looked out, the eyes swivelling to see who was calling. A voice spoke quietly, one that sounded as though the speaker had gravel in his throat.

'Monsieur?'

Inspecteur Apollinaire held up his identity card. 'My name is Inspecteur Apollinaire. I would like to speak with the President.' Richard, who was standing some way behind him raised his eyebrows in surprise, doubting that Apollinaire would be allowed to see the President because he simply asked.

The elderly man roared with laughter until his dry throat got the better of him and he erupted into a phlegmy smokers cough. When he had recovered, he wiped his mouth with a wrinkled handkerchief and smiled at Apollinaire. 'Excuse me, Monsieur. You must forgive my laughter. You cannot see the President I'm afraid.'

'Then who can I see?'

'What's it about?'

'A missing girl.'

They heard the old man sniff and grumble something under his breath. Richard startled and leant forward to Apollinaire. 'Did he say, "another one".' Apollinaire shrugged. Moments later the elderly man released the main gate which opened with a clunk.

'You must speak with the concierge on the front desk. He will have the name of the person you can see, Monsieur. I cannot help you any further.' Richard strode across to the hefty iron gates and pushed one open. Both he and Inspecteur Apollinaire went through onto the grounds, followed by two gendarmes. A long drive led from the gates onto a circular drive which took them to the main entrance. The Elysée Palace was framed each side by gardens; sweeping lawns and well-tended flower beds which were bright with colour.

'Anything like your Buckingham Palace, Monsieur?' asked Apollinaire.

'You've never been to London?'

'Not yet, but my wife wants to visit. She wants to see the Changing of the Guard. She thinks she will be allowed inside the palace, but it is not so, Monsieur?'

Richard chuckled. 'Not unless you have an invitation from the King.'

Apollinaire nodded and pursed his lips. 'I fear it will be the same here.'

At the entrance stood two gendarmes who nodded their heads to Richard and Chief Inspecteur Apollinaire.

'Monsieur?' one of them said. Apollinaire showed his card again and they waved them through. Inside the circular entrance hall the décor was neo-classical with columns of marble and a black and white chequered floor. Inside the door was a desk manned by a concierge who wore an ornate uniform.

'Can I help you, Messieurs?'

Yet again Apollinaire held up his identity card. 'I am Inspecteur Apollinaire from the commissariat on the Rue de Fabert. I would like to speak with someone about the disappearance of a young girl. We believe her father has a position here.'

'The name of the girl?'

'Amandine Lachappelle.'

The concierge reached for a large book and began to flick through it, a frown crossing his face. He shook his head. 'No one here of that name, Monsieur. Do you have the correct name?'

'We believe it may have been her mother's name.'

The concierge drew in a breath and reached for the candlestick telephone. He spoke to an operator and asked for Actifs Individueles. On reaching the person he sought he spoke swiftly then replaced the candlestick receiver.

'Please take a seat, Messieurs. Someone will be with you shortly.' He indicated an area with plush, teal-coloured bucket chairs around an ornate coffee table. 'Can I get you anything?' Both Richard and Apollinaire shook their heads. 'Non, merci,' answered Apollinaire. The concierge went back to his desk.

A few minutes later a woman entered the hall from a room the other side of the hall.

'Messieurs? Please follow me.'

Richard and the Inspecteur rose and followed the woman through the door into what was obviously an office, although it was the most spectacular office Richard had ever seen. His thoughts went to his own office in Scotland Yard which looked exactly like the purpose it was meant for, utility; plain walls, a simple oak desk with a leather chair; bookshelves and a filing cabinet for the cases he had worked on. He lifted his eyebrows and glanced at Apollinaire, whose face was expressionless.

'Please sit down, Messieurs.' The woman indicated two chairs; gilt and red velvet, placed in front of a beautiful walnut desk. She sat the other side. 'I am Madame Felice Marchand, Under-Secretary to President Doumergue. I understand you are investigating the disappearance of a young girl. Is that correct?'

'Not entirely, Madame,' answered Apollinaire. 'The girl is not missing. Perhaps you would permit my colleague, Chief Inspector Owen from Scotland Yard in London to explain the situation.

Felice Marchand's eyes widened, then she frowned. 'Why is Scotland Yard involved?'

'Amandine Lachappelle was taken to Calais by her brother, Pierre...we do not have his last name. We don't think it's Lachappelle. This is the name Amandine gave us. She was comfortable to use the name which is why we think it's her mother's. Amandine became involved in a smuggling operation in Brighton. She was clearly sold to a brothel.' Felice Marchand gasped in horror. 'I spoke to Inspecteur Durand requesting that he investigated her disappearance but no information about the girl was forthcoming. She has been the ward of Lady Camille Divine for more than six months. She has been questioned about her parents but was not willing to give up any information until Lady Divine brought her to Paris a few days ago.

'Amandine told Lady Divine her mother was dead, although we have reason to believe this is not the case. She also said her father worked for President Doumergue and that the President was familiar to her, were friends of the family, often dining in their apartment on the Rue Saint-Dominique.'

Felice Marchand looked shocked. 'This is a terrible story, Monsieur Inspecteur.' She sighed, leaning back in her chair. 'I'm not sure we can help you. No one here has reported their daughter missing. If they had it would have come through me as I am responsible for all staff matters. It also sounds if this story is true then her father, if as close to the President as she claims, would be a well-known name. It would be impossible to hide the abduction of a daughter of one of our most influential politicians.'

Richard nodded thinking they had reached stalemate. There was nowhere else for them to go, and certainly there was no reason for Felice Marchand to hide the truth.

'Madame,' interjected Apollinaire. 'It has been suggested that Amandine Lachappelle has fantasised about her connection to President Doumergue, which,' he inclined his head, 'could be true. However, could there not be a reason why one of our politicians has hidden the fact that his daughter has been abducted. For example,' he sat forward on his chair getting into his stride. 'Have any of your politicians, or those who work closely with the President recently either lost their wife, have divorced, or become estranged?'

Felice Marchand shrugged. 'It is possible.'

'It could be hidden, non?'

'It could be hidden, I accept that. Some of our most senior men might not want the information to be publicised.'

'So I ask you, for the sake of this child, are you prepared to discover if this is true? It might lead us to reuniting a child with her parents.'

Felice sighed and nodded. 'I will do my best, Inspecteur. I will make some enquiries, although it does not mean I will discover the information you require. If the gentleman is determined to keep his private life private,' she shook her head knowing that many of the men in the Elysée Palace had lives they would not want to publicise, 'I think there is little I can do to help you.' She put a hand to her cheek then narrowed her eyes. 'Do you have photograph, Monsieur, of the little girl?'

Richard shook his head. 'We will attempt to find one. It will be sent to you via a gendarme?' He looked at Apollinaire, his eyebrows raised. Apollinaire made one quick nod.

'Thank you, Madame Marchand.' Apollinaire stood and gave her his card and Richard did the same. 'We appreciate your assistance. Please contact us at any time should you discover anything, no matter how small, which will help Amandine Lachappelle find her parents.'

Richard and Inspecteur Apollinaire stood in the Avenue Gabriel and lit cigarettes, Apollinaire his French brand, Richard his favourite English brand. They puffed on them in silence until they had finished, then stood quietly for a few moments more. The gendarmes stood silently some way away, wondering why they were standing outside the President's home.

'Well, Chief Inspector Owen. What are your thoughts?'

Richard paced the pavement for a while, kicking a stone here and there. 'Madame Marchand is the only person who can help us in this case. I feel there is nowhere else to go. If she cannot come up with new information, I'm not sure where else I can go, but I thank you for your efforts.'

'And if the parents are not discovered?'

'If the parents are not found she will be made a ward of court in England and they will decide what will happen to her.'

Apollinaire inhaled. 'Hmm, that seems rather barbaric considering she has been living with Lady Divine. Could Lady Divine apply to adopt her?'

'Perhaps, but the courts will do what they think is best for the child. They don't always make the decisions one would expect.'

Apollinaire nodded. 'A lift, Chief Inspector? I will take you to your hotel.'

'Thank you, Inspecteur Apollinaire, but I'd rather walk. It will clear my head.' He shook his head sorrowfully. 'It's a bad business. I don't feel I've got far with this case.'

Apollinaire smiled at Richard and patted his shoulder. 'Small steps, monsieur. Small steps. It's the only way forward.'

Chapter 17

Richard walked down the Avenue Gabriel, a sunny tree-lined avenue, waving to Inspecteur Apollinaire as he and the gendarmes drove by. He had thought to retrace his steps, but as he had some time to himself decided to change direction and explore the Place de la Concorde. He continued down the Avenue Gabriel, not with any speed but with the intention of soaking up the sights of Paris and giving himself time to think.

First and foremost in his mind was Amandine Lachappelle. Camille had been adamant that Amandine had been speaking truthfully when she told her the story of her parents' connections to the President. If it was the truth, it would appear Amandine's father held a position of some rank at the Elysée Palace. Richard wasn't so naïve as to think politicians did not keep parts of their lives private, some because they didn't want their families involved in their political life, others because they were up to no good. He knew this was how it was the world over.

The second conundrum in his mind was Camille. Richard realised when he was in Brighton following the discovery of Amandine, their friendship was gradually moving into something much more meaningful. The Christmas just past was the first Christmas he had celebrated since Helen died, and had spent it with Camille and her family, and it meant something.

He had fallen for her, there was no doubt in his mind. It wasn't a fling or an infatuation; something they could enjoy then forget about when the time was right. No, it was so much more, and his instinct told him she felt the same.

When they'd kissed, he knew. He hadn't wanted to kiss anyone for many years, in truth not even Helen. There was no love there, no affection. But with Camille...with Camille everything was different. She had been a positive influence in his life and more than anything he wanted to tell her so. Unfortunately there was an obstacle in the way, one that could make the difference between taking their relationship further, perhaps to permanence, and halting it in its tracks before it had even begun.

He heard the sound of the splashing water of the fountains in the Place de Concorde before he saw them, and made his way to the Egyptian Obelisk which stood so proudly in the square. The Obelisk was a present to France from the Egyptian government in the 19th Century and was the centrepiece of the Place de Concorde. Richard stood at its base and looked up towards the golden top where there were hieroglyphics exalting the reign of Ramesses II. I wish she was with me, he thought. Paris...the city of romance. And we *are* together in this delightful city, yet completely apart because of societal rules...and because until he could bring himself to speak with her their future as a couple would not exist.

He turned towards the Seine and from his position he could see the top of the Eiffel Tower. He slowly released a long breath. Honesty, he thought. A relationship cannot proceed without honesty and I must be honest with her, even if it means she feels she cannot associate with me any longer. If I don't tell her, someone who does not have her best interests at heart will ensure she knows. Richard instantly thought of Lord Henry Divine, Camille's estranged husband. He is a bitter man, thought Richard, and will have no qualms about destroying Camille's happiness. I must tell her the truth.

Camille, Cecily, Elsie and the girls arrived back at the hotel just as dinner was being served.

'Oh, my goodness,' cried Camille. 'We must hurry. Perhaps we should have eaten in one of the restaurants we passed on our return, but I feel so exhausted. I don't think I've ever walked so far.'

'Me neither,' moaned Elsie. 'Wore the wrong bloomin' shoes didn't I. Me feet are red raw. I don't know if I can even make it into the dining room.'

'Should we go and change, Madam?' asked Cecily. 'I feel proper mucky. I'd like to wash and brush me 'air before we eat.'

'Yes, we'll change. I would hate to sit and eat feeling like this. Let's go upstairs, but we'll have to get ready in record time.'

'Madame?' The concierge beckoned Camille to the desk. 'I'm sorry to interrupt, Madame, but a letter was left for you at the desk this afternoon.'

'Oh, thank you, Monsieur,' Camille said frowning, wondering who would have written to her. 'Perhaps it's from Richard,' she said under her breath, glancing quickly at the plain envelope. She pushed the letter into her bag and hurried up the sweeping hotel stairs to the suite where she, Cecily and the girls had a hasty wash, then changed into some fresh clothes.

'Oh, that's better,' breathed Camille. 'I feel human again.' She called to Ottilie and Amandine. 'Are you ready, girls? We should go down to the restaurant now if we don't want to miss dinner.'

'Nous sommes prêts, Madame Camille,' cried Amandine in her little voice. 'Et, Cecily?'

'I'm ready too, Madam. And I'm starvin' an' all. I could eat an 'orse.'

They went down to the restaurant for dinner where Elsie and Rose were waiting.

'You made it, Elsie,' said Camille with a smile on her face. She knew Elsie would never miss a meal, although her beautifully curvaceous but slender figure belied it.

'Oh, yeah, Camille. Just stuck me feet in the sink with some salted water. That sorted 'em out. The old remedies are the best.'

Camille chuckled to herself at the thought of Elsie lifting her leg up to the hand wash basin to get her foot into it. 'So I've heard,' she replied with a grin on her face. 'And I'm sure no amount of soreness on your feet will affect your appetite.'

'Not on your Nelly,' Elsie replied. 'I'm ready for a bloody big blow out.'

Ottilie giggled and Cecily nudged her in the ribs 'Miss Ottilie,' she said under her breath, chiding the teenager a little. Camille looked around at the other tables to see if any of the other guests had heard Elsie swear, but it appeared not. They were far too interested in the food on their plates.

'Well, let's order shall we?' said Camille sighing. She was tired from the day's activities and was keen to spend a quiet night in their suite. She had packed a book into her valise and was eager to read it, preferably with a glass of something delicious at her side.

While they were making their way through the second course Ottilie glanced at Camille. 'What was in your letter, Mama?' she asked her brightly. 'Who was it from?'

'Oh, yes,' cried Camille. I'd forgotten about it. Remind me to read it when we return to the suite, darling. I'm so tired I'll probably forget about it again. You must be tired too, and Amandine.'

'Yes, Mama. I'm actually looking forward to going to bed.' She giggled. 'I never thought I'd say it. We walked a long way didn't we?'

'We did, Ottilie. Have you enjoyed yourself so far?'

'Oh, yes, well, apart from poor Madame Tatou disappearing. I wonder what happened to her?'

'Ave you 'eard anything, Madam?' asked Cecily.

'Not yet.'

''Is nibs is a bit quiet if yer don't mind me sayin', Camille,' said Elsie. I saw 'im in the foyer when Rose and me came down for dinner. All pale 'e was. 'E said 'ello but there weren't much be'ind it if yer know what I mean.' She looked around the dining room. 'And 'e's not 'ere is 'e. D'yer think 'e's not well.'

'I must admit I've seen a change in him since we've been here. I must see him before I return to the suite. I understand Inspecteur Apollinaire interviewed the Herouxs this morning, and this afternoon both he and Richard went to the Elysée Palace to discover information about...' Her eyes went to Amandine.

'Ah, I see. I 'ope they found something. Your stay in Paris could be a lot longer than you expected, Camille.'

Before returning to her suite Camille took the lift to the second floor and knocked on Richard's door. He opened it quickly, a frown crossing his face which turned into a delighted smile when he saw her. He had a glass of whiskey and a cigarette in his other hand. His shirt was undone at the neck and his tie hung loosely from the collar. Camille's breath caught in her throat. She had never seen him look so casual, so...undone. She thought it suited him.

'Camille.'

'I'm sorry to disturb you, Richard.'

'You're not disturbing me. I thought I'd have some time to myself. I had an early dinner then came back to my room.' He picked up a book from the coffee table. 'I'm about to get into this.'

Camille gasped. 'It's the same one as I brought with *me*. Is it any good?'

'A bit racy but...' he chuckled. 'Why not?' He invited her to sit down. 'I expect you'd like to know what happened today.'

She nodded. 'I would. How did it go.'

He offered her a brandy which she accepted, then sat opposite her.

'This case is a hard nut to crack.' He pushed his fingers through his hair. 'I feel rather like I'm wading through treacle with this one. It's as though we get so far then, well, in truth grind to a halt. We spoke to the President's Under-Secretary, a pleasant woman called Felice Marchand. We asked her if anyone on the staff had reported the loss of a daughter or perhaps the break-up of a marriage, or a divorce. She said nothing like that had been reported in the last six months, although she also said that many of the politicians and those who work closely with the President would probably prefer to keep their private lives private, some with good reason.'

Camille shook her head. 'So the channel there is closed?'

'Not at all. We, that is Inspecteur Apollinaire and I, left our cards and asked her to do some digging. She agreed and said if she found anything she would let us know. She'd also like a photograph of Amandine. Do you have one?'

Camille frowned. 'Not with me, but we could have one taken. It's a good idea.'

'Perhaps tomorrow?'

Camille nodded. 'We can only hope there are gossips at the Elysée Palace who will be happy to tell her what they know. How was it? The Elysée Palace?'

'Absolutely stunning. I've never seen anything like it. Felice Marchand's office looked like a palace in itself. Makes me think I should get some gilded, red velvet chairs for my own office.'

Camille smiled. 'And how will the villains you apprehend feel about that, d'you think?'

Richard left his chair and went over to the drinks console. 'Another?' She nodded. 'It would probably strike them dumb and they'd tell me less than they tell me now which is already practically nothing.'

'And Madame Tatou? I'm so worried, Richard? There has been nothing from her and I'm very frightened someone has done something awful to her. What did Inspecteur Apollinaire say about the Herouxs?'

'They, like our London bred villains, had little to say. There was *one* thing though. Apollinaire asked them if Janine had returned home the night before she was killed. They said not.'

'Is that relevant?'

'He had asked Madame Tatou if Janine had stayed at her apartment the previous evening. She said not.'

Camille stared at Richard. 'But she must have stayed somewhere.'

'Exactly.'

'Somewhere her parents do not know about? She was hiding it from them.'

'When he pressed them Monsieur Heroux said that Janine was a grown woman and didn't tell them everything she did, which Apollinaire said was rubbish. Families like the Herouxs keep close tabs on all members of their family in case they begin to mix with people of which they don't approve.'

'Such as?'

'Anyone.'

'Anyone?'

'Think about it, Camille. If you were running a family that was up to its neck in criminal activities, would you want other people getting close to you or to a member of your family? None of the brothers are married and they are well into their thirties. Janine was also early thirties and no sign of a romantic interest. Anyone who could be considered to be a life-partner for members of these families would need to be vetted and approved by Monsieur Heroux, and his wife presumably. Can you imagine it?'

Camille looked down. 'Well, actually, Richard, I can. Isn't it how the aristocracy behave? I would not have married Harry had my parents not approved. He had to be a certain kind of man from a good family...and wealthy to boot. If he hadn't been he would have been given very short shrift I can assure you.'

Richard nodded. 'I suppose so. I imagine it's a way of not muddying the waters.'

'Or the bloodline,' said Camille. 'It is really quite barbaric in a way. And even if one were in trade one would never be given the opportunity to become part of the upper echelon.'

Richard sat bent at the waist, knees apart, his elbows resting on his knees. He swirled the brandy around in the glass. 'And what do you think of that,' he asked.

'It was the way I was raised,' she said. 'I suppose the rules of the aristocracy are the rules I became used to.'

'And you wouldn't consider breaking them?'

She stared at him askance. 'Where's this going, Richard? You know as well as I that I have broken rules many times, that my rule-breaking has led others to raise their eyebrows in my direction. I spend the majority of my time with my staff, particularly Cecily, and one of my closest friends, although it took us some time to get there, is Elsie, a former prostitute and now a madam of a brothel. Both she and Cecily, Knolly and Phillips are my family. And you of course. In a way.'

'Friends?'

'Of course.'

She made a doleful smile. 'I'm still a married woman, Richard,' she said quietly. 'Nestled amongst those rules is the one that says a married woman who dallies with another man while she is still married, even though she and her husband are estranged, is a fallen woman, a harlot if you will. Rules mean nothing to me, but if my reputation disintegrates then I have very little. It's the one thing I managed to hold onto when Harry decided I was not to be his wife any longer. He cared little for his own, but then he didn't need to. He held all the cards. And of course there is Ottilie. It would damage her prospects terribly.

'For me to pursue another meaningful relationship I must be divorced and there must be an acceptable amount of time between my divorce and a new relationship so the gossips don't get the chance to sully my name, and my reputation.'

'And then?'

'I'll be truly free to make my own decisions. My life will not alter from how it is now. I'll still retain my income, my name, and even my title.'

'And if you remarry?'

'Ah.' She smiled, her smile reaching her eyes, making them warm and affectionate. She knew what Richard was asking and the thought warmed her. 'If...or when, I remarry I will love that person so very much, the name, the title, and the income, or anything to do with my past life, apart from

Ottilie, will mean absolutely nothing to me. The divorce papers are signed and Harry's solicitor has them in his possession. I don't think it will be long before I'm asked to appear in court. I dread the day because I will be alone and nervous, but I know it is necessary for me to take my life forward. I have not retained the services of a man of letters because there is no need to. I have agreed to everything. Harry has been extremely reasonable.' She raised her eyebrows and shook her head. 'So very unlike him.'

Chapter 18

Camille went back to her suite deep in thought. She agreed with Elsie, Richard was certainly out of sorts. He was always measured and thoughtful, but he looked pale and tired, as though he had the weight of the world on his shoulders.

As she went through the door of the suite, Ottilie, dressed in a nighty and dressing robe and looking thoroughly tired, got out of the chair where she had been dozing.

'I waited for you, Mama, Cecily said I could, to thank you for the most wonderful day and to remind you about your letter.'

'Oh, my goodness,' Camille cried. 'I had forgotten it, darling, thank you. Oh,' she put a hand on her daughter's cheek, 'you look so tired. Off you go, Ottilie,' she bent to kiss her daughter, 'into bed for a lovely sleep. I expect Amandine is dreaming already.'

Ottilie gave a sleepy smile. 'She waited with me but fell asleep. Cecily carried her to her bed.'

Camille gave Ottilie one more kiss goodnight then sat on the chaise and pulled the letter out of her bag.

'Was it from Chief Inspector Owen, Madam?' asked Cecily as she folded their clothes and hung them in the wardrobe. 'You thought it might be.'

'Oh, no, it's not from him. I've just spoken with him.' She slid her thumb under the envelope flap and pulled out a piece of flimsy paper. She unfolded it and began to read. 'Oh, my goodness,' she cried. 'It's about Madame Tatou. Oh, Cecily, you were right. You said it was a coincidence Honoré disappeared just when I was visiting her. Whoever took her is under the impression I'm wealthy. They want me to pay for her return. And a great deal of money.'

'Oh, Madam. What are they asking?'

Camille turned the letter to Cecily who left what she was doing and took the letter from Camille's hands. 'I know I don't speak French, Madam, but I know 'ow much that is in English. It's two thousand pounds. I 'ad a feeling it was what they was up to. It's a fortune. What else does it say?'

'They want me to go the Place de la Concorde tomorrow evening with the money in a bag and leave it on the top step of the Obelisk at seven-thirty. If I comply with their wishes Honoré will be waiting for me at one of the fountains. They don't say which one. We saw it didn't we, this afternoon, the Obelisk. It's the one with the markings on the top and the gold pinnacle. Where on earth am I to get that sort of money?'

'Madam!' cried Cecily. 'You're not goin' ter give it to 'em?'

'But how will we retrieve Honoré if I don't?'

'You must tell Chief Inspector Owen, Madam. And the other inspector, the French one.'

'The letter says no police. No anyone at all actually. I'm to go alone. If they think I'm being followed it will be the end of Honoré.'

'I'm sorry, Madam. You know I always agree with the way you do things, but not today. What you're plannin' is wrong. I know I'm only the maid, but...well...I think you're wrong this time.'

'Do you?

'I do. Look what nearly 'appened to me in Brighton. And Amandine. I got it wrong. I could 'ave got us both killed. If it weren't for Chief Inspector Owen sending 'is constables me and Amandine would 'ave probably frozen to death, and it would 'ave been all my fault. I still 'ave nightmares about it. I owned up to it in the end. I was wrong, what I did. We can't always be right.'

'But my instinct...'

'Your instinct is letting you down this time, Madam.'

Camille folded the letter and inhaled deeply. 'Alright. Alright, I'll go and see Richard. He's probably had experience of this kind of thing before.' She rose from the chaise and pulled a grin at Cecily. 'You're like my guiding star, aren't you?'

'Just want you to be safe, Madam. That's all.' She turned away from Camille, tears threatening, and began to fold clothes again at a tremendous rate. 'These clothes need a bit of a wash,' she said firmly. 'I'd best get down to the concierge in the mornin', see what 'e can do about it.'

'I'll leave that to you, Cecily.'

'Right you are, Madam.'

Camille left the suite and Cecily sunk down onto the bed. No one had called her a guiding star before and it had overwhelmed her. She brushed away the tears running down her cheeks and told herself off for being so silly.

'Honestly, Cecily,' she said to herself. 'Pull yourself together,' but as she continued the little jobs she did for Camille every evening come rain or shine, she couldn't help but smile to herself.

'Camille? Did you forget something?'

Richard invited her into his room again. He was ready to retire, a hotel dressing gown thrown over navy pyjamas. Gosh, she thought. Even in pyjamas you look smart and handsome.

'I received this letter this afternoon. It had been left for me with the concierge. I don't know who it's from. It's a blackmail letter asking for money.'

He grabbed it out of her hands. 'Oh. Right. So this is what it's all about. They knew you were coming to visit with Honoré Tatou and thought they would make the most of it. Twenty thousand francs. Over two thousand pounds in English currency.' He shook his head in disgust. 'Do they have any idea exactly how much this is or did they reach up into a cloud and pull a figure out of the vapour.'

'It's a vast amount isn't it? Where will I get such a sum?'

'You won't', Richard said, frowning. 'You're not going to pay it.'

'Then how will we get her back? You see what the note says. No police. No one. And if they see anyone with me, then Honoré is finished. They'll kill her won't they, undoubtedly the same people who killed Janine Heroux.'

'They want you to go tomorrow evening. We have time.'

'Time for what?'

'To put a plan in place.'

'I'm frightened, Richard. I would do anything to get her back and keep her safe. These people. They don't care who they hurt. They certainly won't care about an old lady who is in their way.'

'You're making an assumption it is the same people who stabbed Janine, but I'm not certain. Don't forget we are still making enquiries into Madame Tatou's friends.'

'And?'

'Nothing as yet. There are telephone numbers with no names and names with no telephone numbers. Very few addresses. And this Guillaume mentioned in the letter. There is nothing written down for him. He is a mystery. She never mentioned him to you?'

'Never. It is something I never expected with Honoré because of her love for Albert. Her faithfulness to him is legendary, yet it looks as though she had met a man who was encouraging her to take their,' she shook her head, frustrated she didn't know more, 'friendship? affair? much further than she wanted to go. There must have been a strong connection between them but I think Honoré rebuffed him and he didn't appreciate it.'

'Perhaps he lost patience. He clearly knew that Albert Tatou had died. It's possible he thought she could now go to him with no obstacles. Maybe she refused and he decided to take her anyway.'

'It sounds like an opera.'

'Hmm, but I'm not sure which is best for her, the Herouxs enemies, which we at least have some knowledge of, or this unknown man.'

Camille frowned. 'But why would he want money?'

'Why does anyone want money? He might be in debt, he might need money to feather his future, who knows. He might be planning to leave Paris; in fact, I'd say he would need to go to another country to escape the French law if it is he who has taken her.'

'It still doesn't feel right though, Richard. He professes to love her.' Camille shook her head. 'I don't know. If it is this Guillaume who has taken her, she must have told him I was coming to Paris, that I am a member of the aristocracy. Whoever has her thinks I'm fabulously wealthy.'

'Which you would have been should you and Lord Divine still be together. That part of their plan has let them down.'

'True. I'm certainly not wealthy now, although I'm not sure *I* ever was. It's Harry who's wealthy, but he is quite, well let's say, 'careful' with money. He would not have given in to this threat.'

'Well, it's one thing he and I agree on. We should never give in to blackmailers.'

'What will you do now?'

'I don't think there's anything we can do tonight. I'll contact Inspecteur Apollinaire first thing. No doubt he'll expect to be involved. He'll know what to do.'

Chapter 19

The following morning Richard went to the Rue de Fabert to speak with Inspecteur Apollinaire and show him the letter that Camille had received the day before.

'Did she see anyone?' asked Apollinaire. 'The person who delivered the letter perhaps?'

'She and her family were sightseeing, Inspecteur. The concierge gave it to her on her return.'

Apollinaire nodded. 'I feel I must take issue with Lady Divine.'

'Oh?' asked Richard, frowning. 'Why would that be?'

'I think you know, Chief Inspector. She interfered in a police investigation.' He shook his head looking cross. 'Surely she knows it is unacceptable to search a premises when she has been expressly told the apartment would be released when the gendarmes and forensics had finished there.'

'Had they finished?'

Apollinaire shrugged. 'Well, yes, Monsieur, but it was still cordoned off. It should have told her something.'

'Yet she found the notebook. She knew it was there somewhere, and your gendarmes did not.'

Apollinaire inhaled deeply, then called to the front desk for one of the gendarmes who arrived in the office within seconds.

'Coffee please, and some of those cakes I brought from Madame Apollinaire's kitchen. They will go stale if I don't eat them.'

'Yes, sir,' the gendarme said smartly, leaving the office.

'And close the door!' Apollinaire called after him. The gendarme returned and closed the door quietly. Apollinaire sat in his chair opposite Richard who had chosen a comfortable bucket chair to sit. His back ached and he knew he had spent too long the previous night thinking about Camille and not attempting to sleep. 'She makes her own rules this lady of yours.'

'Of mine, Monsieur?' Richard said. 'Why do you think she's mine?'

Apollinaire smirked and leant back in his chair, leaning his elbows on the arms and steepling his fingers. 'I had heard that you were on a sabbatical from the British force due to overwork, yet, Monsieur, here you are...working.'

Richard chuckled. 'She's a friend.'

'Just a friend?' Richard shrugged and Apollinaire's eyebrows almost hit his hairline. 'Be careful, Monsieur,' he trilled. 'I hear the British aristocracy are very much like the French were in the 17th and 18th Centuries, and we know from our history books what happened then. I should hate the same thing to happen to you.' He grinned wryly. 'They don't allow commoners into the confines of their society.'

'She's estranged from her husband, Lord Henry Divine. They're divorcing.'

'Yes, I know about that.'

'You do?'

'Of course. I make it my business to find out about the people who are involved in a case. She is involved in this because of her friendship with Honoré Tatou.'

'Not a suspect, surely.'

Apollinaire sniffed a laugh. 'Everyone's a suspect, Monsieur, until the perpetrator is caught. You know that as well as I do.'

'Yes, but...'

'I know about you too, Chief Inspector.'

Richard frowned, then lowered his shoulders and momentarily closed his eyes. He blew out a breath as the young gendarme returned with a tray of coffee and a plate piled high with cake.

'Shut the door!' cried Apollinaire shaking his head with frustration as the gendarme left the office. 'Young people today must have been born in outhouses. They seem to have no respect for doors and for what they're intended.'

Richard nodded. 'Bad news travels fast, Inspecteur.'

Apollinaire passed Richard a cup of coffee and a plate on which sat a cake covered in fondant and sliced through with jam and cream.

'I think you might need this, Richard,' he glanced at him. 'I may call you Richard?'

Richard smiled and nodded. 'And you are...?'

'Nicolas.'

'So. What do you know?'

'Everything, Monsieur. It wasn't difficult to discover who your father is.'

'Was.'

'Ah, I'm sorry.'

Richard lifted the cake from the plate with a tumble of crumbs and bit into it. 'Don't be.'

'You didn't get on?'

Richard sighed. 'Not for a moment.'

Apollinaire nodded observing Richard for a moment. 'Enough of the questions, Richard. There will be time for it when we have solved the two cases...well three if you count the search for Amandine Lachappelle's parents, which is the main reason you're here.'

'Have you heard anything from Felice Marchand?'

'Nothing, but to her credit she agreed to help. The problem we have is if they decide they do not wish for us to know they will close ranks, and Madame Marchand can ask of them as much as she likes but they may not tell her. They have each other's backs, Richard. It is just the way of things.'

'I understand. We must hope there is someone who likes talking behind their hands...or their fans.'

'We need to have a plan for this evening. What did Lady Divine say? I'm sure she does not want to meet the demands of a blackmailer.'

'Actually, I think if she'd had the money she would have paid it, simply to get her friend back in safe hands.'

'She does not have it? But is she not wealthy? Her husband certainly is.'

'Her estranged husband, Nicolas. She has an allowance, a generous one by all accounts but not enough to pay the ransom.'

'Hmm.' Apollinaire thought as he tapped his chin with his fingers. 'I think she must go at the arranged time, but not alone. The blackmailer said no one should go with her, but whoever it is must be naïve to think she wouldn't be watched.'

'Unless they assume she would not go to the police for fear of being controlled. They know that once the police know about a blackmailer they will take over. I'm guessing these people, whoever they are, know she is fond of Madame Tatou and would pay anything to get her back which I'm sure, should she have it, she would.'

'What they don't know about is you, Richard. They don't know that Lady Divine has a friend with her, or that he is a member of the British police. You must tail her. I'm sure you have a good deal of experience. You will have the advantage over them. You do not look like a Chief Inspecteur.' Richard smiled. 'You look like a wealthy man who is in Paris to see our wonderful city, to take in the sights. Dress in a smart fashion, but no suits and ties. A casual approach, I think. You'll fit in very well.'

'And where will you be?'

'Oh, not far behind, Monsieur. In the shadows, amongst the tourists, sitting at the cafés...we'll be there.'

Richard rose to go, still reeling from discovering Inspecteur Apollinaire knew about his past life.

'Is Lady Divine in trouble for crossing the line?'

Apollinaire grinned. 'She is spirited woman, Richard. Personally, I like it. My wife is the same. She runs our home, our children, and me. She is what we need. Without her...life would be difficult. I thank God for her every day. Tell your lady she is not in trouble. This time.'

Richard returned to his hotel room. It was nearly noon but he had no appetite for lunch. He poured a coffee from the coffee pot which had been conveniently left in his room, and lowered himself down into a chair by the window. His back still ached from his recent nights sleeping at the hotel, and he tutted to himself thinking it was probably due to age and his personal concerns other than the rather sumptuous hotel beds.

He watched the street outside, the comings and goings of Parisiennes. Paris had an ambiance about it he enjoyed. There was a sense of joie de vivre, but also a relaxed way about the people there; life was simply for enjoying and any problem would be solved...tomorrow. The many cafés and restaurants were testament to it. They were always full to breaking point and the most popular in the city would often have queues of people waiting outside for a table to become free.

He watched a couple walking on the other side of the street. They had their arms around each other and were laughing, their heads thrown back, the girl's long, dark hair flying in the breeze. How he would have loved to feel so comfortable with Camille, and she with him. Perhaps they would be the same as the couple so obviously in love, to not care she was still officially married to Lord Divine, that Richard had already told her about his former life and she had waved it away as though it would never matter to her, because she loved him.

Camille had said should she ever fall in love with another man she would not worry about her title, that she would ensure she was so in love with him a title would not matter, that not being part of the aristocracy would not concern her. He sipped his coffee and watched the couple until they reached the end of the street and turned the corner. What was it Apollinaire said? He'd said that Camille was spirited, a breaker of rules. Richard wondered if she would not only be prepared to lose her title and everything that went with it, but also accept him, not as Chief Inspector Richard Owen, but Richard Owen, a man with a questionable past.

That afternoon Richard went to Camille's suite. He had seen her and Cecily, Ottilie and Amandine leave the hotel as he had been sitting contemplating how he should proceed to tell Camille that she would have more to consider if they were to make their feelings for each other official; not only the loss of her place in a society in which she was raised, but also her reputation of which she said was all a woman really had. He had remained in his position in front of the window until he saw them return a couple of hours later, laden with carrier bags, gifts no doubt for Knolly, Philips, and some of Ottilie's friends.

They were a happy group, colourful in their dress. He noticed that Camille dressed far more casually than she did when in London. Her usual cloche hat had been eschewed for a straw boater, the ribbon hanging down her back, and her duster coat had been left in her suite. Her bare arms had caught the sun, de rigeur in London because it showed that the owner of those sun-kissed arms had likely travelled to the continent and spent some time there, meaning they were probably wealthy and had some status. It's like a code, Richard thought, the code of the society in which Camille moved and in which she had been raised. He'd pressed his lips together and sighed. Society, he thought. It's all the aristocracy think about.

He knocked on the door of her suite which was opened by Cecily.

'Hello, Chief Inspector Owen. Please come in.' She opened the door wider and Richard went into the main salon where Camille and the girls were unwrapping their purchases.

'Oh, Mama,' squealed Ottilie, 'Knolly will love this.' She held up a straw hat trimmed with faded pink roses and a pink ribbon. 'It'll go with the shawl you bought her for Christmas.'

Camille laughed. 'I'm sure it will, Ottilie, although heaven knows where she'll wear it.'

'She could wear it to church in the spring. She'll look like a flower come into bloom.'

'Mm,' answered Camille as she examined a bag she had purchased in a small boutique on the Champs Elysée. 'What did you get for Phillips?'

'A pair of fancy braces.'

'What!' cried Camille, turning quickly to her daughter. 'Braces?'

'He is rather difficult to buy for. I never know what to buy for a man. It's the same with Papa. And Phillips does wear braces.'

'So he might, but for heaven's sake don't buy Papa braces.' She glanced up and when she saw Richard, smiled. 'Hello, Richard. Do you have any news for us?' He nodded and Camille's smile dropped from her face when she saw his serious expression.

'Girls, why don't you take the gifts into your room. Look, here's the gift wrapping. You can wrap them for when we go back to London. And please, make a decent job of it.' The girls cheerfully put everything back into bags and took them off to their bedroom.

'Would you like me to go with them, Chief Inspector,' asked Cecily, who had been quietly wrapping her own gifts.

'No, Cecily, please stay. It won't hurt for you to hear this.'

Camille and Richard sat in the salon while Cecily made tea for them. She felt nervous. Camille had told her what had been in the letter and she hadn't been surprised. She remembered on one of their other investigations, Chief Inspector Owen had told them over tea at Browns that every crime was usually about love or money. Madame Tatou's abduction had been about money. She didn't for a moment think that it was Guillaume, whoever he was. They needed to find him of course, just to make sure, but even so. No, it was definitely something more sinister. She could feel it in her bones.

She handed the cups of tea to Camille and Richard and sat on the window seat.

'What's this about, Richard?' asked Camille. 'You looked rather serious earlier.'

'Inspecteur Apollinaire has advised me that you should go the Obelisk in the Place de la Concorde with the money the blackmailer has asked for.'

Camille took a sip of tea. 'I thought he would say that.'

'Are you not afraid, Madam?' asked Cecily. 'We don't know who 'e is or what 'e intends. 'E...or she might be carrying a weapon.'

'Lady Divine won't be alone, Cecily.'

Camille nearly choked on her tea. 'I must be alone, Richard, otherwise they will not release Honoré.'

'Inspecteur Apollinaire insists that I should follow you, and they will not be far behind. I am to dress as a tourist. Whoever is behind this will not know we are connected. We will be strangers, Camille. You must not look for me or look behind you. You must act as though you are alone at all times.'

Camille looked startled. 'But what would happen if I did something wrong...make a mistake?'

'You will not do anything wrong, Camille. You will simply take the bag of money to the Obelisk as requested, leave it on the top step then walk away. I and Inspecteur Apollinaire and his men will have already arrived at the Place de la Concorde. He intends to situate his men amongst the visitors and in the cafes. I will simply stroll around the square like any other visitor to Paris, but you must ensure that should you see me in the crowd there must be no recognition, no change of expression or a smile. Nothing.'

'What will happen when I've left?'

'Apollinaire's men and I will wait to see who retrieves it. Then we'll arrest them.'

Camille closed her eyes momentarily and shook her head. This wasn't what she'd planned at all when she'd organised the trip to Paris. It was meant to be relaxing, a trip of culture and fabulous food. It had all turned out very differently.

'This is so very frightening. I know if it goes wrong Honoré will be in even more danger than before. And the money, Richard. Where will it come from?'

'It's not real money, Camille. Apollinaire instructed his men to prepare a bag of cut to size paper and place it in a leather valise. On the top of the paper is an amount of French francs. The valise is good quality so it looks like something you would own and is heavy. It looks the part. I've left it in my room and I'll bring it to you nearer the time. Take a taxicab from the hotel, Camille. I will leave the hotel from the back entrance to ensure if anyone is watching the Hotel Narcisse Blanc they won't see me or connect me with you.'

'What about me, Chief Inspector?' asked Cecily. 'Will you need me for anythin'. I'm not 'appy about Lady Camille going off on 'er own.'

Richard shook his head sadly. 'I'm sorry, Cecily. This is an undertaking for Lady Camille alone. I would advise you to stay put in the hotel and await Lady Camille's return. She will need some care when she returns I'm sure.'

Cecily looked worried but stayed silent. She glanced at Camille, then nodded and sighed.

'As you wish, Chief Inspector.'

Chapter 20

The suite was very quiet when Richard left Camille and Cecily pondering the event that would take place that evening. Neither woman knew what to say. Cecily bit her lip and wrung her hands in her lap. Camille broke the silence.

'You look nervous, Cecily.'

'Yes, Madam, I admit I do feel a bit agitated I must say.'

'Everything will be well.' Camille gazed hard at Cecily.

'But, Madam...'

Camille held up her hand. 'I've been involved in dangerous situations before, haven't I, Cecily?'

'Not like this. This is different this is.'

'In what way?'

'It's....risky. You'll be on your own. Someone might grab you and make off with you, and that will mean both you and Madame Tatou will be missing and we'll be no further forward. Ain't there another way?'

Camille shrugged. 'I don't think there is, no. The blackmailer has requested it is I who goes to the Obelisk and that I go alone. What will happen if he sees someone else drop the bag at the Place de la Concorde? Honoré will be in even more danger and unfortunately I will bear the blame for not being courageous enough to do the deed.'

She rose from the chaise and went over to the console where she opened the cigarette box and took out a cigarette. Lighting it, she took a deep draw and turned to face Cecily, puffing out a plume of smoke. 'Technically I won't be alone. Chief Inspector Owen will be there as will Inspecteur Apollinaire and his men, well-hidden I expect. I rather think they know what they're doing.'

'Do yer?' Cecily mumbled. 'Sometimes I wonder, Madam.'

Camille smiled at Cecily. 'And sometimes we must do things we don't want to do. May I remind you of when you boarded the flight from England to France. If I remember correctly it was something you did not want to do, in fact so worried were you it made you ill.' Cecily looked sheepish. 'And yet you did it because you said, and I quote, 'I always go everywhere with you, Madam,' unquote.' Cecily nodded. 'I am quite determined to do this, Cecily. Saving Honoré from whichever fiend has her is paramount, and I'm looking forward to returning with her here, the Hotel Narcisse Blanc, and into your care. I'm quite sure I shall need it.'

Richard arrived at Camille's suite at one o'clock carrying the valise which contained the fraudulent bank notes on which there was a covering of real francs. He explained that the blackmailer would very likely undo the bag and glimpse inside to make sure the money was there, then make off with it.

'What they'll see is a layer of francs which have been placed neatly on the top of the cut paper notes. What they won't realise is that underneath will be sheets of plain paper, all cut to the size of a franc note.'

'Is this going to work, Richard?' Camille asked him under her breath so Cecily would not hear. 'It seems rather hit and miss.'

'It will work. There will be three thoughts in the blackmailer's mind. The first one will be the hope that you actually deliver the money. The second will be that the bag contains what he wants it to contain. The third will be that he can make a getaway as quickly as possible. He...or she will be on edge as much as we are.'

The taxicab arrived at fifteen minutes past the hour. Camille dressed casually, like a visitor to Paris, her dress a plain cotton shift, her shoes light pumps. She completed the outfit with a straw hat. She knew it was a far simpler outfit than she usually favoured, but she merely wanted to fit in, to be lost in the throng of visitors to the Obelisk. She was just as eager to make a quick getaway as the blackmailer and she looked forward to returning to the hotel with Honoré by her side. The fact the blackmailer did not mention at which fountain Honoré would be left worried her, but she hoped as soon as the valise was in place and she had departed the Obelisk, Honoré would make her presence known.

Inside the taxi Camille's stomach rolled. She had to admit to herself that even though she had realised danger and felt frissons of fear in other investigations she and Cecily had undertaken, she felt most apprehensive about what was expected of her. She knew it was because she was alone; she did not have her faithful maid by her side, the loyal Cecily who was always there to encourage or to make astute observations about the case on which they were working. Camille knew she would not have been brave enough to undertake many of the situations they had undertaken alone. She needed her closest friend beside her. Today was a certain test of her courage.

The Place de la Concorde was as busy as it had been the day before. There were throngs of people admiring the beautiful square and the way the sun sparkled on the Seine. Many stood quietly, staring across the trees, enthralled by the sight of the Eiffel Tower of which the top could be seen from the Place de la Concorde, and in the centre was the great Obelisk with its golden pinnacle.

She left the taxi at the Rue de Rivoli then walked the circular route of the Place de la Concorde, her eyes on the swarming crowd and the top of the Obelisk which glowed gold in the bright sunlight. It was an arresting sight; one from which she could barely take her eyes. As she got closer to the Obelisk she couldn't help but scan the crowd, wondering if she were being watched. She looked towards the fountains aware that if the blackmailer had kept his word Honoré would be standing close to one of them. But which one, she thought.

She made her way through the crowds. Pigeons walked in between groups of people, unfazed, almost tame, hoping for a tasty titbit to be dropped from a paper bag or a child's hand. The bright sunlight blinded her so she took her sunglasses from her bag. The darkened shades blunted the sharpness of the sun's rays and the bright colours worn by the myriad visitors which seemed to blur into one heaving mass. The noise of excited chatter was deafening but Camille felt as though she were moving in a bubble; alone but not alone.

As she got closer to the Obelisk her heart rate increased and her breath came in short, sharp bursts. She felt light-headed so stopped for a moment. She inhaled deep breaths and swallowed hard, wondering where Richard was, and Apollinaire's men who she had been told would be scattered through the crowds at the Place de la Concorde, and sitting at the nearby cafés.

She stepped forward, clutching the valise tightly in her right hand. It was as though she was the only person in the Place de la Concorde. The crowd of visitors seemed to part and she walked towards the steps at the foot of the Obelisk. As she got to the base she couldn't help but look behind her then left and right, but all she could see was people...and more people. No one stood out. She put a foot on the step, leant forward, and left the valise on the step as though laying a wreath, took a step back, then turned and walked towards the fountains where she prayed Honoré was waiting.

She went towards one of the fountains then turned. She saw a boy approach the Obelisk. She saw him step up, open the bag for a brief look inside, then put his hand out to grab the handles of the bag. As he did so a swarm of men ran towards him, including Richard who had appeared like magic from out of the crowd. Camille took in a breath and held it.

The boy glanced up when he saw the approaching men, grabbed the bag and ran. He twisted and turned to avoid the people in the crowd, running towards the Rue de Rivoli where he could avoid them by running across the fast moving road and in between the buildings. He was fast, like a gazelle. Camille's hand flew to her mouth as her breath was caught up in her throat. He was getting away. The men who pursued him were not making any headway, were not gaining on him. Even with the bag of notes this youth assisted him. He was fleet of foot and not so young as Camille first thought.

Suddenly she saw the boy hurtling to one side, floundering on the pavement and looking bemused, not sure why his flight away from the oncoming men had come to a halt. The valise fell to the floor; the notes inside falling onto the pavement were swept along by the light breeze coming off the Seine. Children began to shriek with glee, some amazed when they were fortunate enough to retrieve a franc note.

Camille ran towards where he lay, but before she reached him Richard had him by the scruff of his neck and had hauled him to his feet. Inspecteur Apollinaire came up behind, his face bright red from exerting so much energy which, if his physique was anything to go by, was not a regular occurrence. Other men joined them. One grabbed the youth's arms and held them behind his back while the other pushed a pair of handcuffs on his wrists.

Camille ran as fast as she could to where they stood. She knew they were about to take the youth to the commissariat on the Rue de Fabert, but she needed to speak with him.

'Where is Honoré Tatou?' she asked the youth as she panted from her run. 'Tell me,' she cried. 'Where is Madame Tatou?'

The youth shrugged then shook his head. 'I know no one of that name, Madame,' he answered, his voice strained as though he was in pain. Inspecteur Apollinaire grabbed the youth by the arm and dragged him towards a police vehicle which waited in the Rue de Tivoli.

'What happened?' Camille asked Richard. 'I was so sure he would get away. He was so fast, faster than any of you.'

Richard lifted his chin and Camille turned. Cecily stood on the pavement, her hair dishevelled, her dress torn, and her face sporting a graze where she had hit the pavement. 'Cecily happened,' said Richard.

Camille gasped. 'Cecily! What on earth are you doing here?'

Cecily walked towards them and stood in front of them looking contrite. Her diminutive figure made Camille's heart lurch with affection for her. Camille put an arm around her shoulders and hugged her.

'He was getting away, Madam. I felt I had to do somethin'.'

'Where are the girls? asked Camille.

'With Mrs West, Madam. She's taken them with Rose to the Musée D'Orsay to see Amandine's mother's paintings. She told me her mother has some on the walls there.'

'You're not meant to be here, Cecily,' said Richard, sighing.

'I know, sir, but I was worried. Lady Divine has never done anything like this alone. We always do things together, so I followed. When the taxi left the hotel I ran all the way to the Rue de Tivoli. I don't think I've ever run so far, or so fast, but it was a straighter route than what the taxi could take so I got 'ere first. I saw Madam get out of the taxi and watched 'er as she went towards the Place de la Concorde. I made sure I kept well be'ind 'er, so if someone was watching they wouldn't know I was 'ere for 'er.

'But then I saw a young man running through the crowds like the devil were after 'im...and 'e was carrying the bag what Madam 'ad been carrying, so I knew 'e was the blackmailer. I saw the men running after 'im, but I didn't think they 'ad a cat in ell's chance of catching 'im, so I just sort of threw myself at 'im. I knew I wouldn't catch 'im if I tried to run after 'im. I ain't a bad runner but I ain't that fast. He went down like a stone.' She winced and flexed her shoulders.

'Are you sore, Cecily?' Camille asked her softly.

'I am a bit, Madam. I fell quite 'ard.'

'Well, I think we have a lot to be grateful to you for. Without you the boy would not have been caught. Isn't that right, Chief Inspector Owen?' Camille looked up at Richard, daring him to disagree with her. He tutted, shaking his head then reluctantly nodded.

They walked slowly towards the fountains where Camille prayed Honoré was waiting, but in her heart she knew she would not be there. She felt tears prick her eyelids.

'It would seem they had no intention of releasing Honoré, Richard,' she said, her voice laced with bitterness.

'No. It was a ruse.'

'What will we do? I'm so worried. Do you think he's the blackmailer?'

'Not a chance.'

'Then who?'

'He could be an opportunist, or he's working for the real blackmailers. My guess is the second suggestion. These people are far too smart to carry out their own dirty work.'

'He will be questioned?'

'Extensively. Apollinaire will get it out of him. He seems extremely calm but he has his own way of finding out information. He is an experienced police officer.'

They went back to the Rue de Tivoli and hailed a cab. Cecily had begun to look pale and Camille wanted to get her back to the hotel and run her a warm bath. The swaying of the taxicab lulled Cecily into a sleep and Camille moved her slightly so her head rested on Camille's shoulder.

'Do you think Madame Tatou has been killed, Richard?' Camille asked him, her face etched with sorrow.

Richard paused before answering. 'I assume you want me to be honest with you, Camille?'

'Always. There's no point asking the question if there isn't honesty.'

'Well then let me give you an honest answer. It all depends on who the youth is who took the bag.'

'In what way?'

'He may well have been an opportunist who saw you leave a bag on the steps and wondered if there was anything of any worth inside so he took it; a beggar or a petty thief. There are as many of them here as there are in London.'

'And if he was?'

'Then I would say he was in more trouble than Madame Tatou.'

'And if he is an associate of the blackmailer?'

Richard took a breath. 'Then I think Madame Tatou could be in trouble.'

They were about to leave the Rue de Tivoli when Camille gasped.

'The paintings!'

'Which paintings?' Richard asked, frowning.

'The ones at the Musée D'Orsay, the pictures that Amandine's mother painted. Will they not be signed? She would have signed them surely. All artists do, don't they?'

Richard's expression cleared and he smiled. 'Absolutely. Right, we'll get Cecily settled in your suite and we'll join the others at the Musée D'Orsay.'

They requested the cab driver wait for them outside the Hotel Narcisse Blanc, and once Cecily had bathed and was resting, they left the hotel and got back into the cab.

'The Musée D'Orsay is this side of the Seine,' said Richard, 'near the Rue de Lille. We'll make for there then ask someone to direct us to the art gallery.'

'We might find her real name,' said Camille. 'This could lead us to her, Richard, and if we can locate her she may be able to shed some light on why Amandine has not been searched for, even though she has been missing for more than six months.'

Richard took her hand. 'You see how smart you are? It didn't occur to me that finding her paintings would lead us to the painter and hopefully Amandine's mother.'

'It's seems such a tiny thing doesn't it. That little piece of information which could have got lost in amongst everything else Amandine told me that day in the taxi. It seems so long ago now. I bet Cecily had worked it out. She's very astute.'

Richard raised his eyebrows. 'And very impulsive. She did not know whether the person who picked up the bag would have a weapon.' He shook his head and glanced at Camille. 'I think she would do anything for you, Camille.'

'I rather think she would, Richard, but...I very much feel the same way about her. She and the others in my household. They're special. I want to look after them for as long as they need, just as they have cared for me.' Richard nodded, wishing with all his heart he could be part of Camille's life.

At length they arrived at the Musée D'Orsay. They went to the entrance and spoke with the commissionaire who directed them to the art gallery, hoping they would find Elsie and the girls. They went from room to room, searching each face as they went by, hardly looking at the paintings, until a voice they recognised cut through the other voices in the gallery. It was Elsie.

'Can't make 'ead nor tail of it. It don't even look like a woman do it? How can that be a woman? I like pictures where people 'ave got an 'ead, two arms, and two legs. Can't be doin' with all this stuff.'

Her voice echoed around the gallery and Camille and Richard grinned at each other. 'Do you think that voice might belong to our illustrious Mrs West?' Richard asked Camille.

'If it isn't her, it's her twin. And Heaven forbid there are two of her. Look there they are.'

Elsie and the girls were standing in front of a painting by Degar depicting two addicted absinthe drinkers. The painting showed a shabbily dressed man and a woman sitting on a bench in a drinking den, down at heel and looked dejected, with a glass of absinthe in front of them.

'Look at them two,' cried Elsie. 'They're bloody miserable ain't they? I thought artists painted pretty things.'

'Elsie,' called Camille.

'Mama!' Ottilie cried. 'I thought you were somewhere else today.'

'Yes, but it finished early so Chief Inspector Owen and I thought we would join you.'

'Where's Cecily?'

'She's returned to the hotel. She felt a little under the weather, the heat I think, so she's lying down for a few hours.'

'Oh, that's a shame. She could have seen this with us. Amandine will be so disappointed.'

'We'll come back again. When she's feeling better. I doubt we'll see everything at the Musée D'Orsay in one day. We'll return I promise.'

Ottilie, Amandine, and Rose continued to walk around the paintings, exclaiming about the artists they had learnt about at school and laughing at some of the others. Elsie went across to Camille and Richard and lifted her chin.

'Well. 'Ow did it go?' Camille shook her head. 'Oh, no. You're jokin'. I thought you'd got it all sewn up.'

'So did we. They sent someone else to pick up the bag we think,' said Camille. 'Or...if they didn't, the person who made off with the bag was just a petty thief who saw a bag lying there and decided to take it.'

'Was he arrested?'

'Yes, thanks to Cecily.' Camille proceeded to tell Elsie what had happened.

Elsie gasped. 'She's a plucky little thing that Cecily,' said Elsie in admiration. 'Fancy 'er doin' that for yer. Loves yer don't she? Never known such loyalty from a girl. I 'ope my girls would do the same for me.'

'I'm sure they would, Elsie.' Elsie pulled a face which intimated she wasn't sure. 'Have you seen Amandine's mother's paintings?'

'Not yet. I'm a bit worried about 'em to be honest.'

'Why?'

'They sound a bit...well, let's say...not to my taste if yer get my meaning, not that I've seen anything to my taste. I like nice fings, not miserable old bats and blokes wearing big 'ats and 'uge moustaches. I don't get why that would be interestin' to anyone.'

'Oh!' Camille looked uncertain. 'We need to see them. We want to discover what her signature is.'

'You think it's Lachappelle?'

'We're hoping not.'

'Why? I would 'ave thought it was what you wanted.'

'The name Lachappelle was searched for by the French police in the original investigation and nothing was found, not even an address. It can only mean we were searching for the wrong name.'

'The paintings won't be here though will they,' said Richard. 'This gallery is reserved for the old masters. There must be a new art gallery for 20th Century paintings.'

'I'll ask,' said Elsie before they could stop her. She went across to a commissionaire and tried to speak with him in English but got irritated when he couldn't understand her. She called Rose to her who spoke to the gentleman in fluent French and got the answer immediately.

'It's two galleries away from 'ere,' said Elsie looking annoyed. 'You'd think they'd speak bloody English wouldn't yer? I thought everyone spoke English.'

'Bloody English is spoken in England, Elsie,' whispered Camille. 'It sounds very much as though you'll be happy to leave this particular gallery and go to the 20th Century artists.'

'You're not wrong,' said Elsie as they walked towards the girls. 'Not sure I like this old stuff. Frightens yer 'alf to death.'

They left the gallery and went through each room until they came to the 20th Century artists' gallery where there was a skylight which took up most of the ceiling. It was altogether a much brighter place.

'Oh, this is more like it,' said Elsie. 'Much more my cup a tea.'

Amandine squealed. 'Maman,' she cried. 'Ils sont là. Les peintures de Maman.'

'Oh, look,' cried Camille. 'It's Amandine's mother's paintings.'

They walked swiftly towards them, eschewing the other paintings occupying the walls. Amandine's mother's paintings were beautiful, ethereal, mostly of Amandine as a young child, clutching flowers, a doll, her favourite book. In each one Amandine looked away from the painter, as though her mother had caught her in a moment of contemplation, a secret moment where her thoughts were her own, meant simply for her.

Camille went to Amandine and put an arm around her. 'How beautiful they are, Amandine. You must be so proud of your Maman.'

'Yes, Madame. She is a wonderful painter. I am proud but also very sad. She went away then died. Papa said. He said she died.' Tears filled Amandine's eyes and Camille's heart clenched as she bravely brushed them away. 'I miss her, Madame. I could not talk about her before. I'm so sorry. I should have told you about her. She was so beautiful, so lovely.'

Camille pulled Amandine over to a bench placed in front of the paintings and sat her down. She put both her arms around her to comfort her, resting her cheek on the top of her head. Camille noticed Ottilie glance over and make a little smile, a single tear running down her cheek.

'Where did she go, Amandine?' Camille asked her softly. 'You said she went away. Was there a reason, ma cherie?'

'She and Papa, they argued. One night. We were all in the apartment but not Pierre. Pierre was out. I heard Papa say, 'he will get what is coming to him,' but I don't know who he meant.'

'Not Pierre?'

'No, he and Papa are very close. Pierre looks like Papa.'

'Is he the eldest?'

'Yes.'

'And the others?'

'Red hair, pale skin. A little freckled. They did not like the sun.'

'And you, my darling?'

'My papa's dark looks but my mama's temperament. Everyone said so, even Monsieur President. He said I was the perfect blend of them both.' She made a sob and turned her face towards Camille, soaking the front of Camille's dress with her tears. Elsie looked over and Camille saw her brush away tears. Not so strong, thought Camille. A little girl in distress would break even Elsie's hardened heart.

'What is you Papa's name, Amandine? Would you like to be reconciled with him?'

Amandine glanced up at Camille, biting her lip, her face wet with tears. 'Maman said Papa is not an easy man,' Amandine said in a whisper. 'That he expects perfection, complete loyalty, which is why he and Pierre are so close. Pierre was often rude to Maman. Sometimes I thought he didn't like her. He said hurtful things and always when Papa was not there. I wanted to tell Papa but Maman said no. It would cause too much trouble.' She shook her head frowning, then bit her lip again as though frightened to say what she wanted to say. 'Once...once, he called her a...' she leant towards Camille's ear to whisper into it, 'a whore.'

Camille looked down at Amandine feeling that she was finally putting things in place. This was a story of a family which had been likely pulled apart by infidelity or the threat of it, where the children had taken sides, particularly the eldest boy, Pierre. Camille decided it was Amandine's mother who had found a lover, another life partner perhaps, because Amandine's father was a difficult man, a harsh man, one who wanted things done his way, and her mother could not live her life under his exacting rules.

Camille considered the notion that if Amandine's mother had been a successful painter her father may have resented her success. He saw himself as the head of the family. He worked for the President, perhaps held a position of some status and did not appreciate his wife usurping his position.

'What is your father's name, Amandine?'

'Monsieur Charles Baptiste.'

Camille gasped. 'Monsieur Baptiste is a minister is he not?'

'Oui, Madame. He is a minister...and the President's friend.'

Camille hugged Amandine close to her. 'Shall we look at your Maman's paintings? They are quite lovely and I would like to see them again before we leave.'

Amandine smiled. 'Yes, please, Madame. And thank you for being so kind.'

They joined the others. Richard stood behind Elsie and the girls, his hands in his pockets as he quietly studied the paintings. He glanced up as Camille and Amandine stood next to him. Camille pushed Amandine to the front with Ottilie and Rose, who each took one of her hands in one of theirs and smiled at her.

'Did you discover anything?' Richard asked Camille sotto voce.

'Her father is Charles Baptiste, one of President Doumergue's ministers.'

Richard's eyes widened in surprise. 'Really? An important man it would seem.'

Camille nodded. 'And the signature on the paintings? Was it discernible?'

'Sophie Guillard.'

'So not Lachappelle.' Camille frowned. 'I wonder why Amandine used that name.'

'To protect her, perhaps.'

'Because of who her parents are?'

'I should think it's the most probable reason. With a name like Baptiste, or even Guillard, people would wonder wouldn't they? Both names are famous in their own right. She would be questioned by those who sought to profit from an association with the family; parents of school friends perhaps, or even newspapers or magazines that would not shy away from an article on the beautiful young daughter of a famous Parisienne. With Amandine's family they would be spoilt for choice. Two to choose from.

It would seem they wanted Amandine to lead an ordinary life. It's to be commended I think.'

'I suppose so, but don't you think it has rather backfired somewhat. Because Amandine goes under the name of Lachappelle it has meant we could not discover who her parents are. Any police investigation would fall flat which has been so proved. It's only because we care about Amandine and what happens to her we have persevered.'

'And of course there is another question we should be asking?'

'Which is?'

'Why didn't Monsieur Baptiste and Madame Guillard report her missing?'

Camille nodded. 'I can't believe it's because Madame Guillard did not care about her daughter. Look at the paintings of Amandine. They were painted with absolute love…a study if you like of motherly adoration. And Amandine has only good things to say about her.'

'I agree,' answered Richard, 'but there is a reason for everything and we will need to find out what the reason is if we are to find any success with this case.'

'Will you tell Inspecteur Apollinaire?'

Richard nodded. 'I'll telephone him as soon as we get back to the hotel. Who knows, he may have some information of his own to impart.'

'At least we know where her father is. Legally she should be returned to him immediately.'

'Mm,' said Richard, scratching his chin. 'I'm not sure Apollinaire will sanction it. First we will need to make sure Amandine will be safe by discovering why her brother took her to Calais and left her with Fabrice Ozanne to be taken to England, and also why there has been no search for her.' He took in a breath. 'We've done well, Camille, but we're not there yet. This case is one of the most perplexing I think I've ever been involved with. In London I deal with villains of all stripes; thieves, vagabonds, beggars, even murderers. Their crimes are pretty straight forward, particularly if they're committed in some of the old rookeries. They would give someone up to the police for a penny, but this...this is something else entirely.'

They left the Musée D'Orsay and walked to the Rue de Tivoli before hailing two taxicabs to take them back to the hotel. Richard sat in the front of their cab while Camille, Ottilie, and Amandine sat in the back.

'You have always said that most crimes are committed because of love or money, Richard. Do you think a crime has been committed in this case?'

'When there is a crime one thinks of a perpetrator, the criminal, but the only person who has done something illegal in this case is the brother. He took his sister from her home, telling her they were to go on an adventure which she found exciting. She is a child, of course she went with him, and I'm guessing he knew she would. But he lied to her. One must wonder why he did what he did. There may be a reasonable explanation but I think it will be difficult to find one. He is the only criminal I can see, but until we interview the parents,' Richard shrugged, 'we can't know what the motivation was, or why no one cared enough to report her disappearance.'

Back at the hotel Camille found Cecily sitting by the long window in their suite, nursing a cup of tea. She smiled wanly when she saw them.

'How was the museum, Madam?' she asked in a small voice. 'Was it like in the pictures I've seen?'

'Very much so,' answered Camille with a smile. 'And when we return you shall come with us.' Cecily nodded looking sheepish. Camille sat beside her. 'You're not in trouble, Cecily.'

'I always seem to be in trouble lately,' Cecily answered. 'I got into trouble in Brighton because I did something silly and now I've done something silly again. Chief Inspector Owen is prob'ly fed up with me cos I keep goin' against what he says.'

'But you're not in trouble with me. And Mrs West agrees. She knows how loyal you are. You only did what you did because you care, and Chief Inspector Owen knows it too.'

Cecily looked up at Camille with troubled eyes. 'Does he?'

'I can assure you he does. I rather think he believes you were very brave to do what you did. If the youth had been carrying a weapon you could have been injured, but you put it behind you and did what you had to do and now he is in the custody of the police and no doubt being questioned as we speak. It would not be happening if you hadn't taken such decisive action.'

'Oh.' Cecily looked startled. 'So...you think I'm...decisive, Madam?'

'Indeed I do, and because of it I'd like you to get dressed, if you're not too injured or in pain, and I'll treat you and the girls, Mrs West and Rose to a French afternoon tea. We'll have fancies, pain au chocolat and crème caramel, which I do believe is one of your favourites. Are you well enough to go to the restaurant?'

'Ooh, I definitely am, Madam, and I do so love a crème caramel. I can't even remember the number I've eaten since I've been here.' She almost leapt from the chair and ran to her bedroom where Camille could hear her opening the closet and the small chest of drawers in her room, choosing a dress then disregarding it. She's relieved, thought Camille. Relieved she's not in trouble with Richard and me. She still doesn't trust me enough to know I will always want her by my side in some capacity or other. Even if she were to marry and have her own children I could not think of life without Cecily, or Knolly, and Phillips. It would seem I will have to make it clear to them that their employment...their life, their home with me, is forever.

Elsie and Rose joined them in the hotel restaurant. Camille had ordered a bottle of champagne with which to toast Cecily's bravery and had put Ottilie on her best behaviour not to mention the young waiter who had winked at Cecily.

'I won't, Mama, I promise,' said Ottilie innocently as though butter wouldn't melt in her mouth. 'I shouldn't think she cares about a silly waiter after what she did today. I could never have done such a thing.'

'Without her Inspecteur Apollinaire would not have a suspect in his hands. I would imagine the youth is being questioned as we sit here eating these rather wonderful pastries.'

'D'yer reckon 'e's the blackmailer, Camille?' asked Elsie.

'I don't think so,' answered Camille as she sunk a spoon into a crème caramel. 'He is probably what the criminal fraternity call an associate, or the son of an associate. He looked too young to be anything to be honest. Doing someone's dirty work for them I imagine. Picking up a bag from somewhere surely wouldn't be something a real criminal would do?'

'Oh, I dunno,' said Elsie. 'I know all about associates through. Len 'ad loads of 'em. 'E'd pay 'em ter do the stuff 'e thought was below 'em. 'E said it was worth the money 'e paid 'em so 'e didn't 'ave to risk gettin' caught 'imself. It's 'ow some of these big criminals work.'

'I'm sure it's what happened. I'm eager to find out what the boy says. There is still no sign of Honoré and I'm worried what happened this afternoon has placed her in even greater danger.'

Elsie pulled a breath in between her teeth and shook her head. 'Sorry to say this love, but it pro'bly 'as. These crims, they don't like bein' messed about. It might 'ave been safer to let the boy go.'

'I don't think so,' said Camille after delicately placing her spoon in her mouth. 'The valise was full of paper with only a few bank notes inside. The valise was worth more.'

Elsie pulled a face, her mouth like an upside down crescent before she bit off a large piece of pain au chocolat. 'It's a good fing Cecily did what she did then, cos if they'd seen that, well, I'd say it would 'ave been the noose round Madame Tatou's neck. Money talks yer know.'

Chapter 21

Richard sat patiently in the outer office as he waited for Inspecteur Apollinaire to prepare for the interview with the youth who had tried to run off with the valise Camille had left at the Obelisk. Richard was well aware of how it worked, the questions which would need to be posed to the boy so they would get the answers they were looking for. He had done it himself a thousand times.

He looked at his watch then leant his head back against the chair, trying to relieve the sore muscles in his neck and back before joining Apollinaire in the interview room. Apollinaire had invited him to be part of the interview, an action surprising to Richard, but one for which he was grateful. Honoré Tatou meant a great deal to Camille, and if they could find her it would go a long way to relieving some of Camille's concern for her. What Richard hadn't wanted to say to Camille when she had posed the question about whether Madame Tatou had been killed, was with every day that went by the chances of Honoré Tatou being found and in a safe condition diminished considerably, and she should prepare herself for the worst outcome.

Richard suspected the youth who had taken the valise was in fact connected to the criminals who were holding Madame Tatou and was not an opportunist as Camille had mooted. The youth was probably a small-time criminal in his own right, who was enamoured with the criminals with whom he now associated; like the Heroux and the Bechards, The La Cours and the Vachons who made thousands of francs every year by committing crimes which would not occur to the ordinary man in the street. Yes, it was likely he was a pickpocket, a burglar perhaps, but he had probably been aware that the gangster families in Paris ran hundreds of pickpockets on a daily basis, that they would sniff with derision at a criminal who was trying to make it alone.

Perhaps he had been told if he retrieved the valise and the money successfully he would be initiated into the criminal fraternity in which they held sway, a test to discover if he was worthy of his place with them as an associate. Someone who would be called upon to carry out the work they felt was beneath the family's dignity.

'Chief Inspector?' Apollinaire's voice came from behind the front counter where two gendarmes were sitting filling in paperwork. 'I am ready for the interview, Monsieur.' He frowned when he saw that Richard was not carrying notes. 'Do you not have questions you wish to ask, Richard?'

'I do, Nicolas, but I would prefer to observe initially to see what path the interview takes. You will take the lead of course?'

'I think it best. I am well-known amongst the criminals in Paris. He will know I have a reputation of not giving up until I get what I want.' He grinned at Richard as he walked through the opening in the desk.

'I do not envy him.' Richard chuckled as Apollinaire led him to the interview room.

The youth sat behind a desk with a man who had a file of notes in front of him. The man glanced up as Richard and Apollinaire approached the desk but did not acknowledge them. He was there to do a job just as they were. He wasn't there to make friends. Apollinaire nodded to him and Richard did the same, taking Apollinaire's lead. Apollinaire sat in the chair opposite the youth; Richard in the chair next to him. Inspecteur Apollinaire leant forward and put his forearms on the table, eying the young man as he did so.

'So, young man. I think you have found yourself in some trouble, no?' The youth raised his eyes slowly to look at Apollinaire then lowered them to his hands in his lap.

'Your name?'

'Jacques Noury.'

'How old are you?'

'Sixteen.' Apollinaire nodded but said nothing, simply wrote notes in his file.

'How long have you been a thief?'

The man frowned and leant towards Jacques whispering something to him. Apollinaire took in a breath of annoyance that was heard by everyone in the room.

'Monsieur Tison. You can whisper to your client all you may care to, but he was seen by dozens of witnesses removing a valise from the base of the Obelisk in the Place de la Concorde which had been left there on the instructions of a blackmailer who tried to extort a great deal of money from Lady Camille Divine from London, England.' He turned to Jacques. 'You have heard of her?'

'Why would I have heard of her? I saw a woman leave a bag and I took it. That's it.'

'That is certainly not it, Monsieur,' cried Apollinaire, his voice becoming garrulous. 'You were working for someone else were you not?' Jacques shrugged. 'I will take the shrug as confirmation you were, however if you insist you were working alone you will be charged with blackmail and extortion for which there is a hefty prison sentence. And all for the sake of a valise filled with pieces of paper. A waste of a life don't you think?' Richard sat back in the chair, impressed yet again with Apollinaire who seemed to know exactly the right things to say. Something told him the interview might be rather short.

Jacques turned his head swiftly to look at Monsieur Tison, who flattened his lips then shrugged as if to say, 'They've got you. You may as well submit to them'. Jacques turned back to Apollinaire looking as though he was about to vomit.

'I was asked to do it.'

'By whom?'

Jacques paused looking ill. It was clear he didn't want to tell Apollinaire who had asked him to pick up the valise. 'They'll kill me. They kill people who don't do what they want. I know you know it.'

'I do know it which is why I suggest you tell us the truth and tell us who it was who instructed you to retrieve the valise for them.' Jacques lowered his eyes and swallowed hard. Apollinaire left his seat to stand by the window. 'Would you like coffee, Jacques? And one of Madame Apollinaire's famous cakes?'

'Coffee please. Sir.'

Apollinaire lifted his chin to one of the gendarmes who stood by the door, guarding the room, then returned his gaze to Jacques.

'Look, Jacques. I know more or less where the instruction came from. It would have been one of three, maybe four families who would become involved in something such as this, so really there is not far for me to go. I can question all of them, and I will, if you do not tell me who it was who instructed you. They will walk away, Jacques, of that I promise you. These people,' he shrugged, 'they make sure they're never caught. It is the associates, the underlings if you like, who carry the can. And you will be the one to carry this particular, cruelly hot can, my friend.'

Jacques lifted his gaze as the gendarme brought in a tray of coffee, passing one to Richard, and Nicolas Apollinaire. He placed the tray on the table between Jacques and Monsieur Tison. Richard could see Jacques was wavering. He's scared, he thought. Just sixteen and those evil swine have sent him into this like Daniel into the lion's den.

'I will tell you Inspecteur, but I need to be assured I will not be left alone to be killed by these people. They will find me and send one of their thugs to grab me one dark night and you and your gendarmes will find my body floating in the Seine with its throat cut.'

Apollinaire nodded. 'We will protect you, Jacques. You have my word.'

'What are your thoughts, Richard?' Apollinaire asked as they sat in his office after the interview.

'Do you think he's telling the truth?'

'He gave us one name which we can work on.'

'But he wouldn't give you the other name. Why do you think it was?'

Apollinaire stood and stared out of the window on a view less than attractive, simply the rear of some old buildings and a scrubby courtyard with unattended plants. 'I can only imagine it is because whoever the other person is they perhaps come from a more important family.'

'He's frightened isn't he?'

Apollinaire turned. 'Do you have any idea how many bodies we retrieve every year from the Seine, Richard. You have the Thames in London. You must have the same problem. Criminals know about this, because,' he chuckled, 'they are the ones who dump the bodies in there. And young Monsieur Noury knows it too, which is why he is so frightened.'

Richard shook his head. 'So what now, Nicolas? Where do you go from here?'

'We arrange for Jacques Noury to go to a safehouse for the time being, and I will question the family whose name he gave us.'

'And Madam Tatou?'

Nicolas returned to his seat and rubbed his eyes with his fingers. 'You and I both know that when criminals think they're in danger of being caught they get rid of the evidence. I'm sorry to say it because I know Lady Divine is a friend of yours and she is worried about Honoré Tatou, but there it is. We cannot change what is.'

'At least we know it is not this man Guillaume who sent the letter to Madam Tatou.'

'No, that's right. He is no longer a suspect.' It went quiet for a few seconds. 'I believe you have some news for me regarding Amandine Lachappelle.'

'This gets more complex by the day, Nicolas. Amandine's father is Charles Baptiste, a minister at the Elysée Palace.'

Nicolas Apollinaire raised his eyebrows. 'Really. The girl told you?'

'And her mother is Sophie Guillard, a celebrated artist who exhibits in the Musée D'Orsay's 20th Century gallery.'

'She is celebrated indeed. It would be interesting to find out what has happened to her.'

'We have names now. It will be easier to find the mother with the correct name, but both Lady Divine and I are just as concerned about the why.'

'The why, Richard?'

'Why no one reported her absence.'

A gendarme knocked on the door and poked his head into the office.

'I'm sorry to disturb you, Inspecteur Apollinaire. There is a lady waiting at the desk to see you, a Madame Marchand?'

Apollinaire's expression brightened. 'How timely. Ask her to come into my office, Rauf. I will see her in here.'

The gendarme nodded, then moments later returned with Felice Marchand. 'Madame Marchand, Inspecteur.'

Apollinaire thanked the gendarme then moved a chair from its position against the wall and invited Madame Marchand to sit. He returned to his side of the desk and leant his elbows on the leather top, steepling his fingers.

'Well, Madame, I'm hoping you have some news for us.'

'A little.' She looked uncomfortable. 'Inspecteur, no one knows of the conversation we had at the Elysée Palace. I told no one about what was actually said. If anyone asked me I waved it away saying you had been given incorrect information. I have worked as an under-secretary for many years and although my retirement is not imminent I should like to keep my job until it is.'

Apollinaire nodded. 'Understood.'

'There has been some talk...about one of the ministers.'

'Charles Baptiste?'

Her eyes widened. 'So you know?'

'Only the name, Madam. We know nothing of him, or the position he holds. It matters not. But his daughter is Amandine Lachappelle.'

Felice Marchand nodded. 'Yes, she came to the Elysée Palace often. A sweet girl.'

'She is the child who had been residing in England, taken to Calais by her brother and left on a boat.'

Madame Marchand gasped. 'Surely not?'

'I'm afraid so, Madame. Have you seen any of Charles Baptiste's other children at the Elysée Palace recently? Or his wife?'

'It is what I came to tell you, Inspecteur. Monsieur Baptiste and his wife have apparently not lived together for a year at least. President Doumergue was asking after her some time ago, but it seems Monsieur Baptiste managed to avoid the questions and the matter was dropped. I obtained the information from Charles Baptiste's secretary, Minette, who had been sworn to secrecy by Monsieur Baptiste. She begged me not to implicate her when I told her I should speak to you, that you had been asking questions about his daughter and his wife. I entreated her not to let my conversation with you go any further.'

'There is no reason to implicate her, Madame, but of course she will be questioned if it is necessary. This is something that cannot be avoided if we have cause.'

Felice Marchand sighed. 'I understand, Inspecteur.' She lowered her eyes then glanced up at him. 'There is something else. I did not get this information from Minette, but from another minister, a young man with a talkative nature, who, bearing in mind his position should know better.'

'And what did he have to say?'

'He told me he had seen Sophie Guillard.'

Apollinaire glanced at Richard and nodded. 'How long ago?'

'Just a month or so.'

'And where did he see her?'

Felice Marchand swallowed hard before answering. 'At Le Chabanais, Inspecteur, on the Rue Chabanais in the 2nd Arrondissement. He is apparently a frequent visitor to the establishment. He claims to have seen her there on more than one occasion.'

Richard looked quizzical. 'Le Chabanais? Is it an artists' gallery?'

Felice Marchand coughed delicately and Inspecteur Apollinaire chuckled. 'Some might say so, Richard. It is a brothel, the most celebrated brothel in all of Paris founded by Alexandrine Joannet, also known as Madame Kelly.' Apollinaire frowned. 'You must have heard of her surely, Richard. She was famous the world over at the beginning of the century.'

Richard nodded. 'Yes, I've heard the name, but what was Sophie Guillard doing there?'

Felice Marchand coughed again, wishing fervently that she did not have to say the word in front of two men. 'She is a prostitute, Monsieur.'

'A prostitute? The wife of a government minister?' Richard shook his head. 'It doesn't make sense.'

'Which was exactly my reaction when the young minister told me...I will not give you his name. I went to see Minette and asked her to meet me after work, at a café near the Seine, where we could talk. She was not happy to share what she knew, but when I told her about Amandine she relented.'

'And what does she know, Madame?' asked Apollinaire.

'Charles Baptiste told Minette his wife had had an affair with another artist, that they'd had trysts in his studio. I know of the man, Javier Leon. The Elysée Palace is often the venue for events for the great and good of Paris. The artist is an up and coming young painter whose popularity has increased a thousand-fold since he exhibited at the Musée D'Orsay and he has been invited to the Elysée Palace on more than one occasion. He is young and extremely handsome. Sophie Guillard is much younger than her husband, Monsieur Baptiste.'

'Is there proof?'

'Proof of her working at Le Chabanais, Monsieur?' frowned Madame Marchand, not understanding the question. 'She was seen, Inspecteur. She plies her trade in the Louis XVI room, dressed appropriately in costume...when she is dressed of course.'

'Non, Madame, you misunderstood. I meant is there proof she had an affair with Javier Leon?'

Felice Marchand shrugged. 'That I do not know. Her husband discovered what he said was an affair after having her followed. She spent many hours at Monsieur Leon's studio and Monsieur Baptiste was convinced of the affair. He threw her out of the apartment, which is government owned, so she had no say over the matter. From there I don't know what happened to her, but I think you will agree, a woman will only go to a brothel to work if she has no funds and there is no other employment open to her. She will not have made a living from her art. She is not well-known enough, and she is female. We know that male artists make more, although why that should be one can only guess.'

Richard had listened carefully to what Felice Marchand had told them. Another avenue had opened up for them to investigate, but he felt their first port of call was Charles Baptiste. What he and Inspecteur Apollinaire had heard from Felice Marchand was hearsay after all, and they needed proof and evidence. The only way they would get it was straight from the horse's mouth.

Chapter 22

Richard and Inspecteur Apollinaire sat quietly in the foyer at the Elysée Palace in the same chairs they had occupied previously. Apollinaire had made an appointment for them to interview Charles Baptiste. At first he had been told an appointment that evening was out of the question because it was too short notice, but when he'd mentioned he was an Inspecteur of the Paris police and it was an investigation regarding Amandine's safety one had been swiftly organised. Minette, Baptiste's secretary impressed upon them that finding an appointment so quickly was unusual, and should not be expected in the future. Apollinaire had seen red but kept his counsel, knowing he would achieve more with honey than vinegar.

'Messieurs?'

They both looked up at the same time. In the doorway stood a diminutive woman of an indeterminate age. Her jet-black hair was swept off her face into a tight chignon making her already distinct cheekbones stand out in sharp relief.

She was dressed severely in a black calf-length skirt and crisp white blouse buttoned to the neck, the sleeves of which had been ironed so precisely the creases looked as though they had been sewn. The name, Minette, did not suit her, Richard thought.

'Madame,' said Inspecteur Apollinaire, bowing his head in greeting. 'I am Inspecteur Apollinaire, and,' he gestured towards Richard, 'this is my colleague from England, Chief Inspector Richard Owen.'

Minette nodded, her coiffure not moving. 'Monsieur Baptiste is expecting you. Please, follow me.'

She turned on her heel and went back through the door. Richard followed Apollinaire, and as he did so he glanced towards the commissionaire who raised his eyebrows as if to say, 'I don't envy you.' Richard chuckled to himself, deciding the interview with Monsieur Baptiste would not be an easy one, particularly with what they had to tell him, if indeed he did not already know about Amandine and her whereabouts.

They were shown into a large, beautifully appointed room. There were four long windows at the other end of the room, each dressed with sumptuous fabrics; the curtains were floor length gold velvet, held back by huge gold tassels. On the floor were Turkish carpets of the finest vintage, and the walls were decorated in gold flocked wallcoverings. In front of the window was a huge walnut desk behind which sat Monsieur Baptiste; a broad, heavy featured man with a full head of bushy dark hair flecked with grey. He was not an immediately attractive man and Richard could not help wondering why a young woman such as Sophie Guillard would find him appealing. Baptiste rose from his chair and welcomed them to the Elysée Palace.

'Gentlemen, please, sit down.'

He indicated two gold chairs upholstered in gold fabric placed in front of the desk.

'Now, what is this all about?' He frowned, the expression making his face look even more heavily featured. 'Minette tells me you wish to speak with me about my daughter, Amandine. I cannot imagine what about.' Richard glanced at Apollinaire, deciding to let him take the lead. Richard had no authority in Paris and Monsieur Baptiste would have been in his rights to refuse to answer any questions.

'Monsieur Baptiste,' began Apollinaire. 'We are grateful to you for seeing us at such short notice.' Baptiste bowed his head once in acknowledgement. 'Do you know where your daughter is, sir?'

Baptiste laughed. 'Of course. She resides with her maternal grandmother.'

'She does not, sir.'

Monsieur Baptiste narrowed his eyes as he looked from one to the other of the men sitting in front of him. 'She was placed there because my wife was unable to take care of her. She needed a woman's touch so I sent her to Madame Guillard to be cared for.'

'When was the last time you saw Amandine, Monsieur Baptiste?'

At this question the big man faltered, got up from behind his desk and went across to the drinks cabinet in the corner of the room. He poured a generous glass of wine, offering the bottle to Richard and Apollinaire who refused the offer, then walked across to the window. He sighed.

'It was at our apartment on the Rue de Varennes. I know...I have rather neglected her. It must be,' he pulled a face, 'three or four months perhaps.'

'It is closer to seven months, Monsieur, but I must tell you she has not been at the residence of Madame Guillard.'

Baptiste turned back to them ready to fight his corner. 'But, yes, I sent her there. She has been living there while my wife...my wife followed her own path.'

At this Apollinaire and Richard proceeded to tell Monsieur Baptiste what had happened to Amandine, that his eldest son Pierre had taken her to Calais and put her on a boat set for England.

'She travelled alone?' he cried.

'She was with a man called Fabrice Ozanne.'

Baptiste gasped. 'Fabrice! That reprobate? His father was a minister until he was kicked out for incompetence. Why, why was she with him?'

'We think your son sold her to a gang of criminals. She was intended for a man and his wife who had lost their own daughter, to replace her, if such a thing can be achieved. The wife was French and distraught at the loss of her child. The gang saw an easy way to make some money by selling Amandine on to them.'

Monsieur Baptiste sat heavily in his chair and threw back his glass of wine. 'You say...you say my son, Pierre did this?'

'Yes sir. Amandine told us the full story of how he told her they were to go to England on an adventure. That they would go together and she could sent a carte postal to you and her mother to let you know where they were. He abandoned her on the boat and Fabrice Ozanne took over from there.'

'You should thank him, Monsieur Baptiste,' Richard interjected. 'He saved Amandine from an even worse fate than the one she faced.'

'You mean...'

He slammed his glass down on the table and put his face in his hands.

'This is my fault,' he said, glancing up at Apollinaire and Richard. 'I should have checked her, should have made time for her, but being a minister...there is no time. No time for family, for children, for a normal life. My sons live with my brother on his farm. I thought it best. I didn't want them getting into trouble in Paris where there is so much temptation, but it wasn't right for Amandine. She needed a gentler hand. Madame Guillard is a fine woman,' his voice changed, 'even if her daughter is not.'

'And your wife, Monsieur Baptiste. You are aware of where she is?'

He face turned bright red and he grimaced with anger. 'Living with that damned artist,' he spat, his dark eyebrows coming together in a knot across his eyes. 'He was after her from the moment he set eyes on her…and she him. He couldn't get enough of her. I dreaded the events we had here for our Parisienne artists because I knew he would be included. There was nothing I could do so I had her followed. She went to his studio many times.' He inhaled and shook his head in sorrow. 'I loved her. The life we had was good but she wanted something else, someone else, a man her own age who would give her everything I could not.'

'We don't think she lives with him, Monsieur Baptiste.'

Baptiste startled. 'So where is she?'

This was a question that both Richard and Inspecteur Apollinaire had anticipated. They felt strongly they could not tell Monsieur Baptiste where his wife was, or how she earnt her living until they had questioned Sophie Guillard. They had made a pact before going to the Elysée Palace that they would not tell him until they were sure she was working at Le Chabanais as a prostitute.

'We're not sure, Monsieur, but we are fairly certain she does not live with Monsieur Leon.'

'You know his name then?'

'Of course, Monsieur. We make it our business to know.'

There was a heavy silence. Both Richard and Apollinaire knew Monsieur Baptiste would be suffering a certain amount of shock after everything he'd heard, but the question had to be asked.

'Would you like to see Amandine, Monsieur Baptiste?'

Baptiste looked startled. 'She is in Paris?'

'Yes, Monsieur. She is at the Hotel Narcisse Blanc with the person who has been caring for her since her escape, a temporary guardian, Lady Camille Divine, who is on holiday here from London. She brought Amandine with her. She will have much to tell you.'

Chapter 23

Camille and Amandine sat on the chaise in front of the window of their suite while Cecily paced up and down, wringing her hands together and glancing every so often at Amandine. Camille knew why she was so agitated.

'Cecily,' she said softly. 'My dear.'

'I am happy, Madam, of course I am…but I s'pose I thought we would go back to London as a four rather than a three.' She stopped pacing and sat heavily on a chair; her face etched with sorrow. 'I've tried not to think about it really. I know how hard you and the Chief Inspector have worked to find Amandine's parents, and the French policeman, and I know it's the right thing.' She shook her head. 'But I've got used to things being the way they are in Duke Street.'

'But you can see if we find Amandine's parents she must be reunited with them? It doesn't mean we'll never see her again. She is part of our family now and we will remain in touch with her, I promise.'

Cecily nodded. 'I know, Madam. I know you're right. I'm just bein' selfish.'

Camille's heart melted. 'No, Cecily. I've never known you to be selfish. Never that. You have come to love her…we all have. But she has her own family and I could not rest if we had not done everything we could to find them and to make sure she is safe with them. It is far and away the right thing to do.'

'But what about the boy, Madam? That Pierre?' Amandine looked up when Cecily mentioned her brother's name and Cecily looked sheepish. 'Surely he will be punished for what he did,' she whispered leaning forward to Camille, even though Amandine could not understand what she was saying.

'His father, Monsieur Baptiste is none too pleased with him from what Chief Inspector Owen told me. But you must remember that Amandine's brother is his son. He is just fifteen, perhaps sixteen now, between a boy and a man. It is a challenging time in anyone's life. For all we know there might be a reason why he felt it was necessary to get Amandine away.'

'But he sold her, Madam!' cried Cecily.

Camille scratched her chin, pondering the fact that Amandine's brother had rather coldly left her on a boat to England to be escorted by a man she had never met before. 'Well, yes there is that. I wonder how much it was and where it went.'

'Prob'ly kept it for himself I shouldn't wonder,' replied Cecily. She rose from her chair and began to tidy the room, although it didn't really need it. A knock on the door halted her and she looked up at Camille and took a shaky breath. 'That's 'im I s'pose. I'll get the door.'

Monsieur Baptiste almost filled the doorframe. He stepped quietly into the suite, followed by Richard and Inspecteur Apollinaire. When Amandine saw who it was she fled from the chaise and almost flew into her father's arms.

'Papa,' she cried. 'Papa, is it really you?'

The girl's bedroom door opened and Ottilie stepped into the salon, a smile on her lips, a tear running down her cheek. 'Is it Amandine's father,

Mama?' she asked Camille as she went across to her, wrapping her arms around her. She leant forward and whispered into Camille's ear. 'I don't want her to go.'

Camille nodded sadly. In her heart she knew the family would never be quite the same again. They had become so used to Amandine's girlish giggle, the way she sat at the huge table in the kitchen looking for all the world as though she had never been anywhere else, watching Knolly cook with such delight. Even Phillips had fallen for her. She wondered what Knolly and Phillips would say when they returned to Duke Street without her.

'Yes, Ottilie. This is Monsieur Baptiste, Amandine's father.'

Ottilie frowned. 'But Amandine's name is Lachappelle.'

Charles Baptiste glanced over to Camille and Ottilie, and after untangling himself from his delighted daughter, he made a bow to Camille and smiled warmly at Ottilie.

'Lady Divine,' he said in perfect English. 'I am so happy to meet you.'

Camille inclined her head. 'And I you, Monsieur. We are so pleased we have found you at last.' Camille invited him to sit. 'I rather think Amandine is delighted to have found you too.' They both laughed at the little girl who had grabbed Ottilie and was dancing around the room with her. Ottilie couldn't help but laugh.

'I heard your daughter mention Amandine bears the name of Lachappelle.'

'Well, yes. It has posed some problems for us I must say. I'm sure Chief Inspector Owen has already told you he began an investigation to look for you more than six months ago. We all assumed Amandine's parents would bear the name of Lachappelle, as she does. She seems quite comfortable with it. Not once has she ever mentioned the name Baptiste.'

'Her mother and I thought it would be safer for her to use her paternal grandmother's maiden name, Irene Lachappelle. She is gone now of course. We have many criminals in Paris who would think nothing of kidnapping a young girl and holding her for ransom. Amandine was at a boarding school for a time but Sophie and I were never happy for her safety when she was away from us, so we changed her name to Amandine Lachappelle and enrolled her into a private school near where we lived.'

'The apartment on the Rue de Varennes.'

Baptiste raised his eyebrows. 'Why, yes. We have a government apartment there, but no one lives there now. I go there from time to time to make sure all is well. It is still in my ownership as it were, but the boys are with my brother on a farm in the south, and Amandine was sent to Madame Guillard's.'

'Why did Madame Guillard not inform you Amandine was no longer with her?'

Charles Baptiste suddenly looked uncomfortable. 'Madame, it is a question I must ask my son, Pierre. I understand he went to Sophie's mother to tell her he had permission from Sophie and me to remove Amandine from her care and to return her to us. Of course, it is not what happened. It would seem Pierre took her to Calais to go to England on an "adventure".'

'Did he know Fabrice Ozanne?'

Baptiste nodded. 'They spent some time together at the Elysée Palace. Fabrice's father was a minister until he was kicked out for some behaviour or other that did not fit with the President's view of things. One must be careful when one is in the political world. A clean slate is the best sort of slate to have at the Elysée Palace.'

Camille nodded and glanced at Cecily who had been listening intently, her face darkened with disquiet.

'Cecily, would you mind sending for refreshments for myself, Monsieur Baptiste, Chief Inspector Owen and Inspecteur Apollinaire. Ask the girls if they would like something...and please, my dear, something for yourself.' She glanced at Richard and Apollinaire. 'Do sit, gentlemen. Make yourselves comfortable.'

Cecily bobbed a quick curtsey, 'Yes, Madam,' and left the room.

Camille pulled a stiff smile at Monsieur Baptiste.

'May I ask if this is why you and your wife are no longer living together? Amandine thinks her mother is dead, Monsieur. Why would it be so?' Camille glanced at Richard and he looked uneasy to say the least.

Again, Monsieur Baptiste showed signs of discomfort. 'How must you think of us, Lady Divine? I see you have your own daughter with you, Ottilie is it not? Sophie and I have behaved less than is acceptable over the last year. Many things came to light which neither of us found easy to deal with. There have been mistakes on both sides.'

'But it is your children who have suffered, Monsieur Baptiste.'

At that moment Cecily returned with a maid. They both carried large trays of tea, coffee, and the ubiquitous French pastries. Cecily dismissed the maid which made Camille smile, and poured the coffee or tea to request. The expression on her face said everything, and Camille did not need to ask her what she was thinking.

'I see you are a woman who speaks her mind, Lady Divine. I appreciate it but you are telling me something I already know. Sophie and I have neglected the children in our own way, I because of my political ambitions, and Sophie, I believe, was not satisfied with her life with me and the children. I am under the impression, although of course I cannot be certain, she found another to take my place.'

'Yet without proof I understand you asked her to leave your home. Amandine should not have been sent to her grandmother. Surely, even if your wife was no longer residing in your family home, Amandine should have stayed with her?'

'I could not allow it,' said Baptiste as he sipped his coffee. 'Her affair means she is a woman of questionable morals. How could I allow Amandine to live with her?'

Camille felt anger rising in her chest. Was this not a similar situation to the one she had experienced with Harry? He had taken the lead and made the rules, even though he had been the one who had wronged her by having an affair, and both Ottilie and Camille had suffered because of it. She knew she must not allow her own experience to colour her judgement, but here she was again, with a man who insisted his own beliefs should not be questioned.

'Monsieur,' Camille said as politely as she could. 'Amandine should be with her mother, not with a woman who I'm sure had Amandine's best interests at heart, but who was easily duped by your son. If we had not found Amandine she would be living with the couple who had bought her.' Baptiste coughed, almost spilling his coffee. 'I'm quite sure Chief Inspector Owen and Inspecteur Apollinaire have not had time this evening to avail you of everything that happened to Amandine, but I can assure you it is quite shocking.' Camille's voice got higher and firmer the closer she got to the end of her sentence.

She stood and helped herself to more coffee as Cecily stood by as still and cold as a statue. Camille continued.

'May I suggest, Monsieur, that Amandine remains with me until the end of my stay in Paris.' Cecily smiled. 'It will give everyone time to decide as to what will happen next. Unfortunately, I don't know for certain when I will be returning to London, but you have my word Amandine will be at the forefront of our thoughts and intentions.' Unlike your own, she thought. 'I believe Chief Inspector Owen intends to search for your wife. I have found myself in a... let us say, similar...situation, Monsieur Baptiste. The child must come first regardless of our position.' She sat on the chaise again with a determined expression on her face and Cecily was relieved and certain that Camille would argue her case vociferously.

Charles Baptiste glanced at Richard and Inspecteur Apollinaire. Richard nodded to confirm what Camille had told him was correct, and Apollinaire simply shrugged as if to say, 'There's little point in arguing with someone like Lady Divine'.'

Baptiste put his cup down on the saucer and returned them to the tray. 'As you wish, Madame. But if by the end of your stay in Paris Sophie has not been found, I expect Amandine to be brought to the Elysée Palace. Clearly you and your family have an affection for my daughter. I wish to thank you for it.'

Camille made a short nod and Baptiste stood to leave. He called to Amandine, using the term of affection, which was probably what her family called her, Camille thought: Amie. Amandine ran towards him and put her arms around his waist.

'Papa? Are you leaving?'

He bent towards her and kissed the top of her head. 'I must go back to the Elysée Palace, Amie, but you will stay with Lady Divine until your Maman has been found.'

'But...Papa, you said she was dead.'

'I said she was dead to me, Amandine, because I was angry with her. I'm sorry. I should have been clearer. She is not dead to you. She is still your mother.'

'Will we all live together as before?' she asked him pleadingly, her eyes bright with hope.

'We will see, ma cherie. We must hope the Chief Inspector from London finds her and then we will see.'

Baptiste left the suite as Amandine ran to the window to watch him climb into his car. When she turned back to them tears rolled down her cheeks.

'I want my Maman,' she said quietly. 'So much. I've missed her.'

Camille felt tears pushing at her eyelids. It was the first time Amandine had ever said it. She went over to the window and put her arms around the little girl.

'Of course you do,' she said softly to Amandine. Chief Inspector Owen and I will do everything we can to find her and then you will be reunited.'

'Will it be soon do you think?' Amandine asked, desperation in her eyes. 'And what about Pierre? Is he in a great deal of trouble?'

'I think we must allow your father to speak with Pierre to discover what his intentions were. In the meantime you will stay with me, Ottilie, and Cecily. We are a family, and we remain so until your own family are together again.'

Camille looked up at Ottilie and lifted her chin, encouraging her to take Amandine into the bedroom.

'It's late, and you should be in bed. Ottilie will take you. Don't worry, Amandine. All will be well. We'll do our best to return you to your family once more.'

When Ottilie and Amandine were in bed Cecily sent out for some hot milk for them, then went to her own bedroom to rest. She was certain

Chief Inspector Owen and Inspecteur Apollinaire would want to discuss with Camille what had happened that evening. As she sat by the window with a book a small smile twitched on her lips. Amandine was still with them as part of their family, and Cecily was sure Camille would not let her go back to the family who had not served her well until she was certain Amandine was safe and would be well-cared for should she return to Monsieur Baptiste and Madame Guillard. Perhaps I can hope, she thought, that Amandine will always be in our lives somehow, even if Camille and Chief Inspector Owen agree to her returning to her family. We are still close and we all still love her. It can never be taken away.

'Well?' said Camille to Richard and Apollinaire. 'What do you make of it?'

Apollinaire spoke up first. 'I think my work is done here, Lady Divine. We have found Amandine Lachappelle's father. She has a parent she will go to when the time is right. I have another pressing investigation which I am sure you will wish me to continue.'

Camille nodded. 'Of course, Monsieur.' She sighed. 'With each passing day I lose hope. What will happen now, Inspecteur Apollinaire?'

'Tonight we will call on the family Jacques Noury has been working for.'

'Tonight?'

'Of course. We must move quickly now we have the information. My gendarmes are already situated at the address, unseen of course, but I assure you they are there. They await my instruction to move in. It will happen before midnight.'

Camille wrung her hands and sat heavily on the chaise. 'Will you keep us informed please, Inspecteur.' She blanched. 'Whatever the outcome.'

'Of course, Madame. I wish you both good evening.'

He left the suite after bowing to both Camille and Richard who had sat quietly listening to all that was said. He took a silver case out of his jacket pocket and pulled out a cigarette, offering one to Camille who refused.

'We know where Sophie Guillard is, Camille.'

Camille looked astonished. 'You do? Why did you not say?' she asked frowning. 'We could have reunited Amandine with her mother.'

'You may not wish them to be reunited when I tell you where we believe her to be.'

'Which is where?'

Richard rose from the chair and went across to the chaise so he could speak with Camille without fear of being overheard by Ottilie, and particularly Amandine.

'At Le Chabanais,' he said sotto voce.

Camille gasped. 'The brothel?'

'The very same.'

'But why?'

Richard shrugged. 'Who knows. Presumably, she needed an income. Paintings don't sell well on a regular basis, particularly if the painter is a woman. She needed somewhere to live and something to live on. Presumably at Le Chabanais she has both.'

'You know the King's father, Edward VII, was a regular there. He had his own room and a chair made especially for him.'

'A chair?' grinned Richard.

'A special chair,' said Camille laughing. 'And even Marlene Dietrich went there.'

'What was she doing there?'

Camille raised her eyebrows. 'Heaven knows.'

'So, you see, we could not mention it to Charles Baptiste until we were certain. It would ruin Amandine's chances of being with her mother, or for her mother and father to reunite. We need to be utterly certain before we give away that kind of information.'

'A reputation could be ruined.'

'Exactly.'

'But if she were not a courtesan what would she be?'

Richard shook his head and cleared his throat. 'As I'm not familiar with places like Le Chabanais it's a puzzling question for me to answer, but I suppose they have chaperones, minders for the girls, attendants. Just because the minister Felice Marchand told us of saw Sophie Guillard there, it does not mean she's a working girl.'

'Felice Marchand? The under-secretary from the Elysée Palace?' Richard nodded. 'She helped you then?'

'As much as she dared, I'd say.'

Camille looked thoughtful. 'Shall we go to the bar in the hotel? I'm feeling rather claustrophobic in the suite this evening.'

'Of course. A liqueur de café would go down nicely.'

Camille knocked on Cecily's door to let her know she would be going out for an hour or so.

'Come in, Madam,' Cecily said as she answered Camille's knock.

'Are you alright, Cecily? It's been quite a day.'

'It has, Madam, but I just wanted to thank you.'

Camille smiled. 'Thank me. Whatever for?'

'For not letting Amandine go to her father until you've found her Ma. I don't think it would be right. 'E's already neglected 'er, and didn't even know she was missing which means he'd 'ardly thought about 'er. You've been more of a parent than either of her real parents 'ave.'

Camille shut the door behind her and went into the bedroom, sitting on the bed.

'You know she must stay in Paris, Cecily.'

'Yes, Madam, I know. I've got it settled in my mind she prob'ly won't come back to England with us…but I needed to know she'd be safe and what 'appened to 'er before won't be allowed to 'appen again.'

'I can assure you she will be safe. She won't be released from our care until we have reassurances. I've already decided to charge Inspecteur Apollinaire to make a check on her from time to time, but I want to wait until he's found Madame Tatou. Before we go home I'll have a meeting with him to ensure it's what will happen.'

Cecily smiled. 'I knew you would, Madam,' she whispered. 'I know you care about Amandine as much as I do.'

'I think we all do,' said Camille, smiling. 'Ottilie, Knolly, and Phillips love her. And Chief Inspector Owen cares for her too. How could we not?'

'I knew you thought the same as me, Madam. 'It's why we work so well together.'

Chapter 24

Inspecteur Apollinaire left the Hotel Narcisse Blanc with a feeling of satisfaction. Some cases he undertook were like that; the pieces would fit together like a puzzle just waiting to be created. In truth he had done very little, but he knew if Chief Inspector Owen and Lady Divine were to achieve the reuniting of a family they had some work to do. If Sophie Guillard was indeed working as a prostitute Monsieur Baptiste would be duty bound to reject her. The same went for if she were having an affair. Her husband could not be seen to condone such behaviour. He was a politician and his behaviour and that of his family must be seen to be exemplary, even if behind closed doors the situation was very different.

The newspapers had already had a field day with the murder of Janine Heroux and the abduction of Honoré Tatou. He had expected Janine's murder to be big news, but how they had discovered Madame Tatou's disappearance Apollinaire had no idea. He was sure it must have begun with a loose-lipped gendarme who had just happened to mention to someone a woman had been kidnapped and her close friend, Lady Camille Divine had been known to be visiting her at the same time. The newspapers of course had put their own spin on it, as they always did, marking him out as the incompetent Inspecteur who had yet to find a suspect, never mind arresting anyone for the murder or the apparent abduction.

Thankfully, the newspapers hadn't got hold of the blackmail story. After Madame Tatou's disappearance had been reported upon, Apollinaire had called his staff into his office to remind them anything they were called to do in terms of cases and investigations were classified and on no account should anyone on his staff, from gendarmes to office staff, talk about investigations to anyone, not even family members. He couldn't help noticing some of the staff looked sheepish. He was aware of who the gossipers were on his team, and some of them in particular turned puce, particularly when he told them what the reprimand would be.

He hailed a cab from the Boulevard de la Tour which took him to the Avenue Rapp, a famous, tree-lined street, with celebrated buildings which drew visitors to Paris in their droves, simply because of the fascinating buildings and apartments. The controversial French architect, Jules Lavirotte had designed a short span of the street with the most sumptuous residences. Apollinaire was headed for one of those buildings where he knew the family of Lucas Vachon owned an apartment.

As he drew into the avenue he spotted his men. Some were simply sitting at cafés, some loitering on the corner of the avenue, smoking and reading newspapers. Others were more strategically placed by the fire escape on the back of the building, for example, or with clipboards at the front of the building, pretending to be Arrondissement staff inspecting the trees that lined the avenue. He knew them all. Apollinaire smiled to himself. Should Lucas Vachon attempt to escape he would need the skills of Houdini.

Chapter 25

Camille and Richard met for breakfast in the hotel restaurant while Elsie, Cecily and the girls had agreed to go to the Champs Elysée to do some shopping. The excitement in the suite was palpable.

'I can't wait,' Ottilie squealed as she and Amandine got ready. 'It's just such a shame Mama won't be coming with us. She loves to shop.'

'Why can she not come?' asked Amandine. 'There is nothing more important than shopping, no?'

Ottilie laughed. 'You're quite right, but when Mama and Chief Inspector Owen have breakfast together it's usually because they're discussing something important.'

'Your Maman. She is a clever woman. My Maman never spoke to my Papa in the way yours did. And he did not get cross.' She raised her eyebrows. 'Which is unusual.'

Ottilie sat on the bed which was covered in the clothes she had tried on and discarded simply because she wanted to look as fashionable as the Parisienne girls who would be also shopping on the Champs Elysée. She'd been told by her friends at school the Champs Elysée was never quiet, never still, always bright and colourful, and they would probably need to queue to eat at one of the cafés or restaurants. As it was she had still not decided what to wear.

'Was he very strict? Your Papa I mean.'

Amandine nodded. 'Oh, yes, he is fierce. It is what my Maman always said about him, that Papa was like a tiger. She said it was because he was trying to protect our good name.' Amandine shrugged. 'I don't know what it means. He wasn't so harsh with Pierre. I think it was because he was the eldest son. Maman said Papa had high hopes of him following him into the Elysée Palace to work with President Doumergue.'

Ottilie inclined her head and looked thoughtful. 'I think it means he is trying to protect your family's reputation. Mama often talks about reputation. She says it is important in society, 'that one's reputation is fragile and should remain squeaky clean'. Why I really don't know.' She shrugged and when she saw the clothes she'd left on the bed, winced at what she thought Cecily would say when she saw them. Does Pierre want to work at the Elysée Palace?'

'He does not.' Amandine shook her head. 'But I would love to. Pierre wants to be a painter like Maman, but he dare not tell Papa. Papa says artists are idlers who do not wish to do an honest days' work. It's what he says. He has no time for them. None at all. Even Maman's painting,' she pulled a face, 'he has no time for them. And he does not like the artists who go to the Elysée Palace for events the President holds for them. Papa says the events should be for people who deserve it, not for people who give nothing to the country but daubs of paint.'

'What does your Mama say? She is an artist after all.'

Amandine touched the side of her nose. 'She says nothing. When I've asked her she says, 'I know better than to cross your father'.'

Ottilie looked astonished. 'Oh, dear.'

'Is your Papa fierce like mine?'

Ottilie wrinkled her nose. She wanted to be loyal to her father but she knew, as young as she was, he was a selfish person who expected his word to be the last. His behaviour towards Camille had astonished her and she had often cried into her pillow because all she wanted was for things to go back to the way they had been. She had learnt it would not happen now. 'I wouldn't say fierce, but he is rather bossy. He's a Lord you see, and Lords help to make the laws in our country. Mama says because he makes the laws of the country he expects to make the laws at Kenilworth House. It's the house where he lives. I live there too sometimes, but I'd much rather live at Duke Street with Mama, Cecily, Knolly, and Phillips...and you of course.'

Amandine sat on the stool in front of the dressing table.

'I have loved living with you and Lady Divine. And Cecily and Knolly and Phillips. They are all so kind to me, so caring.'

'Was your grandmother not caring?'

'Yes, but she is old. I was sent to bed at six o'clock in the evening because she said it's when she had to be in bed when she was ten, but it was many years ago. I tried to explain to her things had changed since then but she would not listen.

' I could hear the other children playing outside in the courtyard with their hoops and skipping ropes and it would make me cry. Some of them were allowed to go to the cafés nearby and buy pastries. I would have loved to go with them but she refused. I love Grand'Mere but she treated me like a baby. When Pierre came for me and said we were going on an adventure I nearly exploded with excitement, thinking I would only be away from Grand'Mere for maybe two nights, but...' she looked down, 'it wasn't like he said it would be.'

Ottilie looked sympathetic, dreading the thought anything so terrible should happen to her.

'Was it very awful?'

Amandine nodded looking sad. 'Yes, it was. Like a nightmare. When I saw Pierre on the side of the port where all the people were I thought I was seeing things, that the boy I saw walking away from the boat was just someone who looked like him. It felt like a dream. I had thought he was on the boat with me, that we were going together. And then the man came and told me I would be alright, that I was going to England and I would have a lovely time.'

'Who was the man? Was he a friend of yours?'

'No. I didn't know him, but he said his name was Fabrice Ozanne and he knew my brother, Pierre. He said we were to go to England to meet some nice people. Oh, Ottilie, I did not want to go, not without Pierre.'

'And then what happened?'

'After the boat we got onto a coach which took us to Brighton. We went to a dirty house in the town, a hairdressers. Fabrice had an argument with the lady there. I don't know what about. She gave him a key and told him to take me to a house on the beach. It is where your Maman and Cecily found me.'

'With Fabrice?'

'Yes, but someone killed him.' Ottilie gasped, her hand flying to her mouth in horror. 'I didn't know what to do. I went into the room and Fabrice was lying on the floor...with blood.' She shook her head as though shaking the images out from behind her eyes. 'It was horrible. I picked up a knife that was on the floor, then your Maman and Cecily came into the house.'

'It must have been very frightening.'

'Yes.' Amandine nodded. 'I'm so glad it was your Maman and Cecily who found me. I don't know what would have happened if they hadn't.'

It went quiet until Ottilie went across to the dressing table and sat next to Amandine, putting her arms around her.

'You don't need to worry anymore,' Ottilie said quietly. 'You're almost my little sister and I'll make sure you're alright. Mama and Chief Inspector Owen have found your Papa and they will find your mother too. Mama always does what she says she's going to do. She always keeps her promises.'

'Does she?'

Ottilie nodded sombrely. 'Always.'

Camille and Richard sat at a table for two, a pot of delicious hot coffee between them, and honeyed pastries and pain au chocolat on a cake stand begging to be eaten.

'Gosh, they're so tempting,' sighed Camille, 'but I should really cut down.'

'I don't think you've got anything to worry about,' said Richard as he bit into one of the pastries. 'One won't do any damage.'

'Do I have your word on that, Chief Inspector Owen?' Camille said with a sparkle in her eye. 'I shall blame you if my waist expands even half an inch.'

'You have my word,' he said, bowing his head.

Camille lifted a pain au chocolat from the stand with a pair of silver tongs and put it on her plate in front of her. 'This is the last one,' she said. 'No more for me after this one.'

'Do I have your word on that, Lady Divine?' Richard said grinning. Camille didn't answer him but simply bit into the pastry allowing the crumbs of flaky pastry to fall gently to her plate.

'I thought ladies were meant to cut cakes up and eat little bits at a time.'

'I'm in Paris, Richard. Things are much different here.'

He raised his eyebrows. 'So it would seem.' He brushed his mouth with a napkin and sat back in his chair. 'So, Lady Divine. What do we do now?'

Camille took a sip of coffee placing her cup back on the saucer with a soft chink. 'About Sophie Guillard?'

'Indeed.'

'I almost want her to remain lost,' said Camille, 'because if we find her at Le Chabanais and she's doing what we think she's doing,' she glanced at Richard, 'which isn't a given, 'he bowed his head in agreement, 'we must tell Charles Baptiste.'

'Which means he will not allow Sophie Guillard within a mile of Amandine.'

'Exactly. Amandine should be with her mother, not her grandmother, and certainly not her father.'

'You think not?'

Camille frowned. 'The grandmother is quite elderly from what he told me. Amandine is so young and she's coming into womanhood. She needs a mother for that time of her life. And what I think about Charles Baptiste is that he is a garrulous man with exacting standards which are too high for most, and puts his political career ahead of his family.'

'Many men do it.'

'It doesn't make it right, Richard. The poor girl. Can you imagine what all this has done to her. She has no stability. She cannot rely on anyone to do the right thing for her.'

'Except you,' said Richard.

Camille made a moue of annoyance.

'She's a child and I have treated her as I treat Ottilie. Ottilie comes first in everything. It's a pity Amandine's parents didn't do the same. Her father was quick to leave Amandine with me until it's convenient for him to have her. I have a feeling it will never be convenient which begs the question, what will happen to Amandine if he rules her mother is unsuitable. Being responsible for a child will interfere with his political ambitions.'

Richard shrugged. 'We don't know anything about Sophie Guillard except hearsay. I think we should speak to her first before we judge her.'

Camille nodded and took another sip of the fabulous coffee they served at the hotel, relishing its deep flavour and aftertaste. 'This is so good,' she said, sighing. She drained her cup and looked at Richard. 'I agree with you. I would like to speak to her.'

'You know there is only one way we're going to do it, don't you?'

Camille stared at him, then closed her eyes and sighed. 'Oh, Richard, no, please. She won't do it.'

'She cares for Amandine, doesn't she?'

'Yes, but, she doesn't see herself like that anymore. She calls herself a businesswoman, and with respect, if one can be respectful about such a place, isn't Le Chabanais a rather high-end establishment. Its clients include royalty, and the most popular entertainers from the stage and screen. Elsie isn't...like that, and what on earth would she say?' Camille sat back in her chair, almost a look of relief etched across her face. 'Elsie doesn't speak French. She couldn't go there. And for what reason would she go?'

'To ask for a job.'

Camille covered her mouth with her napkin to stifle a laugh. 'She's a bit old wouldn't you say? She's the same age as me and I think that's getting on a bit for a working girl.'

'But she's still attractive, Camille. I'm sure she would have a certain allure for some men.'

'You?'

'No, of course not.' He tutted, frowning, and shook his head. 'But she has a look about her. She knows how the business works. With more cosmetics and the right clothes I think she could do it. An English girl at Le Chabanais would cause quite a stir don't you think? She could play a part. A naughty, but well-connected member of the aristocracy.'

'Who doesn't speak French? Most of the ladies of aristocracy do, bearing in mind the majority of them were educated at the Sorbonne. She'll stand out like a sore thumb.'

Richard wasn't listening. 'And may I suggest you go with her...as a sort of....manager.'

'What!' cried Camille, rather too loudly which drew questioning glances from the other guests. She drew in a breath and stared at Richard with astonishment. 'You want me to be her Madam?' she hissed.

'No, not a Madam, a manager. Someone who oversees her interests.' He glanced at Camille, raising his eyebrows as if to say, 'Well. Will you do it?"

Camille threw her napkin onto the breakfast table, leant back in her chair and folded her arms. She blew out a breath of frustration.

'Oh...I suppose it's the only way if it means there's a chance Amandine can be with her mother. To be honest I didn't really have a plan for how we would get into Le Chabanais to speak with her, and I know we must. We really need her side of the story. We've only heard Charles Baptiste's part and he seems to be a difficult man who wouldn't listen if his young wife were trying to explain something to him. I already feel sorry for Sophie Guillard.'

'Until we speak with her we won't know how to proceed, Camille. It's important. This case, and it is a case even though we are emotionally involved, needs to be wrapped up.'

'And Honoré Tatou? What about her?'

'I would trust Inspecteur Apollinaire.'

'Do you?'

'Yes. He's extremely efficient.'

'Have you heard anything about what happened last night?'

'Not yet, but I'll telephone the station as soon as I go back to my room. He has information he did not impart to me. Of course he doesn't have to tell me anything. I am a Chief Inspector but out of my jurisdiction. I have no authority here.'

'She is my friend, Richard,' Camille said softly. 'I feel responsible for her. She's elderly and vulnerable and...I feel as though I'm letting her down.'

'You're not letting her down. What can you physically do?'

'Find her.'

'And how do you propose to do it?'

'We, Cecily and I, when we went to her apartment found some Bach remedies. Do you know what they are?' Richard shook his head. 'No, I've not heard of it.'

'They were discovered by a Dr Bach, who believes the natural world can heal. He distils plants into remedies. It is a new science, and Honoré had some in her closet cabinet. Yesterday, when the girls were taking a nap and Cecily was reading, I went to an apothecary at the corner of the Boulevard de la Tour and asked the gentleman there if he had heard of them. He had. I asked him what the particular remedies Honoré had were for.'

Camille proceeded to take three little brown bottles from a small satchel hung over the back of her chair, placing them on the table in front of Richard. 'These are the bottles we found, Rock Rose, Scleranthus and Mimulus.'

'And what are they for?'

'Mimulus is for fear of known things.' Richard frowned as Camille brought the bottle to the front. Richard unscrewed the top and smelt it, pulling a face. 'The apothecary said it's taken when the reason for the fear or anxiety is known. So, there was something in Honoré's life she was worried about. And this is Scleranthus. It's for the inability to choose between two alternatives.' Camille threw up her hands. 'What ever could it mean?' She pulled the last bottle forward. 'This is Rock Rose.'

'What's this for?' asked Richard, sniffing at the bottle.

'Terror and fright.'

He stared at her. 'Oh, dear.'

'There was something in Honoré's life that was frightening her, Richard. It breaks my heart to think a woman of her age was so frightened she felt it necessary to find something to help her deal with whatever it is.'

'Do you think they work?'

Camille shrugged. 'Who knows, but perhaps she felt they did, and if it is the case then they can only be a help to her.'

Richard nodded and lit a cigarette. He instinctively felt there was more to Honoré Tatou's disappearance than was immediately apparent. An attempt to extort money from Camille was one thing, but it seemed as though something else was going on, or at least had been before Madame Tatou had been abducted.

'I'll speak with Inspecteur Apollinaire about this, and also find out what happened last night.' He grinned at Camille. 'Perhaps you could have a chat with Mrs West, Camille.'

Camille rolled her eyes. 'I suppose I must, but I'm telling you now, she won't like it.'

Chapter 26

What!' Elsie cried when Camille explained to her what was required of her. Elsie was tired and dusty after a full days shopping at the Champs Elysée, and Rose was out of sorts due to eating too many sweet things.

'As if I 'aven't 'ad enough of a day without you springing that on me, Camille. You know I don't do that anymore. I'm a businesswoman, not a whore.'

Camille had gone up to Elsie's suite under the auspices of a visit and a female chat, only to find Elsie laying on the bed with a damp flannel covering her eyes.

'Are you ill, Elsie,' asked Camille, concerned at her friend's condition. She had never seen Elsie quite so done in before.

'Nah, I'm not ill, Camille, just bloody worn out. Them girls,' she sat up allowing the flannel to fall on the floor. 'Where do they get their energy. We went into every shop, and I mean every shop on the Shamps a Wotsit. Most of the shops didn't 'ave what they was lookin' for anyway, but no, that didn't matter, they 'ad to go inside. I'm sure Cecily's as done in as I am.'

'She did look a little tired I must admit.'

'And me feet. They've swollen to double the size of what they was. Look.'

Elsie slid her feet out from underneath her and showed them to Camille who winced. 'Yes, they do look rather sore.'

Elsie stared at her. 'They ain't 'rather' sore, Camille. They're bloody sore. I'm gonna 'ave to soak 'em in the sink again. And then I've got Rose to deal wiv. Oh, she's in a right mood she is. Jus' cos I wouldn't buy her this coat she wanted. My God, it was a year's takin's, Camille. Bloody ridiculous.'

Camille sat on a chair and crossed her legs, allowing Elsie to rant and rave about how awful things had been that day.

'So, did you have a good time?' she asked Elsie.

'Oh, yes, we 'ad a wonderful time. I loved being with the girls and Cecily. She's a sweet'eart ain't she?'

'She is.'

'And what about you? What 'ave you and his nibs been up to?'

Camille rolled her eyes. 'We didn't spend the day together, Elsie. Chief Inspector Owen went to the commissariat on the Rue de Fabert to speak with Inspecteur Apollinaire about Honoré.'

'And?'

Camille looked distraught. 'I haven't heard anything.'

'You will, ducky. 'Is nibs won't let yer down.'

'Actually Elsie there's something I need to speak with you about.'

'Yeah, I thought so. You've got that look on yer face.'

'What look?' asked Camille, frowning.

'The look that tells me yer want me to do somethin' for yer. Your face speaks volumes Camille. You don't 'ave to say anythin'. Your face 'as got a mind of its own.'

'It's important, Elsie.

'So's my feet. Come into the closet while I put me plates of meat in the sink. You can tell me in there.'

Camille followed Elsie into the bathroom and watched with astonishment as she filled the washbasin with water, lifted her skirts then her leg, and sank her toes into the warmth.

'Ooh, that's lovely that is. I've wanted to do this all day.' She glanced at Camille. 'Alright then, Camille, spill the beans.'

'Chief Inspector Owen, and I, think it would be a good idea to go to Le Chabanais to speak with Sophie Guillard who seems to be working there.'

'Elsie frowned. 'Right. So why don't yer go then.'

'You know what it is?'

'Course I do.'

'The Chief Inspector and I can't go because...well...we have no familiarity with establishments like Le Chabanais.'

'Right. This Le Chabanais, it's only a whorehouse ain't it?'

'Yes.'

'Am I right in thinkin' you want me to go there?'

'Yes.'

'I don't know if you've forgotten, Camille, but I don't speak the lingo.'

'No, but I do.'

Elsie shook her head, frowning. 'Sorry, Camille, you've lost me.'

The Chief Inspector thinks you should go there as a member of the British aristocracy looking for a job. I would accompany you as your...manager.'

'What!'

'I know. I suppose it *is* a bit left field.'

'Left field my arse. It's up a chimney and round the flippin' corner if you ask me.'

'Why?'

"Cos you'd never pass as a madam,' Elsie cried. 'You say manager, I say madam. And like I said, I don't do that anymore.'

'Please, Elsie. It's the only way we'll get to speak with Sophie Guillard and it's not as though you'll actually be expected to...well, you know.'

'Lay on me back, yer mean?'

'Yes.'

'What makes yer think she'll speak ter me?'

'We want you to say your name is Lady Amandine Lachappelle, at least I'll say your name is Lady Amandine Lachappelle. I'm quite sure once Madame Guillard hears it she'll want to know who is using her daughter's name.'

Elsie swapped over her feet, placing the other one in the water with a sigh. 'You should do this, Camille,' said Elsie. 'It ain't arf nice.'

'Will you do it?'

Elsie took her foot out of the basin and sat on the edge of the bath, drying her feet on a towel.

'I remember telling you once that if you ever needed my 'elp I'd give it to yer. Remember that?'

Camille nodded. 'I do.'

'And you let me take Rose to the little 'ouse on the beach of yours in the spring.' Camille nodded again. 'I'd like to take 'er there again, with you and Ottilie, and Cecily, and Amandine if she's still with you.'

'Your wish is my command.'

Elsie grinned. 'Alright. I'll do it.'

Chapter 27

Elsie stood in the middle of the floor in Camille's suite, surrounded by myriad dresses that had been tried on for size and discarded.

'The problem is, it's me bosoms,' said Elsie patting her top half as Cecily, Ottilie, Amandine, and Camille looked on in amusement. 'They don't match the rest of me.'

'You're slim hipped, Elsie, but your bust doesn't quite fit in.'

'No, I know it don't. And your boosoms ain't as big as mine so everthin's just that little bit too tight, but I don't s'pose it matters. I won't be wearing it for long will I?'

'I think the red one looks best, Mama,' said Rose. 'It sort of matches you.'

'Which one?' asked Elsie looking around her feet at the pile of dresses. She bent and picked one up. 'D'yer mean this one?'

'Yes,' the girls said in chorus. 'That's the one,' cried Rose. 'It looks lovely. The sparkles are divine.'

'Oh, divine, eh,' said Elsie. 'That's why Lady Divine bought it I s'pose. I'll wear this one then, Camille,' said Elsie. ''Ave you the shoes to match?'

'I do,' answered Camille. Cecily ran to the closet to get them and Elsie slipped them on her feet. 'Cor,' she said, wincing as she pushed her toes into them. 'Bit tight. Oh, well, they'll 'ave to do. And what about a bag?' Cecily passed her the matching bag as Elsie glanced at herself in the cheval mirror. 'Oh, yes, I look proper posh. Not something I would buy meself, but yeah, I reckon it'll do the trick.' She turned to Camille. 'And what about you, Camille?'

Camille pulled a black dress from the closet. It wasn't as ostentatious as the one Elsie wore, but it seemed to fit the character she was trying to portray, an employee, yet one who knew her business.

'You're the one who needs to stand out, Elsie because you're the one who wants to work at Le Chabanais. I work for you on this occasion don't forget.'

'Oh, yeah,' said Elsie, grinning. 'So yer do. I'm goin' ter enjoy this,' she said, plonking a bright red hat on her head and sashaying up and down the room as the girls and Cecily giggled.

'Don't enjoy it too much,' said Camille, a smile playing on her lips. 'It's only for one night.'

They left the Hotel Narcisse Blanc in a taxicab and asked for the Rue Chabanais to which the driver lifted his eyebrows and looked pointedly at Camille.

'Madame?'

'We're meeting a business associate, Monsieur. If you would rather stop at the end of the street we'll understand.'

He shrugged. 'Whatever you say, Madame.'

'But if you stop outside we'll pay you extra,' said Elsie, lifting up her bag and rattling the coins inside hoping he would understand her.' She glanced at Camille. 'These shoes are already killin' me, Camille,' she said. 'Don't think I can walk far in 'em.'

The driver stopped directly outside and Camille paid him with extra coin from Elsie. He nodded and thanked them, and Camille asked him if he could return for them in an hour to which he agreed, no doubt thinking he would get an even bigger fare.

They stood on the pavement and looked up at the building. It was unremarkable in appearance, the front a dreary grey, a building that stood directly on the pavement with no gardens to soften the harshness of the almost utility appearance.

'Blimey,' said Elsie. 'This ain't what I was expecting. Bloomin' ugly ain't it?'

'Mm,' said Camille, frowning. 'I agree. I thought it would be much showier than this, but perhaps it's the point. They don't want it to stand out from the other buildings.'

'Bit daft. I should think everyone in Paris knows what it is.'

Camille nodded. 'True. Let's go inside.'

'D'yer think they'll let us in?'

'I'm not sure, but we'll use your credentials as a member of the aristocracy. Hopefully, it will sway them.'

'If it don't we've 'ad a wasted journey.'

Camille knocked on the door with a gloved hand. The door was opened by a butler who had unfortunately forgotten to put on his trousers.

'Oh, my Lord,' said Elsie under her breath, glancing at Camille. 'E ain't got any trousers on.'

'So I see,' said Camille, her eyes wide. 'I'm quite sure it's not the only shocking thing we'll see this evening.'

The "butler" showed them into the foyer which was a room made to look like a stone cave.

'May I help you, Mesdames,' he asked them.

Camille awarded him with one of her most sparkling smiles. 'We're here to see the owner, Monsieur,' she answered. 'We have a proposition for him.'

'A proposition?'

'Yes.'

'Do you have an appointment?'

'Er no, but 'er we are acquainted with someone here?'

'Who is that may I ask?'

Camille could have kicked herself. They were not acquainted with Sophie Guillard and she realised that lying about it could have them kicked out before they'd made any headway. 'Monsieur, is it not true that one likes to keep a little about oneself undisclosed, a little secret perhaps. I can tell you that Madame,' she inclined her head towards Elsie, 'and I are from the English aristocracy, and that Madame,' again she inclined her head in Elsie's direction, ' is an artiste in the skills of an aristocratic courtesan.'

Realising that Camille was speaking to the butler about her, Elsie stuck out her chest and gave him what she thought was her most alluring expression.

'Wait here, Madame,' the butler said before turning and going through an entrance at the back of the cave. As he turned Camille and Elsie saw that his derriere was utterly bare. Even Elsie was shocked.

'Don't care what they do 'ere do they?' she said to Camille, shaking her head. 'And I've seen some things in my time.'

'He has quite a nice bottom,' said Camille wistfully.

'Camille!' cried Elsie who then gave a salacious grin. 'Yeah, 'e has ain't 'e.'

Moments later the butler returned. 'If you would like to come this way, Mesdames.'

Camille and Elsie followed him. He took them to the back of the cave and through an entrance. The entrance led to a small vestibule which smelt of tobacco, and then into a bar. Camille narrowed her eyes as she tried to see through the smoky haze. There were a few men sitting at the tables, most smoking pungent cigars which accounted for the smoke cloud hovering just under the ceiling. There was a clink of glasses as the barkeeps served customers at the bars, some with scantily clad girls hanging off their arms; others were groups of men who were ordering large trays of drinks with glasses filled almost to the brim with brandy or whiskey.

There was an array of bottles at the back of the bar which was lit with small lights. Absinthe was clearly on display, its green colour announcing its prominence amongst the other spirits. Camille knew the "green fairy" could be highly addictive although she had not tasted it herself. She wondered if this was how the owners of Le Chabanais emboldened the working girls to disport themselves in front of the brothel's customers, encouraging them to spend more and more money.

'Mesdames,' said a strong male voice behind them which made them both turn. 'How can I help you?'

'Could we 'ave a drink first?' asked Elsie. Camille began to translate but the man held up his hand to stop her.

'I speak English, Madame,' he said. 'Your friend wishes for a drink?' Camille nodded. 'Then let's go to a table where we can talk business. I understand you have a...proposition for me.'

Anxiety crept up Camille's neck inch by inch as they walked to a table. She felt out of her depth, wondering what on earth she could say to this man to convince him she and Elsie were who they were about to say they were.

They sat at a small round table near the bar, and the man, who introduced himself as Monsieur Michel Vachon clicked his fingers. A member of staff attended to him immediately.

'Three brandies. The best cognac.'

'Yes, Monsieur,' the waiter answered before darting away to the bar.

Michel Vachon turned to them and smiled. He was a devastatingly handsome man, dressed in the finest of clothes, and Camille realised that Elsie was instantaneously taken with him. Camille turned to her and frowned, trying to stop her from pushing out her chest and looking lascivious. She was meant to be playing the part of a member of the aristocracy.

'Now, Mesdames. What is this business of which you speak?' The waiter arrived with a tray of drinks and served them separately, Camille and Elsie thanking him, unlike Michel Vachon which was brought directly to Camille's notice. He's arrogant, she thought, and rude. I might enjoy a bit of verbal sparring with Monsieur Vachon. Camille spoke up.

'Monsieur Vachon, thank you for welcoming us to your little establishment.' His eyebrows rose at the word 'little' and he settled back into his seat as though wondering what was to come next. 'We have come to Paris to offer you the services of my business partner, Lady Amandine Lachappelle.' She saw him frown. 'We are from England as I'm sure you have surmised. Lady Amandine is an artiste in...in erotic dancing and a purveyor of the sports enjoyed by men.' Vachon nodded looking amused. 'We have heard your establishment is the finest in all of Paris, and of course, Madame Amandine would not wish to display her talents anywhere other than the best Paris can offer. We think she will be unique amongst your current...stable...of girls.'

Vachon leant forward. 'And are you in the same business, Madame?'

Camille recoiled. 'I am not, Monsieur. I am Madame Amandine's manager.'

'Her madam,' he said, which was clearly not a question, more a statement.

Camille lifted her chin. 'Not exactly.'

'That's a shame, Madame.'

'Why?'

'Your burnished skin would attract many clients. Many of our celebrated customers are fond of company who hail from the far continents.'

Camille bristled. 'I hail from London, Monsieur. Not so very far away.'

He flashed her a smile that would have melted many a heart, but not Camille's. 'Indeed.' He rose from the table rubbing his hands together. 'In that case, perhaps Madame Amandine would like to make her way to the Louis XVI room. My personal assistant will show you the way.'

'May I accompany her?' asked Camille.

'You may, but Madame Amandine will need to show what she can do, so I'll expect you back here within, shall we say, ten minutes, once you have decided my 'little' establishment is worthy of her.'

'Oui, Monsieur,' answered Camille, hoping they would find Sophie Guillard before Elsie was expected to entertain any of the clients.

Vachon turned to go but then thought of something and turned back. 'Oh, by the way, you did not say who it was you knew who visited here.'

Camille gave him a steady look. She thought quickly and a name suddenly came to her. 'Rudolph Valentino,' she said with confidence as she looked Vachon right in the eyes.

He shrugged and nodded. 'Yes, he has been here. Merely as an observer you understand. We hope it helped him in his roles.' Camille nodded then looked quickly away, thanking someone, somewhere Valentino's name had sprung to mind. 'My assistant will be here in a few minutes. Please.' He smiled the sparkling smile again which Camille knew he was fully aware of and the effect it had, particularly on Elsie. 'Make yourselves comfortable. Drinks on the house. You should try the absinthe.'

'Not likely,' Camille said under her breath.

'I've 'ad that,' said Elsie quietly, leaning towards her.'

'And how was it?' asked Camille chuckling.

'Got a funny taste to it. Not my thing. Made *me* go a bit funny an' all.'

'It wouldn't take much to make you go funny, Elsie.'

Elsie gave her a look and they both laughed.

'What's going ter 'appen now,' Elsie asked her.

'I think you're expected to perform.'

'Oh! Right.'

'Wrong, actually. You won't of course.'

'I'd rather not, Camille. I'm a bit tired.'

Camille glanced quickly at her. 'Darling, don't be silly. It's not going to happen. We're simply going to find Sophie Guillard and tell her what's happened to Amandine.'

'What if she don't care?'

'She will, I'm quite sure of it.'

'Yeah, but what if she don't?'

'Then I'll apply for guardianship.'

Elsie gasped. 'You'd do that?'

'I certainly would. She's become one of the family and I want to do right by her. If I am insecure in my feelings for her safety then she will not stay here and I will entreaty Chief Inspector Owen to be an advocate.'

'He'd do that?'

'Of course.'

They were both startled into silence as a young woman approached their table. She wore a black dress to just past the knee which was elegantly fitted to her slender shape, and black shoes. Her blonde hair was caught up in a chignon secured with a diamante barrette. Her lips were bright red which accentuated the paleness of her face.

'Mesdames. I have been instructed to show you the Louis XVI room, where Lady Amandine will be working. Please follow me.'

Both Camille and Cecily rose from their chairs and did as they were instructed. The young woman led them to an ornate staircase which was situated behind a sliding partition in the bar, decorated in a trompe l'oeil fashion that made it invisible to the naked eye, leading to the rooms upstairs where business was carried out.

'Come this way please,' the woman said in perfect English.

They followed her up the gold staircase complete with golden dolphins ridden by mermaids carved on the balustrade. Elsie turned to Camille who was behind her and widened her eyes. Camille knew what she meant. It was astonishing.

Above them was a landing painted in an underwater scene of blue and green. There were mermaids and mermen depicted everywhere, even on the ceiling, all in sexual union, between fronds of seaweed, open clamshells and the wreckage of ships.

'I feel rather hot,' said Camille as she followed Elsie up onto the landing.

The woman opened a door for them someway along the landing, then to their surprise pushed them both into what seemed to be a janitor's cupboard. She glared at them, her hands on her hips. 'Who are you, and please do not give me the story about one of you wanting to be a courtesan here. It is hogwash. I want to know who the hell you are.'

Camille smiled at Cecily. 'I think we've found who we've been looking for. Madame Guillard if I'm not mistaken.'

Sophie Guillard looked taken aback. 'Yes, I am Sophie.' She frowned. 'But I don't understand. Monsieur Vachon said you were applying for a job here, but you used the name Amandine Lachappelle. It is my daughter's name.'

'Yes, we know,' said Camille. 'We couldn't think of another way to find you except to use Amandine's name.'

'But why do you need to find me?' Her hands flew to her mouth. 'Oh, my God, it's Amandine isn't it. Something has happened to her.'

Camille patted her down. 'No, Madame Guillard, she is perfectly safe, but we need to speak with you at length.'

'Not 'ere though,' said Elsie. 'You must come to the Hotel Narcisse Blanc so we can tell you what's 'appened. We 'ave Amandine there. She's stayin' with us.'

Sophie Guillard frowned. 'But why? She is staying with my mother. Charles said she could stay there as long as I didn't have contact with her and I have kept to the agreement.' She coloured slightly. 'I...I tried to keep to the agreement. At first I railed against it. We shouted at each other; I told him it was barbaric to keep me away from my daughter. I went to my mother's and she allowed me access.

'She could see how much Amandine and I were suffering. I went to see her every other day but Charles discovered our ruse and forbade me to go, saying I was a harlot and he did not want a harlot to raise his child. He insisted I kept to the agreement. I didn't want to of course, it almost broke my heart in two, but I would do anything to keep my sweet Amandine safe.' She frowned and shook her head. 'She doesn't deserve this. Amandine is so innocent. I believed her to be safer in her boarding school in the south but Charles did not agree. There were incidences. The school is home to the children of many famous people and became a target for abductors. Of course I was worried. It's true I wanted her home; I couldn't bear to be parted from her, but Charles...he always has the final say.' Tears gathered at her eyelashes and she brushed them away. 'It would not do for Michel to see me crying. He is already suspicious.'

'Why is 'e suspicious?' asked Elsie.

'Because he knows my situation. He knows about Amandine which is why I think he allowed you up to the rooms. He doesn't allow anyone up here unless they've paid, and he doesn't know you. You could be anyone.'

'Are you an' 'e, yer know?'

'No, no, please don't think that.'

'I think we should go,' said Camille. 'My guess is he's expecting Elsie to do the deed and we didn't come here for that. We came to find you.'

Sophie nodded. 'What should I call you?'

'I'm Elsie West,' answered Elsie, 'and this,' she thumbed to Camille, 'is Lady Camille Divine. Amandine has lived with her for the last six months.'

Sophie gasped. 'Six months?'

'More,' said Camille. 'She needs her own Mama.'

Sophie reached for Camille's hand, then one of Elsie's. 'Thank you,' she said, her eyes sparkling with tears. 'Thank you for taking care of my sweet Amandine.'

'We've seen yer paintings of 'er,' said Elsie smiling, her own eyes beginning to water. 'They're lovely, really beautiful.'

'Thank you. All my paintings are of her. Charles says my work is too sentimental but I don't care.'

'When will you come?' asked Camille.

'Tomorrow. Tomorrow morning. Shall I ask for you, Lady Divine?'

'Yes. I won't say anything to Amandine. You'll be a lovely surprise for her.'

Sophie showed Camille and Elsie down the stairs, but instead of going through the sliding door into the bar, she turned right and went down a dark corridor leading to a curtain at the end. She pulled back the curtain and unlocked the door.

'The service entrance,' she explained. 'We use it for when any of our clients become unruly or unmanageable.' Camille raised her eyebrows and Sophie smiled. 'It happens.'

Camille nodded then thought of something. 'Are you a working girl, Sophie? What is your role here?'

Sophie chuckled. 'I could never do what they do. I wouldn't know where to begin. This place…this place is extreme in every sense. No, I'm Michel's assistant that's all.'

Camille nodded and she and Elsie went out into the night.

They avoided loitering on the street for fear of being thought of as touting for work as they waited for their cab, and simply walked up and down, Elsie praying it wouldn't be too long before the taxicab arrived.

'I'm sorry, Camille,' she said. 'These shoes are goin' ter 'ave to go. They're pinching my feet somethin' wicked.' She bent down and prized the shoes off which left her in her stockinged feet.' Elsie sighed with pleasure as she put each foot down onto the warm pavement.

'Are you going to walk the street like that?' asked Camille.

Elsie chuckled. 'Look Camille, after what we've just seen I don't think a pair of trotters in stockings are goin' ter get anyone goin'.'

Camille smiled. 'I suppose not, but there are some very strange people in the world.'

'Don't I know it,' replied Elsie.

Camille grinned to herself. 'Yes, I suppose you do.'

Once inside the Hotel Narcisse Blanc Elsie joined Camille in her suite for a much needed drink. Cecily was on hand to fuss around them. She had been on tenterhooks all evening and was visibly relieved when the door opened and Camille and Elsie arrived.

'Well, Madam?' she asked as she poured drinks for Camille and Elsie. 'Did you find 'er?'

'We did, Cecily,' said Camille, sipping the martini that Cecily had expertly prepared for her. The ice tinkled alluringly in the glass, and she sat down gratefully onto the chaise, thanking all that was Holy she was back in her suite with Cecily and the girls.'

'My Rose alright?' asked Elsie. 'She was whacked after today.'

'Fast asleep, Madam,' replied Cecily as she passed a glass of whiskey to Elsie. 'They all are. Think it wore 'em out.'

'Pour one for yourself, Cecily,' said Camille.

Cecily's eyes brightened. 'Is it alright for me to 'ave one of them martini's like you've got. I love the glass what they come in, and the noise of the ice. I've never 'ad a martini before.'

'Of course,' answered Camille. 'Your choice, Cecily.'

Cecily prepared her drink and sat next to Elsie. She sipped the martini and winced, then decided she liked it and sipped again. 'Well, Madam? What did she say? 'Ow did yer find 'er?'

'Our ruse worked,' Camille frowned, 'at least I think it did. We met the current owner, a Michel Vachon, who accepted our story that Elsie wanted a position at the brothel.'

'You should a seen him, Cecily,' sighed Elsie. 'E was so 'andsome.' She took a swig of whiskey. 'Now, if *'ed* 'ave suggested testing out my skills, I'd 'ave gone for it. I'd a shown 'im a thing or two that's for sure.' Cecily giggled.

'Elsie!' cried Camille.

'Oh, come on, Camille. You fancied him too.'

'I did not 'fancy' him as you so indelicately put it.' She took a sip of her martini. 'He was handsome I grant you, but he's the owner of a brothel. Hardly the sort of man one should be setting their cap at.'

Elsie pulled a face. 'I'm the owner of a brothel too, more than one as it 'appens, but you're *my*

best friend.'

Camille looked surprised. 'I am?'

'Yeh, you are.'

'Anyway,' continued Camille, sighing. 'Monsieur Vachon agree to allow Elsie and me to go up to the Louis XVI room...'

'The what, Madam?' Cecily interrupted.

'The Louis XVI room, where they...they,' she tutted, 'ply their trade.'

'What were it like?' asked Cecily, her eyes agog.

'We didn't get to see it,' said Elsie. 'The woman what was showing us round was none other than Amandine's mother, Sophie Guillard.'

'Is she a prostitute?' asked Cecily, clutching her conical-shaped glass so hard it looked in danger of cracking.

'No, she isn't,' replied Camille. 'She's Michel Vachon's assistant. She looked extremely smart. Very elegant in fact.'

'So what will 'appen now?'

'She's coming here tomorrow to see Amandine, and to allow us to tell her what has happened to Amandine in her absence.'

'Did she know Amandine were missing?'

Camille shook her head. 'She did not. I think the woman is heartbroken. Monsieur Baptiste has a lot to answer for, particularly the behaviour of his eldest son. What he did was unacceptable.'

'What if he finds out Madame Guillard's been 'ere, Madam. You know what 'e's like. 'E might turn funny.'

Camille made a pout of disgust. 'He can turn as funny as he likes, but I invite whomever I please into my own suite of rooms. Long gone are the days when I must ask a man for permission to do anything.'

'Quite right,' agreed Elsie looking a little worse for wear. 'We ain't be'olden to no man, not when we've got funds of our own.'

'*You've* got funds of your own, Elsie. Unfortunately, I still rely on Harry's generosity.'

'You should come and work for me, ducks,' cried Elsie, laughing into what was her fourth glass of whiskey. 'You'd earn a shedload a money with your looks.'

'Er, no I don't think so, Elsie,' said Camille, shaking her head at her in frustration. 'And I think you've had quite enough of that.' She inclined her head to the glass in Elsie's hand.

'Yeah,' said Elsie, rising from her chair with difficulty. 'You're prob'ly right. Can I leave Rose 'ere?'

'Of course.'

'I'll come back tomorrow mornin'. I want ter see what 'appens when Sophie Guillard gets 'ere. Poor little lamb will be so excited.'

Elsie staggered to the suite door and opened it. 'Abyssinia,' she said with a wave of her hand, then hiccupped and giggled to herself.

When Elsie had left the suite Camille dragged herself from the chair and yawned.

'I'm done in too, Cecily, and so must you be. It's been a long day and I think we'll have an early start in the morning. I don't know what time Madame Guillard will arrive.'

'I'm not sure Mrs West will make it, Madam. She didn't 'alf knock that whiskey back quick. Think she'll 'ave a bad 'ead in the mornin'.'

'I'm sure you're right. Go to bed, Cecily. A six o'clock start I think.'

'Very well, Madam. Goodnight, Madam.'

'Goodnight, Cecily.'

Chapter 28

Camille ordered breakfast to be delivered to the suite and asked Cecily to join her. The girls were still in bed, their little bodies making soft bumps under the covers. Camille had gone into the room earlier to check on them and thought how sweet they looked in the land of nod.

Rose had shared Amandine's bed as they were both smaller than Ottilie, and they snored softly, their heads touching on the pillow. The three girls had become so close, and Camille worried that if Amandine was claimed by Sophie Guillard which would of course be the perfect outcome, the friendship between them would become fractured. And then of course there was Cecily. Her triumph at finding Amandine's mother took a dip and her stomach rolled. Cecily had become a mother, of sorts, to Amandine, even though they did not share a language. From the first time they had met in a cell in Brighton's police station they had formed a bond. Camille feared that bond would soon be broken.

At breakfast Cecily was unusually quiet. Her spark was nowhere to be seen and Camille knew she was thinking about Amandine and what would happen when Sophie Guillard arrived. Just as they were finishing breakfast there was a knock on the door. Camille frowned and Cecily jumped in her seat.

'Surely it's not Madame Guillard arriving already,' Camille said frowning. She looked at her watch. 'Just seven. Gosh, she's keen.' Cecily nodded and got up to answer the door. It was not Sophie Guillard. It was Richard.

Camille's look of pleasure was plain to see. 'Richard. You're an early bird. Why don't you have some coffee?'

'Thank you, I will,' said Richard, pulling a chair over to the breakfast table. 'I thought you should know Janine Heroux is being buried today.'

Camille steadied her hand as she poured the coffee for Richard and another for herself. 'Oh, dear. Oh, dear that poor girl. And her family.' Her plan to tell Richard she and Elsie had found Sophie Guillard was completely forgotten. Richard shrugged but said nothing. Camille sat at the table again and eyed him. 'You want me to go, don't you?'

Richard shrugged and smiled. 'I can't force you to go, Camille, but it would be helpful. Inspecteur Apollinaire will attend, as will I, but of course, none of us will be together. Take Cecily with you if you'd rather. Perhaps Mrs West could keep an eye on the girls.'

Camille rolled her eyes. 'Only if she isn't nursing a sore head.'

Richard laughed. 'Another one?'

'Well, you know how she likes to get her fair share.'

'And everyone else's by the sound of it.' They both laughed, attempting to lighten the moment a little.

'What time is the funeral,' asked Camille, praying it would be in the afternoon. She was desperate to see Amandine reunited with her mother.

'It begins at two o'clock.' Camille sighed with relief. 'It will leave from the Rue Saint-Dominique at two, and the hearse will take the coffin to the Chappelle Notre Dame de las Medaille Miraculeuse.'

Camille nodded. 'I know it.'

'You do?'

'It's famous for the nun who claims to have had three meetings with the Virgin Mary; a Catherine Leboure. My parents took me there years ago.'

'They're going to have a Mass there for Janine, or Marthe as Madame Tatou knew her.'

'It will be a pleasure and a privilege to visit there again. I just wish it was under happier circumstances.'

Richard nodded sadly. 'And what about last night? Did you have any luck with finding Sophie Guillard?'

'We found her, Richard.'

He smiled. 'So the ruse worked.'

'Indeed it did and extremely well. The only thing I'm concerned about is the owner, a Michel Vachon. Sophie Guillard said he was suspicious of our arrival, particularly as we used the name Amandine Lachappelle. Sophie explained that Monsieur Vachon is aware of her circumstances. She had to tell him when she applied for the job as his assistant.' Camille shrugged. 'But if we hadn't used her name we would not have found Sophie. It was because of the name she was alerted to us. She wasn't happy in the beginning, rounded on us, asking what game we were playing, but as soon as we explained she was astonished. She thought Amandine was still with her mother.'

'So what now?'

'She's coming here, to the Hotel Narcisse Blanc to see Amandine. There is a lot to discuss. She must be made aware of everything that happened to Amandine since she last saw her. Apparently, Monsieur Baptist forbade Sophie from visiting Amandine at Sophie's mother's house, but she broke the rules he'd implemented. She could not bear to be away from her daughter. The visits were discovered by Charles Baptiste and he put a stop to them.'

'Why did he impose such a harsh regime?'

'Because he said Sophie was a harlot. He believed she was having an affair with her artist friend didn't he?'

'And was she?'

'We didn't have time to ask. If we had stayed at Le Chabanais much longer Elsie would have been expected to perform her 'arts' to prove she was up to the job.'

'Something within the realm of her expertise I would have thought.'

'Only if it had been with Michel Vachon. She fell for him, hook and line.' Camille gazed into the distance. 'He was rather handsome I must confess.'

'Handsome or not I'm sure I recognise the name. Inspecteur Apollinaire mentioned it when we spoke last.' He rose from the chair and placed it back against the wall. 'Will you attend the funeral, Camille. With Cecily of course.'

Camille nodded. 'We'll be there, but first I must rouse Elsie and tell her what's happening, then await the arrival of Sophie Guillard. We must find a way through this, Richard. The best outcome would be if Amandine could live with her mother. A girl needs her mother,' she said wistfully, 'and I rather think her father is a little too forthright for such a sensitive girl as Amandine. She's a child and needs a gentle hand to guide her. No, we will see this through to the bitter end, and if Monsieur Baptiste will not listen to his wife, then I'll make sure he listens to me.'

Sophie Guillard arrived at the suite at ten o'clock. Camille had decided not to tell Amandine, should there be a change of arrangement. It was only two days before Amandine had thought her mother dead. It is what she had believed since she'd been left at her grandmother's. She had mourned for her, grieved her absence, and Camille wondered what effect it would have on her when suddenly confronted by her mother's arrival.

'Come in, Madam,' said Cecily quietly. Camille was watchful of Cecily as she was aware that her maid would have mixed feelings over the discovery of Sophie Guillard.

'Where is she,' whispered Sophie.

'In her room with my daughter, Ottilie.'

'A beautiful name.'

'Thank you. Should Cecily tell her she has a visitor? She'll likely think it's her father.'

Sophie looked surprised. 'He's been here?'

Camille nodded. 'It has taken us months to find you both. Amandine told us nothing while she was staying with me at my house in London. It was only when we came to Paris she began to talk about her family. Unbeknown to us our visit here was the best thing we could have done. She clearly felt comfortable in her home city.' Camille nodded to Cecily who went into Ottilie and Amandine's bedroom. Moments later both girls entered the salon.

'Maman!' Amandine cried. She ran across to her mother and threw her arms around her waist, squeezing her tightly. Tears ran copiously down her cheeks as she cried, 'Maman, Maman, you are not dead.'

Sophie pushed Amandine away gently from her and sat in a chair, holding the little girls arms, then brushing away her tears from her cheeks, ignoring her own.

'Amandine, mon cherie, why did you think I was dead?'

'Papa. Papa said you were dead to him. It's what he said to me and the boys, so we thought you were dead. When you stopped coming to Grand

Mere's house to see me I thought it must be true. I didn't like to ask Grand Mere because I thought she would get upset. I didn't see Papa. He did not come to the house.'

Sophie looked angry, her frustration with her husband clearly visible. 'He did not visit you?'

'Non, Maman, not once.'

Sophie threw her hands up in the air then pulled Amandine to her.

'Why do men do these things? They make the rules, make promises they never mean to keep. No wonder it all went wrong. He said he would visit, promised me he would take care of you. He accused me of terrible things, things that never happened.' She looked into Amandine's eyes and stroked her hair, speaking softly to her daughter. 'Did Grand Mere treat you well, Amandine. I know she can be a little strict.'

'She was kind, Maman, but she is strict sometimes.'

'So why did you leave her, my darling, if she was kind to you?'

'Pierre. Pierre came to the house and said that you and Papa had given him permission to take me from the house because you both wanted me back. When we left Grand Mere's he said we were to go on an adventure...to England?'

'England?'

'He took me on a train to Calais where we got on a boat, but then I think Pierre left the boat, but didn't take me with him. A man came and said he would look after me.' Amandine began to sob and Sophie hushed her.

'No more, no more, darling. You can tell me another time. You've told me enough for today...all I want to hear for the time being.' She closed her eyes momentarily then glanced up at Camille. 'Those boys. After everything I've done for them. When their mother died I took care of them all, tried to help them in their grief. This is how they repay me.'

'You aren't their mother?' asked Camille gently.

Sophie shook her head. 'Their mother died many years ago when the youngest boy was a baby. Pierre is the eldest. He's sixteen now. The youngest,' she shrugged, 'about twelve. I haven't seen them for a while. Pierre is his father's favourite. Charles wants Pierre to follow him to the Elysée Palace, to become an intern there and then go into politics. Unfortunately, it is not what Pierre wants. It has caused trouble in the family. Pierre is very wayward, very opinionated, and rude. He did not take to me because he thought I was trying to take his mother's place. He looked down on me, sneered at me. This thing he had done...I thought it even beyond him. Amandine is the only child Charles and I have together.'

Camille sat in front of her and reached for Sophie's hand which was shaking with nervous energy.

'Where did you meet?'

Sophie look down. 'Please don't judge me,' she said in English, knowing Amandine wouldn't understand.

'I would never judge you, Sophie. We all do what we have to do, what we want to do, and what we need to do sometimes.'

'I was taken on as the boys' nanny. Charles could not cope with them all. They needed a woman's hand. I had to live in because Charles was away so much, often away at night. The boys could not be left alone and he had no one to help him. His own mother had already died by then.

'I had been there for about a year when we both realised we had feelings for each other. He was so sophisticated, so strong, so intelligent. It attracted me to him. My own father was a poor man, a good man, my mother hardworking. We lived a simple life on a small farm just outside of Paris. There was little reward for the work they put in. Perhaps I should have been contented with that life, perhaps married the boy next door who was sweet on me, but I wanted more.

'I was good with children, I love children, so signed to an agency in Paris.' She pulled a sad face. 'It was fate I suppose. We were married soon afterwards. Amandine came along quickly. It was the happiest day of my life, and I believe one of the happiest for Charles. We had a wonderful life together. I think Charles was one of President Doumergue's favourites. He used to visit us at the apartment and I would cook for them. I think the President liked my simple rustic food. He said the fine dining food at the Elysée Palace gave him indigestion.' She chuckled at the memory. 'The President was kind to us. I liked him.'

'But it went wrong?'

'When Amandine went to school I had nothing to occupy me. I thought perhaps we would have another child but it did not happen. I took up painting again. On the farm I would take my paints to the fields and woods, and paint there. I loved it. It calmed my soul. Charles was not pleased. He said I should concentrate on *his* career, become a better hostess to further his ambition. I didn't think it was necessary. Charles was rarely at home and when he was he worked on his papers, only coming out of the office to eat. I took up painting and to my surprise quickly found a following.' She smiled, a gleam in her eye. 'I suddenly realised it was what I wanted. To be a painter, to display my work, and in front of me I had the perfect subject. Amandine.'

Amandine looked up at the mention of her name. She had climbed onto Sophie's lap and pushed her face into her mother's neck. Camille wondered what would happen when Sophie left.

'What are your plans, Sophie?'

'I'd like to take Amandine with me, Lady Divine. I'll forever be grateful for what you have done for her, for me. You took care of my darling, kept her safe when I could not,' she inclined her head, 'was not allowed to, but it will change. If you have no objections I would like to take her with me.'

Camille glanced at Cecily who stood by the window, frowning. She knew what was going through her mind.

'But surely you won't take her to Le Chabanais?'

Sophie looked shocked. 'Mais non, Madame. She will come to the apartment with me.'

'The apartment? The one you shared with your husband?'

'I've been living there, Madame. Charles does not know it. I needed somewhere to live and the apartment had been my home. *I*...had made it a home, not just a place to be. Charles is there so little he did not even notice. He came to the apartment a few times but didn't stay. I hid until he was gone. It is a large property. There were plenty of places I could go to hide. I needed somewhere to stay and the apartment was perfect.' Camille smiled thinking Sophie had more about her than she'd previously thought. She would have done exactly the same thing. She glanced at Cecily again who looked relieved.

'And will you hide now, Madame Guillard?' Camille asked her.

'Certainly not. Whatever my husband has said to you, Lady Divine, I did not have an affair. I had no interest in Javier Leon other than as an artist. It is true I went there when Charles asked me to leave, but I had nowhere else to go. Monsieur Leon offered me a place of safety in his apartment where he has a studio. I thought about going home, but it would have been too far away from Amandine and it would have broken my heart. My husband had already decided I was having an affair so I believed I had nothing to lose. I stayed with Javier for a short while until I knew the boys were away on their uncle's farm, and Amandine was at my mothers. It is when I got the job at Le Chabanais as Michel Vachon's assistant. I had no alternative. Living on the streets in central Paris is the same as asking to be murdered.'

Chapter 29

Camille booked a taxicab to take her and Cecily to the Rue Saint-Dominique which was where the cavalcade would leave before going for Mass at the Chapelle Notre Dame de la Medaille Miraculeuse. She had suggested to Richard that she and Cecily simply go the chapel but he had suggested she would see a great deal when observing the family from the street and advised her to join the procession.

In the cab Camille turned to Cecily, then took one of her hands in her own.

'Are you alright, Cecily?'

Cecily nodded brightly, but it wasn't convincing. 'Of course, Madam. Why would I not be?' Cecily turned her face towards Camille who simply gazed at her. She saw Cecily swallow, then tears gather at her eyelashes. 'Oh, Cecily, I'm so sorry.'

'I didn't think it would be today, Madam. I thought Madame Guillard would do what Monsieur Baptiste did and leave Amandine with us. I…I wasn't prepared for it, see.' She looked down again. 'I don't know when I'm ever goin' ter see Amandine again. She's with her Ma now.' She glanced up at Camille. 'And I do know it's where she should be, Madam, honestly, I do know that.' She sighed. 'It's just so bloomin' 'ard. To see 'er go out of that door near broke my 'eart, but Madame Guillard was very kind to me when Amandine told 'er 'ow close we were. She even gave me a hug and thanked me.'

'I know,' Camille said gently, 'and I know how much you cared for her, but you're right, she should be with her parents. Both of them ideally, but at least Sophie Guillard knows the story and is prepared to be strong where Monsieur Baptiste is concerned.'

'Do you think he'll make her leave the apartment?'

Camille chuckled. 'I have a feeling Sophie Guillard won't let it happen, so...we should be happy for them shouldn't we? She has found some power from somewhere, and I promise we'll invite Amandine...and Sophie if she wishes, to spend some time with us at the beach house in Brighton. Would you like that?'

Cecily smiled, her eyes suddenly brightening. 'Oh, Madam, it would be wonderful. We'll have so much fun.'

Camille nodded; glad Cecily had cheered up. She needed her to be on her metal for the next couple of hours. Honoré Tatou needed to be found, alive and unscathed hopefully. Camille knew that Cecily was eagle eyed and often picked up things she, Camille, missed.

'Miss Ottilie wept buckets, d'int she, Madam, when Amandine left?'

'Yes, I was worried about leaving her, but Elsie assured me she would take care of her, and Rose of course, who was similarly distressed. They were more like sisters than friends, and do you know, I never once heard them argue.'

'Blimey,' said Cecily. 'Me and me sisters and brothers argued all the time, mostly about who was gettin' the most food.'

'Really,' said Camille, wondering at the life Cecily had led before she had gone into service. 'And who did?'

'Well, it weren't me, Madam, I can assure you of that.'

The procession would be long. People had already begun to line the pavements, waiting for the family to make an appearance before Janine Heroux's funeral. The hearse, a long vehicle with glass on each side so mourners could see the coffin, was to be pulled by four black horses. Each one had a black plume of feathers on its head decorated with gold. The wheels of the carriage were also gold which sparkled in the afternoon sunlight. Around the carriage stood six men in matt-black long-tailed coats, and wearing shiny top hats. They had their heads bowed; their black-leather clad hands clasped solemnly in front of them. There wasn't a sound from the crowd, but the anticipation was palpable.

'There's a lot of people here, Madam,' said Cecily. 'She must've 'ad a lot of friends.'

'Not according to Honoré. She was apparently a rather quiet person who preferred reading to socialising.'

'Friends of 'er parents then?'

'Possibly, although one wonders how one could count any of the Herouxs as a true friend. They have an unenviable reputation.' She spoke sotto voce aware she could be overheard by someone who was determined to listen to their conversation.

'D'you think it was someone 'ere who killed 'er?' Cecily whispered.

'I think it's why we're here, Cecily. Chief Inspector Owen places a lot of faith in your powers of perception, even more than mine I'd say. He believes if there's something to spot you'll be the one to spot it.'

'That's nice of 'im. 'Ope I don't let 'im down.'

'I'm sure you won't. Just keep your eyes on the event.' A wave of low chatter began at the front of the crowd and seemed to sweep over the gathering like a cloud of mist, gathering pace as it reached the back. It was precisely two o'clock and the family had begun to emerge from the apartment building. 'Look,' said Camille. 'There's the family, the Herouxs.'

Cecily nodded. 'They're a nice looking bunch. Reckon they've got their mother to thank for that. She's very h'elegant. 'E looks a bit stern if you ask me.'

'Well, he has just lost his daughter, Cecily.'

'I know, Madam. But 'e looks stern, as though 'e's angry about somethin', rather than sad which is what I would 'ave expected. Look. His wife's in floods of tears, poor woman.'

'Yes, one can't help feeling some sympathy for them, even if they are criminals. I can't imagine...well, I don't want to.'

The Heroux family lined up on the pavement waiting for the coffin to be brought out of the building.

'They must 'ave 'ad 'er in their apartment,' said Cecily, her eyebrows knotted together. 'Their daughter I mean. Bit unusual ain't it? Don't most people go to the undertaker. They could afford a funeral 'ome an' all. Look at the clothes, not the sort I could afford.' She glanced up at Camille. 'There must be money in nicking stuff.'

Camille bent down to whisper in her ear. 'They do more than that I can assure you.'

Cecily's eyes got larger. 'Ooh, 'eck. That don't sound good.'

As the coffin was brought out by four men dressed the same way as the men guarding the hearse, Monsieur Heroux and this three sons stepped forward and helped the undertaker's men slide the coffin onto the bier of the carriage. The coffin too was black, mahogany Camille had no doubt, with gold handles. On the top of the coffin was a display of exquisite cream lilies and roses. As the coffin disappeared into the hearse there was a cry of anguish from Madame Heroux who would have collapsed if her daughter, Angelique, had not supported her.

'Oh, dear,' said Camille as two of the undertaker's men climbed up onto the box seat behind the horses and encouraged them to move off. In front of the horses walked two men, one behind the other, professional mourners who kept the procession at a sedate pace. The remaining two men climbed into the passenger seats of two cars waiting behind the hearse to take the family to the Chapelle Notre Dame de la Medaille Miraculeuse.

'What do we do now, Madam?' asked Cecily.

'We follow, Cecily. We follow, and we watch.'

The procession began to move off, following the hearse and the cars as it traversed at a sedate pace down the Rue Saint Dominique. Camille and Cecily managed to find themselves a position near to the side of the cars, Camille determined to observe the passengers inside.

'What do you think, Madam? asked Cecily. 'Have you seen anyone who shouldn't be here?'

'I've just noticed Michel Vachon.' She frowned. 'I can only assume the trade in which he is in brings him into contact with families like the Heroux.'

'A criminal then?'

'Well, yes, Cecily. One wouldn't be in that kind of business unless one were familiar with the criminal fraternity. The difference with Le Chabanais is it doesn't hide its intentions. It is as much a club for the celebrity crowd as it is a brothel. Michel Vachon knows this, and Mrs West and I saw it. When one goes inside it has a club atmosphere; a bar just like any other, smoke-laden, awash with alcohol of course, but there was also an undercurrent.'

'What of, Madam?'

'Something not quite right, a sleaziness if you will. It is wedded to anticipating and delivering sexual favours to rich men...and women, there were women there too; those who can afford to spend hundreds of Francs on buying an hour or more of one of Michel Vachon's girls.

'Mrs West told me about the butler. He weren't wearing any trousers, and his under things was a bit strange.'

Camille chuckled. 'They were certainly strange. Very odd indeed. There seemed to be nothing covering his...latter part.'

'His bum, Madam?'

Camille's lips twitched. 'If it's what you call it.'

'Bet 'e got cold then, 'specially in the winter.'

The procession continued slowly to the Chapelle Notre Dame de la Medaille Miraculeuse. Camille spotted Richard who had moved to be just near them. Inspecteur Apollinaire was nowhere to be seen.

'What are we looking for, Madam? Trouble is I don't know any of these people. They've all got the same sad faces, the look you'd expect from them, being as they're at a funeral.'

Camille sighed. 'You're right, Cecily. I'm not sure what we should be looking for either.'

'What about the family, Madam? Shouldn't we start with them?'

'Why, Cecily? Would they not look the same as the other mourners, worse if anything of course. They might be criminals but I'm sure they loved Janine.'

'But maybe not all of 'em loved 'er as much as they should 'ave, or as much as someone might expect 'em to.'

Camille turned to Cecily wondering what she meant. Cecily was squinting into the interior of the vehicles and pulling a face. 'Careful, Cecily. We don't want them to see us observing them. And why do you say that?'

Cecily straightened up and stared into the distance, watching the procession as it snaked its way to the church. 'Not sure, Madam, but I'll keep looking and let you know what I think afterwards if it's alright.'

'Of course,' answered Camille. 'But don't forget what Chief Inspector Owen says. It doesn't matter how small something is. If it has occurred to you he would like to know about it.'

'I remember, Madam, don't worry. Once I get me eye in things seem to fall into place, but I ain't sure yet. They said they thought it was one of the families 'ere in Paris, didn't they, one of the criminal ones, who they thought had killed Janine?'

'That's right.'

'Hm. I s'pose they would say that wouldn't they?'

'What d'you mean, Cecily?'

Cecily glanced up at her. 'Ave you ever read a penny dreadful, Madam?'

Camille shook her head. 'I can't say I have. Whatever's a penny dreadful. They sound awful.'

'They were little books what you could buy for a penny. People don't seem to 'ave 'em now, but in my last post, yer know, the old lady what I used to work for before I came ter you, she 'ad a stack of 'em in 'er library. I was shocked really, Madam to tell the truth. I didn't think an old'un like 'er would 'ave read something like it, but she said she loved 'em. Not sure they do 'em now though.'

'What were they about and why have you suddenly thought of them?'

'They were all about murders and mysteries, and sometimes there were ghosts.'

'I see. And they have reminded you of our current situation.'

'They 'ave, Madam.'

'Why?'

'Because it was often the person what you would least expect who would be the one what 'ad committed the crime. I read one where a girl was killed and everyone thought it was 'er betrothed what 'ad killed 'er, because he wanted to get out of the engagement. They was high society, but it weren't 'er betrothed.'

'Who was it?'

'It were 'er father who had wailed and grieved the most at her passing, made a big show of it, but 'e'd done away with her because he'd done something unacceptable to 'er what fathers shouldn't do to their daughters,' she looked away, her face turning pink with embarrassment, 'if you get my meaning, Madam?'

'Er, yes, I do get your meaning. And you're telling me people found this kind of reading entertaining?'

Cecily nodded with enthusiasm. 'Oh, very much so, Madam. Everyone likes tales of intrigue and mystery...and if there's a bit of murder thrown in for good measure, well, all the better for it.'

Camille shook her head. 'I'm astonished. Where did you learn to read, Cecily?'

'At the ragged school. I went there for quite a time until me Ma and Pa said I 'ad to go out and get work.'

'And how old were you then?'

'Thirteen, Madam. I worked as a scullery maid for the old lady, Mrs Summers it were, until she died. Then I came to you at Kenilworth House.'

'And because of the stories in these penny dreadfuls you think we're looking in the wrong place?'

'It's something I'm thinking about, Madam. It's what d'you call it a...a, oh, I don't know the word.'

'Do you mean a theory?'

Cecily snapped her fingers. 'That's it, a theory.' She grinned. 'I'm working on a theory.'

The procession wound up the hill following the hearse and the horses with the black feathered plumage. As it went by people on the pavements stood still and lowered their heads, paying respects to a stranger, although Camille surmised many would know whose coffin it was. The French newspapers had been full of the story and it had even made its way to English newspapers according to Richard, who had had contact with the courts about Amandine and the whereabouts of her parents. The English newspapers, much like the French ones, had painted the story as luridly as they could, to entice more readers, Camille thought. That case seemed to be closed, the mystery solved, thank goodness. Camille prayed Amandine would be permitted to stay with her mother in their apartment. It was the correct decision, but she was ready for a fight with Charles Baptiste should the occasion arise.

The Chapelle Notre Dame de la Medaille Miraculeuse loomed up ahead of them. Cecily was surprised it was a comparatively plain building with an almost sandstone coloured exterior. Over the lintel, above the door, which was supported either side by two columns, was an inset arch, much like a cartouche which had the carving of a nun and a child and the words "J'ai ete etablie gardienne'.

'What does that mean, Madam?' asked Cecily, pointing up to the carving.

'It translates roughly to I am established as your guardian.'

'Oh, that's nice.'

'The church honours the Heart of Jesus Christ and the miracles which took place here in the 19th Century. A nun was said to have spoken to the Virgin Mary three times. In the middle of the century an epidemic of cholera broke out causing thousands of deaths. One of the fathers of the church requested holy medals be made as a protection for the people of Paris. They were given out by the Daughters of Charity. I suppose it brought people comfort. It was seen as a miracle when those who had been struck down by the disease began to heal. There are many medals now. Parisiennes hold them still as talismans I assume.'

'I reckon we need a miracle, Madam, if yer don't mind me sayin', to find Madam Tatou.'

Camille nodded; her face etched with sadness. 'I think you're right, Cecily. Perhaps coming here today will help us. I'll be praying for Honoré.'

'So will I, Madam. So will I.'

The procession waited in the street, parting like the Sea of Galilee as the coffin was taken from the glass hearse and carried into the church. Behind the coffin were Janine Heroux's parents. Her brothers and sister followed on. Both Madame Heroux and Angelique were wearing short black veils to cover their faces which Cecily found frustrating.

'Wish they weren't wearing those bloomin' veils,' she said sotto voce, as much to herself as to Camille. 'They're gettin' in the way.'

'In the way of what?' whispered Camille just as she spotted Richard in the crowd.

'In the way of their faces. I need ter see them ter see what they're thinking.'

'Perhaps they'll remove them once we're all inside the church.'

'Bet they don't, Madam' replied Cecily who seemed a little frustrated. 'I want ter see their eyes.'

'What about the father...and her brothers? You said you thought the father looked stern rather than sad.'

'I did, but I can see him closer now. He is stern but I think it's just his natural face. His eyes are terribly sad. I can see some regret there. Maybe some shame? I dunno. Maybe I'm reading him wrong.'

'What about the brothers?'

'They're all handsome aren't they, 'specially the younger one. Their eyes are lowered. They don't want ter look at anyone. The tears are real, Madam, I'm sure of it.'

'Which leaves us with the mother and the sister.'

'What happens after the funeral?'

'The same as when a member of any society passes away I expect.'

Cecily blinked rapidly. 'Ooh, no, Madam, I don't think so. When someone from the rookeries goes there ain't all this palaver. He or she is put in a wooden box which 'as more 'n likely been used for someone else, and left on the kitchen table.' She blinked, deep in thought. 'That's if they've got a table.'

Camille pulled a face of surprise. 'Really. But aren't they buried in the box?'

Cecily sighed thinking Camille didn't know much about the poor in society. 'Not always, Madam.' She turned to Camille. ' I know you don't understand, Madam, but there ain't no money for nice coffins and 'orses wiv feathers on their 'eads. The box gets put on an old cart, maybe a coal cart and the owner of the coal cart, if that's what's used, usually 'as an 'orse. The 'orse pulls the cart to the church, St Giles mostly, a few words is said, then they get buried. There's no stone and no flowers. Sometimes there's a wooden cross, a couple of bits of wood what's bin nailed together, and if someone can write they write on it. That's it. Then everyone goes down the pub and gets plastered.'

Camille shook her head in disgust. 'They can't afford a proper burial but they can afford to get drunk?'

Cecily chuckled. 'They can always afford to get drunk, Madam. My Pa never 'ad no money, but 'e was always drunk.' Camille put her arm around Cecily and gave her an affectionate but rather sorrowful hug.

The inside of the Chapelle Notre Dame de la Medaille Miraculeuse was exquisite. Cecily was spellbound, her eyes wide at the sight in front of her.

'Oh, Madam,' she sighed. 'It's beautiful.'

The mourners began to fill up the pews and Camille knew they would need to hurry to a seat if they were to have one at all. She'd never seen so many mourners and she wondered if they wanted to be there, or were there simply to appease an influential family like the Heroux. In the circles in which they moved she was certain many people acted in ways to ensure their own safety, rather than because it was something they actually wanted to do.

They managed to find two seats together near the front. Camille began to look around the mourners hoping to see Richard. She spotted him on the other side of the aisle near to the back of the church. She glanced at Cecily whose mouth had dropped open at the exquisite artwork on the walls and above the altar, a beatific smile on her face.

'I never knew anythin' like this existed,' she said, her voice hushed. 'We ain't got nothin' like this in St Giles.'

Camille sighed as she looked up at the hand-painted frescoes on every wall. The altar was situated underneath a sculpted arch above which was a blue and gold fresco of a nun and a child. Below this were painted angels in blue and gold, and below the fresco sculptures of the Virgin Mary with her child, the young Jesus. There were balconies above their heads, and as Camille's eyes went towards the beautiful ceiling, she saw Inspecteur Apollinaire and whom she assumed were his men, all in plain dress, but all searching the mourners' faces.

The only noises in the church were low whispers between the mourners, people making themselves comfortable on their chairs which weren't particularly comfortable, and the rustles of the Order of Service. The organ struck up a hymn and everyone stood to sing. It was mournful and sorrowful, and Camille felt her heart clench.

The service was long, the eulogies heart-breaking. Loud weeping came from the front pews which became louder when each of the brothers took their turn to go to the lectern and speak about their sister, Janine, and how much they loved her and would miss her. Monsieur Heroux also stood and spoke about his daughter, his tanned face a mask of misery. Camille and Cecily watched each one closely; Camille listening to their voices for any inflection that did not ring true, but there was nothing.

Camille and Cecily were glad to be outside when the service was over. The bright sunlight hurt their eyes as they got used to the brightness after the gloom, and as beautiful as the church was neither wanted to stay there much longer. The sorrow felt by the family had been palpable. The weeping had not diminished for a moment, and many of the mourners had been swept up in the tide of grief that washed over everyone.

'Phew, ain't I glad to be out of there,' said Cecily, flapping her face with the Order of Service. 'Thought I was goin' ter melt it was so 'ot. And the sadness. I didn't think I could bear it much longer.'

'Or me,' said Camille. 'Wasn't it awful?'

'We won't go to the wake will we, Madam?'

'I don't think we should go, but I've been wondering...could you perhaps manage to get inside the apartment as a waitress? You know what to do don't you?'

Cecily gasped with apprehension. 'But I ain't got a uniform, Madam. What if I'm caught out?'

'Why would you be? You could say you left it at home, or perhaps hadn't been given one to wear. I've been to many events like it. No one takes any notice of the waiting staff.'

'Charmin', Madam. And you're forgettin', I don't speak French.'

Camille chortled. 'You know I didn't mean it like that. I just meant you could slip in, and slip out unnoticed, because of your advanced detection skills.'

'Actually, Madam, I don't think you meant that...but,' Cecily sighed. 'I'll give it a go. If I get caught I'll make a run for it, bearing in mind I can't give 'em an explanation why I'm there.'

'That's my girl,' smiled Camille, giving Cecily's narrow shoulders a quick hug. 'A brilliant plan as usual.'

Cecily gave Camille a look she was sure no maid should ever give her mistress. Camille simply laughed.

Chapter 30

The apartment was like nothing Cecily had ever seen before. She had been astonished when she'd first worked at Kenilworth House, Lord Henry Divine's stately home where she had become Camille's personal maid, but it was as one would expect, not particularly fashionable, wood panelling in most of the rooms, and portraits of Lord Divine's ancestors, the eyes of which seemed to follow her around the room. She had always felt as though she were being watched and would often scuttle out of the rooms as fast as she could, particularly if she were alone. The Heroux's apartment was a different prospect entirely. It was beyond fashionable. Cecily didn't know how much things cost but even she could see opulence did not come cheap. She shook her head.

'Ow the other 'arf live, she thought.

She had been amazed at how easily she'd managed to inveigle her way into the wake. She could have said she was a guest and no one would have known she wasn't known to Janine, a friend perhaps; none of the mourners were asked. Camille's idea of her acting as a waitress had been a good one because it meant she could go around the room, offering drinks and food to the guests and listen in on the conversations without causing suspicion. She knew she wouldn't understand what they were saying, but the tone of voices and hand gesticulations often said more than words.

Luck had been on her side too. The staff had been asked to wear uniforms the Herouxs had provided because they were embroidered with a crest bearing the Heroux name. Cecily thought it was all a bit overdone. No one cared what was on the collars of the waiting staff but who was she to question it. It had got her into the apartment without a question being asked of who she was and it was all that mattered, that is until she saw Charles Baptiste, Sophie Guillard's husband, and Amandine's father.

Cecily gasped when she spotted him and turned away from the clique of men he was talking to. He was holding court as though he were an old friend of the Heroux's, his right hand nursing a large glass of whiskey, the other a huge cigar. She noticed the catering manageress, a sour-looking woman with iron-grey hair and a downturned mouth frowning in her direction, so she left the room and went to the kitchen, grabbing one of the large platters of petit fours. The last thing she wanted was to be questioned by her. It would have certainly blown her cover.

Back in the salon she offered the platter to the Heroux's guests, listening intently to what was being said, the inflections, the expressions on their faces. The men did most of the talking, mostly in low voices as befitted the occasion. She hovered a little, then went to another group whilst at the same time looking out for the family. It was then she spotted the Herouxs who were sitting near the fireplace; Madam Heroux and her daughter, Angelique and the three brothers who were almost enclosing the women with a shield of muscle. They were tall and well-built. Were they protecting the women? It wouldn't have been unusual, thought Cecily. They'd lost a daughter and a sister so would have been distraught, but there was something about the way they were sitting that didn't look natural. It looked more like a barrier than protection.

The two women had removed their veils. Mrs Heroux was red-eyed and held a handkerchief near to her face. She had used cosmetics that morning; Cecily could see marks of tears as they had rolled down her cheeks and caused a pale line in her rouge. She looked somewhat dishevelled, undone, as though she had rushed to ready herself that morning. Cecily frowned.

Angelique was a different prospect altogether. She sat on the edge of her seat, her knees together, her hands in her lap. She was elegantly dressed in a beautiful black dress. She made a demure tableau, the dress being cut to the neck and hanging almost to the floor, but also designed to hide her figure. It was cut in the princess design; a style Cecily knew all about because of Lady Camille and the women who had visited Kenilworth House. A dress for a funeral, Cecily asked herself? I don't think so. Madam would never wear anything like it and I always go by 'er. She never gets anything wrong. I need to get closer, thought Cecily.

She left the salon and went out to the kitchen again. She was just about to reach for a tray on which there were glasses of red wine when someone stopped her.

'Qui es-tu?'

Cecily stopped in her tracks and turned to face the sour-faced catering manager? She didn't know what to do. She only knew it was a question because the woman's voice had gone up at the end, but she didn't know what the question was. She was also aware as soon as she opened her mouth the game would be up. A girl's voice from behind the catering manager called out. Cecily looked behind the woman's back and saw one of the other waitresses.

'Tout va bien, Madame. C'est la nouvelle fille. Lisette est tombée malade hier soir.' The catering manager nodded and flapped her hand at Cecily to get along. Cecily grabbed the tray and went into the salon, thinking she should soon find a way to escape the apartment before she was asked anything else. There's something not quite right in there though, thought Cecily. One more look. It's all I need and I'll be able to work it out.

She made her way back into the salon and walked directly towards the family. She stopped in front of them and offered them the tray of red wine. One of the brothers shook his head and made a motion with his hand for her to go away.

'Non. Non, merci.'

'Oui, Monsieur,' said Cecily in a low voice. It was all the French she knew and she hoped she'd got away with it.

Cecily lay the tray down on the console in the salon. When she thought no one was looking she made her way to a small cloakroom allocated for the waiting staff. She ripped off her headdress, changed back into her own clothes and left the apartment by the front door. Two men had been left to guard the door, but they'd imbibed so much wine they couldn't have cared less who left and who stayed. She left as she had arrived, looking like a guest, a long-lost friend perhaps of the unfortunate Janine.

Back out on the pavement of the Rue Saint-Dominique Cecily felt elated. She'd done it, a proper, dangerous investigation which could help Lady Divine and Chief Inspector Owen discover who had killed Janine Heroux, and hopefully return Lady Divine's dearest friend to her.

Honoré Tatou had been missing for nearly a week and Cecily knew from reading the penny dreadfuls at Mrs Summer's home that nothing was as it seemed. She'd had a hunch and she'd acted upon it. She congratulated herself and decided she deserved a treat.

She went into a boulangerie and bought herself a crème caramel tart, eating it as she walked back to the Hotel Narcisse Blanc. She savoured its sweetness, the beautiful creaminess of the crème, the stickiness of the caramel, and the soft texture of the pastry.

She giggled to herself, hoping Angelique Heroux wasn't fond of crème caramel tarts or pain au chocolat. Everyone knew you had to be careful about eating sweet things when you were pregnant.

Chapter 31

'She's pregnant?' cried Camille. 'But she's not married.' Camille frowned. 'And only nineteen I understand. Are you sure, Cecily?'

'As sure as I am about 'ow tasty the crème caramel tart was I've just eaten. I went into a bakers and treated meself for bein' so brave and ate it walkin' along the street. Sorry, Madam, I know you prob'ly don't approve but I was dead 'ungry and I thought it would calm me nerves.'

'Would you like some of Honoré's Bach remedies? I think it would help. They're meant to alleviate tension and fear.'

Cecily frowned glancing at Camille quizzically. In no event did she want to forget what she'd just eaten by drinking something that looked like poison. 'No thanks, Madam. I'm alright.'

'If you're sure.'

'I'm sure.'

'So what 'appened?' asked Elsie who was still in the suite when Camille had returned. 'As anyone spoken to the Chief Inspector yet, or that French policeman?'

'Not yet,' answered Camille. 'I don't think Richard has returned to the hotel. He might have gone to the commissariat on the Rue de Fabert with Inspecteur Apollinaire. I believe the Inspecteur had something to tell him.'

'What was it like in the apartment, Cecily,' asked Elsie. 'Was that Michel Vachon there?'

'Oh, Elsie,' cried Camille.'

'I'm only askin',' Elsie said, grinning. 'Was 'e, Cecily?'

'I don't know, Madam. I don't know who he is. All I wanted to see was Madame Heroux and her daughter, Angelique, and I got to see everythin' I wanted to.'

'Which was?'

'The women, the mother and daughter.' Cecily shook her head, unable to explain what it was that had drawn her attention to both the women. 'I dunno what it was, just somethin' about them.'

'Instinct perhaps?' said Camille.

'Don't know about that, Madam. Not really sure what that is. All I know is that when I saw them walking into the church with them veils over their faces it was like they was tryin' to hide somethin'.'

'Female mourners often wear veils, Cecily. I don't think it's anything unusual.'

'Well, the girl *was* tryin' to 'ide something,' said Elsie. 'She's got a bun in the oven and she don't want no one to know about it. I shouldn't think 'er parents want anyone to know either. They might be criminals but it sounds like they're sort of proper if you know what I mean. Bit like me really. I'm in a funny business, but if anyone messed with my Rose, well, I'd bloody kill 'em wiv me bare 'ands, that I would.'

'I wonder who the father is,' said Camille. 'I think Chief Inspector Owen should know about Angelique's pregnancy, and Inspecteur Apollinaire. Particularly him actually. He might be able to throw some light on it.'

'Not unless 'e was there, ducks,' said Elsie, getting up to leave. 'By the way, I'm glad to 'ear about Amandine. I know you're goin' ter miss 'er, 'specially you, Cecily, but she's with 'er Ma now, and it's where she should be ain't it, with her own?'

'I agree, Elsie, but Cecily will miss her most...and Ottilie I suppose. We were a real little family.'

'My Rose cried her flippin' eyes out when she found out Amandine 'ad gone, but I like the idea we can all meet up at the little 'ouse in Brighton, all girls together like.' She grinned at Camille. 'Unless 'is nibs turns up.'

'He won't,' said Camille, smiling. 'It'll be just us girls.'

'Glad to 'ear it. Bloody sick of men. They gets what they want then off they go into the wild blue yonder to sow their wild oats with some other poor silly gel. Can't 'elp feelin' sorry for that poor kid what's been left with a baby and her just a kid 'erself. Someone should be made to pay.'

Chapter 32

Inspecteur Apollinaire lent back in his chair and sighed. He leant forward and rested his elbows on his desk, rubbing his eyes with his thumb and forefinger. Finding no comfort from it he leant back again, then stood up from behind his desk and went over to the window in his office. He could see the sun's rays struggling to peer through the rather dry, scrappy trees in the courtyard outside the window. He sighed again and shook his head. He was frustrated with life. His good name as an Inspecteur had been dragged through the mud by the newspapers because he was yet to arrest anyone, not only for Janine Heroux's murder, but also the kidnapping of an elderly lady, Honoré Tatou who had been missing for days. They had clearly received yet another story from someone on the inside, and he could not fathom who it was who had no loyalty to their team...to him. And it hurt.

The narrative had been ramped up with huge, lurid headlines which shouted his incompetence to his fellow Parisiennes, and also to his superiors. He had been called to a meeting to discuss the situation, and something told him he was about to be hauled over the coals, or worse, replaced by another Inspecteur which would kill his career path stone dead.

His wife had also had occasion to speak to him. She wondered why the investigation seemed to be at a standstill.

'You must do something, Nicolas,' she'd said, 'and fast. The people on the streets of Paris are worried. They think there is a kidnapper out there, ready to whisk them away to who knows where. It's getting embarrassing for me. My friends are asking, 'Why has Nicolas done nothing?' and I have no answer for them.'

He'd tried to placate her but she was having none of it. Nicolas knew when his wife began to complain things were bad. Very bad indeed.

The meeting with his superiors was scheduled for eleven o'clock that morning but before then Richard Owen had agreed to go to the commissariat to discuss what had happened when the raid had taken place at the Avenue Rapp.

When the youth who had tried to take the valise from the step of the Obelisk, Jacques Noury, had been questioned by Apollinaire, he had been put under a not inconsiderable amount of pressure to give them a name, one that could lead them to discovering the whereabouts of Honoré Tatou. The raid had gone to plan with one omission, the person Apollinaire and his men had been hunting had not been there. Apollinaire surmised that because the pick-up from the Obelisk had gone so badly wrong the suspect had made a run for it. Apollinaire had been distraught because his best lead so far had escaped. It turned out the suspect had the skills of Houdini after all.

'So who was the suspect?' asked Richard.

'Lucas Vachon, the grandson of one of the Vachon brothers. They run a similar operation to the Herouxs. The Vachons are a huge family with it seems each one of them with a finger in the criminal pie.' He raised an eyebrow to Richard. 'I include the women in that statement. They are as bad if not worse.'

'Lady Divine's maid went to Janine Heroux's wake.'

Apollinaire sat up in his chair, a look of utter surprise crossing his face. 'How in God's name did she manage it? Who told you?'

'Lady Camille Divine left a message for me with the concierge at the hotel which I received when I returned after the funeral. Lady Camille hopes the information will help you. Cecily, her maid, posed as a waitress, pretended she had been hired to attend with the catering company.'

'And?'

'There was a guest there who we would probably not expect bearing in mind the Heroux's line of work.'

Apollinaire shook his head, frowning. 'Who?'

'Charles Baptiste.'

Apollinaire sat back in his chair, then called to the gendarmes in the outer office.

'A tray of coffee please...and biscuits.' He grinned at Richard. 'It's time for my mid-morning snack.' His expression changed and he stared at Richard with a look of resigned acceptance. 'I'm not so surprised, Richard. The Herouxs may be criminals but they are an important family in Paris. One crosses them at one's peril, and our Mr Baptiste likely feels the same way. Everyone is wary of displeasing them. They will kill at the drop of a hat. Perhaps Baptiste was forced into it. The President would certainly not have wanted to attend so he sent Charles Baptiste instead.'

'You saw the photographers? It was like the funeral of a movie star.'

'We know how to do grief in France, Richard. And families like the Herouxs will want to make sure everyone knows they are well-connected and wealthy enough to have such a funeral for one of their own.'

'They certainly did that. Did you or your men spot anyone of interest?'

Apollinaire shook his head, his mouth a hard line. 'No one. I thought maybe the other families would be there, but sadly, no. They know when to stay away.'

'There's something else,' said Richard, leaning forward to take a cup of coffee from a tray a gendarme had left on the desk.

'Oh,' said Apollinaire, dipping two biscuits together in his coffee.

'Angelique Heroux. She's pregnant.'

This small piece of information got Apollinaire's interest. 'Pregnant? The girl is nineteen and without a beau. How did she get pregnant?'

'The usual way I should imagine,' chuckled Richard.

'But...no one is allowed within a mile of the girls. Heroux would not allow it. I explained why. He guards them jealously because of the dangers of making an acquaintance with the wrong person. Even the brothers are not allowed to date unless they have Monsieur Heroux's permission.'

'Someone did. Someone got close to Angelique Heroux. You don't get someone pregnant without getting rather close to them. Even I know that.'

'We must find out who the father is,' said Apollinaire, biting into his biscuits like a man possessed. 'It might come to nothing, but then,' he nodded, 'it might mean everything.'

Moments later there was a knock on the door and a gendarme poked his head into the room.

'Inspecteur, I apologise for interrupting but there has been a development.'

'What is it, Rauf. My snacks are sacred.'

'A body, Inspecteur Apollinaire. It was found by some sightseers who spotted it in the Seine.'

'Has it been retrieved.'

'It has been contained, Inspecteur. You will want to go the place, sir?'

'Indeed, Rauf. Get a car around to the front.' He pulled his jacket from the back of his chair and retrieved his hat from the top of the coat stand. 'Richard...you will join me, yes?'

Richard hesitated, the biscuits and coffee he had just consumed roiling around the bottom of his stomach. His thoughts went to Camille and how she would feel if the worst had happened. 'You think it's Honoré Tatou?'

'I sincerely hope not, Richard,' said Apollinaire pulling on his jacket, his thoughts going to tomorrow's newspaper headlines. 'It would be a disaster for everyone.'

Gendarme Rauf drove Inspecteur Apollinaire and Richard to the place by the Seine where the body had been spotted. Two sightseers had seen something rolling around in the river. At first they thought someone had thrown an old coat into the water, but to their horror realised there was a person inside it.

When Apollinaire and Richard arrived, a middle-aged couple were sitting on the ground on the Pont de Bercy, the woman leaning against the railings her face in her hands. The man with her had his hand on her back to comfort her. Apollinaire approached the couple and introduced himself.

'Madame, do you need a doctor? We will take you to the nearest hospital. You could be suffering from shock.'

'Non, Monsieur, I'm alright. I've seen a dead person before, but not in the same way of course. We hadn't expected to see something like this on our trip. I feel very sad.'

'Perhaps return to your hotel, until you feel better.' He glanced at the man. 'A medicinal brandy perhaps?' The man nodded and helped the woman to her feet. Rauf proceeded to take details from them before they left and Apollinaire and Richard made their way to where the body had been spotted, not quite underneath the bridge.

The coat the sightseers thought they had seen had become caught on a piece of metal protruding from under the bridge, just beneath the water.

'This is odd,' grunted Apollinaire.'

'Why do you say that?' asked Richard.

'Usually some attempt would have been made to weigh the body down but not in this case.'

'Perhaps he fell in by accident.'

Apollinaire bent over the body which had been pulled clear of the water by the gendarmes. Apollinaire turned the body over. 'I don't think so, Monsieur. His head's been bashed in by something heavy.' He made a face of disgust then turned the body onto its back. He pushed his hand into the coat pockets finding nothing, then into the inside pocket, pulling out a wallet.

'Hm, whoever killed him doesn't mind us finding him and discovering who he is. Let's see.' He opened the wallet and pulled out some photographs and other paper paraphernalia. 'Now why doesn't this surprise me,' he said.

'Who is it?' asked Richard. 'This isn't the man you were after is it?'

Apollinaire nodded. 'The very same, Lucas Vachon, the name Jacques Noury gave us.' He glanced at Richard. 'You see, Richard. His plan went wrong and it is something that won't be forgiven. He made a mistake. Gave the job he should have done himself to a boy. The families won't accept it.'

'You don't think his own family killed him do you?'

'It's possible, Monsieur. It's always possible.' He lifted his chin to the gendarmes who went to a large police vehicle and produced a stretcher on which they lifted Lucas Vachon's body. 'Oh, and what do we have here?' He laid two small sodden photographs on the flat of his hand and showed Richard.

'Two women?'

Apollinaire nodded. 'You don't know who they are do you?'

'Do you?'

'Indeed. This one is Angelique Heroux.' He pointed to the sopping photograph of a beautiful blonde-haired girl with luminous eyes in an exquisite face. 'And this is Janine Heroux, the woman whose body has recently been laid to rest, Monsieur.' The photograph was of an older woman who was also attractive but did not have the looks of her younger sister.

'A coincidence?'

Apollinaire pursed his lips. 'I do not believe in coincidence, Chief Inspector Owen.'

Chapter 33

'So,' said Richard, pulling out his silver cigarette case, and after lighting one gave a long draw on it. He was galvanised now. The discovery of Angelique Heroux's pregnancy and the finding of Lucas Vachon's body in the Seine pointed to a family feud, and he was sure Apollinaire would be feeling the same. 'What do we have, Nicolas?'

'We have two dead bodies, a disappeared woman, and a pregnant girl.'

Richard felt slightly deflated. 'When you put it like that it does sound rather vague.'

'Not at all,' said Apollinaire, glancing at the clock. 'I missed my appointment with the high-ups. I'm in no doubt in even more trouble.'

'You were at a crime scene. They can't berate you for that.'

'You would be surprised what they can do, Monsieur. My future hangs by a thread. Do you not feel the same at times?' Richard shook his head and Apollinaire shrugged. 'Then you are fortunate.'

'Do you think it's connected?'

'Of course. As I said there are no coincidences in the criminal world. The deaths were not accidents. They, whoever *they* are, took the lives of Janine Heroux and Lucas Vachon for a reason. We must find out what the reason was. It is the answer to everything.'

'Do you have a theory?'

'I do. Do you?'

Richard smiled. 'Maybe. I suppose I'm wondering why a member of the Vachon family would have two photographs in his wallet of Angelique and Janine Heroux, two sisters of a rival family.'

'Exactly, Monsieur, and it is what I intend to find out.'

Apollinaire did not wait for the summons to attend another meeting. He explained to the Prefet de Police that he was making progress on the case and thought his attentions were better placed elsewhere. The Prefet had simply nodded then got back to his paperwork. Inspecteur Apollinaire blew out a puff of relief and closed the door to the Prefet's office gently behind him. Richard was still waiting in Apollinaire's office when he returned.

'You wish to come with me, Richard?'

'If you have no objections.'

'None at all.' He gave Richard a warm smile. I would appreciate your input. Two heads are better than one. Is that not what they say in your country?'

'They do, Nicolas.'

Once again Gendarme Rauf drove Inspecteur Apollinaire and Richard to the Boulevard de la Tour.

'What do you make of all this, Rauf? You have a theory?'

'Yes, Inspecteur.' Apollinaire nodded. 'What is it?'

'That Lucas Vachon was seeing both the Heroux women. There would be no reason to have a photograph of each of them in his wallet unless he were.'

'Do you have a sweetheart, Rauf?'

The young gendarme began to turn red and Apollinaire laughed. 'Come now, Rauf. We are all men here. There's nothing you could say which would embarrass us. I'm right am I not, Chief Inspector Owen?'

'Indeed, Inspecteur.'

Rauf glanced at Inspecteur Apollinaire. ' I do have a sweetheart, sir. I'd like to marry her. One day.'

'And do you have a photograph of her?'

'Yes, sir. At home. On my night table.'

'Good. Good. Remember what I told you before, Rauf. Make sure you don't mess it up.'

'I'll do my best not to, sir.'

The Avenue Rapp's well-swept pavements shone in the bright sunlight and Richard squinted wishing he'd worn sunglasses. Apollinaire looked up at the impressive building as he got out of the car and glanced at Richard, raising his eyebrows.

'What do you think, Monsieur? There is money here is there not?'

'I think these are expensive apartments.'

'You'd be right, some of the most expensive in Paris. And they don't try to hide the fact. Serious money lives here.'

The trio entered the vestibule, Apollinaire leading, Richard and Rauf following. A commissionaire rose from his seat behind a desk as they entered.

'Monsieur?'

Apollinaire showed his identity card. 'The Vachon apartment, sil vous plait?'

'I will call on the interior telephone, Monsieur. To let them know you are here.'

'As you wish, but which floor are they on?'

'Top floor, sir.'

Apollinaire shrugged and pulled a face. 'Of course they are,' he muttered. He lifted his chin to Rauf who took the stairs and made his way to the top floor. 'In case someone decides to leave suddenly,' he explained to Richard.

The commissionaire made his phone call and spoke quietly to whoever answered.

'Take the lift, Monsieur. The lift opens into the hall of the apartment. I will press the button from here. There is no other way for you to get there other than using the lift.' He glanced at Apollinaire's paunch. 'Unless you wish to use the stairs, Inspecteur which will take you to the front door of the apartment.' Apollinaire made for the lift.

The lift doors opened into a tastefully decorated hallway, not large, but Richard could see the furniture and décor was worth thousands. He glanced at a piece of art on the wall, a Degar, and shook his head. An original he was sure. So crime does pay, he thought.

A butler came out to greet them. 'Messieurs. Please follow me.' He led them into a gloomy room which smelt of strong tobacco. They stood quietly, waiting for a greeting.

'You have heard the news, Inspecteur Apollinaire,' said a voice from a chair near an impressive fireplace. The blinds in the vast windows had been lowered to reveal just slivers of light from below them. The room was depressing with only the dim light from a table lamp relieving the melancholy.

'Of course, Monsieur Vachon. I'm sorry for your loss.'

An old man sat in the beautiful wing chair. He wore a silk smoking jacket and a tasselled hat in a matching design. In his hand was a huge glass of whiskey. Richard could see by the yellow stains on his fingers smoking was his main occupation. He took a long swig of whiskey before speaking.

'He was a stupid boy. I always told my brother his grandson would get into trouble one day. Of course we think the children of our family are perfect and he would not listen. That boy played with fire all his life.'

'Your great-nephew?' Monsieur Vachon nodded. 'How old was he, Monsieur?'

'Thirty-two, the same age as my grandson, Michel, a different prospect altogether.'

'He runs Le Chabanais does he not?'

'He does, and very successfully too. He is a shining light. We are proud of him.' He glanced up at Apollinaire for the first time. 'Why don't you sit, Inspecteur, and your associate. You'll get backache standing there like that.'

'Merci, Monsieur.'

'Drink?' Apollinaire shook his head. 'So, Inspecteur, why are you here? My brother and his family live in the apartment below this one. Why are you not there?'

'Because you are the head of the business, Monsieur. And I need you to be candid.' The old man bowed his head in acceptance. 'Who killed Lucas?'

Monsieur Vachon took another swig from his glass and stared at Apollinaire and Richard with rheumy eyes. 'My eyesight is very bad, Monsieur, but it seems you've been eating too many pastries, my friend. Your outline has expanded somewhat since the last time we saw each other.'

'Thank you. Who do you think killed Lucas?'

Monsieur Vachon took in a deep breath and pressed his thin lips together. He closed his eyes momentarily then opened them again, staring into the distance as though he wished Apollinaire had disappeared.

'You don't have to look far.'

'Meaning?'

'Have you not been investigating a case recently? I get the newspapers delivered every morning, Inspecteur. Seems you are in a certain amount of trouble for your ineptitude.'

'The Herouxs?'

'They don't like it when someone messes with their property. The Vachons feel the same way of course.'

'The girls?'

'One was not enough for Lucas.' Monsieur Vachon turned to Apollinaire. 'I warned them he was playing with fire, that he would bring the Herouxs down on us like an earthquake. They did the next best thing. They took Lucas out, and do you want to know something, Inspecteur?' Apollinaire nodded. 'I would have done exactly the same. He should not have gone there, not with them.'

'They are attractive girls.'

'It doesn't matter!' Monsieur Vachon shouted, leaning forward in his chair. He settled back again as though the exertion was too much for him. 'It doesn't matter. They are untouchable. I told them. I told him, but he would not listen. Just called me names, was insubordinate. Not a nice boy. Not nice at all.'

'You think he deserved it?'

Vachon took another swig. 'He needed to be put down, Inspecteur. He was a runt. They saved me the job.'

Apollinaire and Richard climbed into the car. Rauf appeared from the building after standing in the corridor for the last half hour and joined them.

'Did you see anyone, Rauf.'

'No one, Inspecteur. No one left or came. There was no one below either.' Apollinaire nodded, seemingly satisfied.

'What do you think, Richard?' Richard lit a cigarette, offering one to Apollinaire who refused. 'I'm not allowed to smoke. She'll smell it.' Gendarme Rauf turned to look out of the window, grinning to himself.

'Lucas Vachon was seeing both women at the same time and he is the father of Angelique Heroux's child.'

'And Janine Heroux?'

Richard shrugged. 'If the women found out about each other I would suggest it was either Lucas Vachon or Angelique Heroux, or one of their associates. Would they kill one of their own themselves? You heard what Vachon said. He would have done away with Lucas Vachon himself if the Herouxs had not. He would not have the strength to do it. He would have simply paid one of his associates to do it. I can't imagine any of them dirtying their hands. And Angelique is pregnant. Could she have killed her sister?'

'They are not close in age. Janine was much older. I get the impression Angelique was a happy accident after having the four older children. There would have been jealousy between the women I'm sure of it.'

'One of the brothers perhaps? At Angelique's bidding?'

'Mm, no...I don't think so. Rauf? What are your thoughts?'

Gendarme Rauf swallowed hard at suddenly being dragged into the conversation. He faltered for a moment then gave up his theory.

'Angelique Heroux discovered Lucas was seeing Janine at the same time as he was seeing her. She was pregnant and expected Lucas Vachon to do right by her but Lucas refused, so Angelique either did it herself or got someone else to do it. She realised Lucas had strong feelings for Janine and thought he would leave her. She recruited one of her father's associates perhaps, paid him enough to ensure his silence.'

Richard nodded. 'Sounds eminently plausible to me. Angelique is the one who stood to lose the most. Perhaps Lucas was more enamoured with Janine. They were closer in age. Janine would have been more experienced, more mature.' He nodded. 'Yes, I'd go with it if it was my case.'

'And so we shall,' said Apollinaire. 'Well done, Rauf. We'll go to the Heroux's. I'm going to get tough and little miss butter-wouldn't-melt will tell me today. This case needs to be finished. I'm getting tired of it, tired of them getting away with murder. To the Heroux's residence, Rauf.'

'Yes, Inspecteur.'

The tableau was a repeat of the one before, Apollinaire seated with Rauf standing behind him. Richard stood to the side. He was interested in what the Herouxs had to say, particularly where Honoré Tatou was concerned.

'You're here again, Inspecteur,' said Monsieur Heroux. 'I hear you've been to the Vachon's.'

'Nothing escapes you does it, sir?'

Heroux sniffed and sat down, pulling his beautifully cut and pressed trousers over his knees to protect them. 'It does not.'

'I'd like to speak with Angelique.'

'She's sleeping.'

'I understand she is with child, Monsieur Heroux.'

Heroux eyes widened. He swallowed hard and regained his previous composure. 'Nothing escapes you either, Inspecteur. We have tried to protect her.'

'You know who the father is?'

'Do you?'

'Yes.'

Heroux shifted slightly in his chair. 'The boy has befallen an accident I hear?'

'His body was hauled out of the Seine.'

Heroux nodded. 'Best place for him.'

'Angelique, Monsieur Heroux?' Apollinaire's voice had gone up a gear and was laced with gravel. Richard glanced at him in surprise. This was a new Apollinaire, a more determined Apollinaire. 'I must see her today. Please do not think we don't know what has happened, Monsieur.'

Heroux rang a small bell placed on the table next to him. The housekeeper appeared in the doorway.

'Wake Angelique and tell her to come here.'

The housekeeper wrung her hands. 'But, Monsieur, Miss Angelique is indisposed. She is not well today.'

Heroux turned to her and keeping his voice low said, 'I have asked you to wake her and to bring her to me. Please do as I ask.' The housekeeper nodded and scuttled off. Within minutes Angelique Heroux joined them in the salon and sat next to her father.

Her hair was scraped back off her face which was free of cosmetics. Her clothes were unkempt, as though she had slept in them all night and had not bothered to change. She looked huge in the baggy clothes, unlike at Janine's funeral where her dress had been cut to accommodate her growing pregnancy, and not far from her time, Apollinaire decided. This was not the Angelique he'd seen previously. Apollinaire decided to get to the point.

'Miss Heroux, did you kill your sister?'

Angelique gasped and Monsieur Heroux looked enraged. 'Inspecteur! That is not a question to ask a pregnant woman.'

Apollinaire ignored him. 'Angelique,' he said, softer now. 'You were seeing Lucas Vachon were you not?' She nodded miserably. 'As was Janine.' She nodded again. 'Did Janine know about you?'

'I don't think so,' she said in a small voice.

'How did you find out about her?'

'His wallet. He had a photograph of her in his wallet. I did not understand. It was the day I planned to tell him about the baby.'

'Did Lucas know about the baby?'

'She nodded. 'I told him the same day. I screamed at him he was to be a father yet he was playing around with my sister. Janine, Saint Janine. He'd laughed and said she was no saint. I knew what he meant.'

'Why did you call your sister a saint, Mademoiselle?'

Angelique shrugged. 'Because she was. So good. Except she chose the wrong man to love.'

'As did you?'

Angelique nodded and burst into tears. 'I did not mean for them to kill her, just to frighten her off, but she fought back and she was stabbed. I asked them to frighten her, just to frighten her. I told them to tell her to stay away from Lucas Vachon, that the Vachon family did not like him seeing a woman from the Herouxs, a rival family, but it went wrong.' She stared up at Apollinaire imploringly, copious tears running down her cheeks. 'Please believe me, Inspecteur. I did not tell them to kill her, just to frighten her. How could they do that to her?' Her father sat with his eyes closed as though he could not bear to hear what she was saying.

'Who are *they*, Mademoiselle?'

Monsieur Heroux's eyes suddenly sprung open. 'Quiet, Angelique,' he said querulously. He turned his attention to Inspecteur Apollinaire. 'I think you should leave, Inspecteur.'

Apollinaire shook his head. 'Your daughter will need to come to the commissariat, Monsieur. You can attend her if you wish.'

'Is this necessary? She is near her time.'

'She will receive every courtesy, Monsieur Heroux, I assure you.' Heroux sighed and nodded in submission.

Chapter 34

Richard strolled through the streets of Paris, wondering at his life, and at the lives of others. He had been utterly astonished at the fabulous apartment of the Heroux's; the art, the sculptures, clearly bought with stolen money, yet for all their wealth Richard could not imagine changing places with them. Why would anyone want to live like it? he thought.

The Herouxs had wealth, could afford anything money could buy, yet the trials of life were not inescapable no matter how much they had. They had one daughter dead, and another about to be hauled off to the cells. In reality, Monsieur and Madame Heroux had lost both their daughters and would perhaps be responsible for a baby at a time of life where one would perhaps expect a little peace. There would never be peace for these people, he decided, not the Herouxs and not the Vachons.

He had offered to walk to the Hotel Narcisse Blanc when he realised Angelique Heroux and her father would be accompanying Apollinaire to the commissariat. And he wanted to see Camille. The holiday she had planned for herself and Ottilie had not turned out the way she had expected, and even though Apollinaire's hunt for Janine Heroux's murderer had been solved, it did not help them find Honoré Tatou. Richard bit his lip, hardly seeing the wonderful sights of Paris he passed as he walked. He felt himself praying for Honoré Tatou's safe return even though he was not a religious man. He had seen far too much of people's wickedness to encourage a strong faith.

As he walked into the foyer of the hotel the concierge called him to the desk.

'Monsieur, Monsieur Owen?' Richard nodded in surprise. 'Lady Divine requests you go to her suite on your return, Monsieur. It is important I think.'

Richard nodded and ran up the stairs to the second floor, taking two at a time. He hardly had time to knock before the door flew open.

'Richard, thank goodness.' Camille stood in the doorway dressed as though ready to go out. 'I've had a note from someone, left at the desk downstairs as before. The writer wants to meet us at the Eiffel Tower.' She showed the note to Richard.

'It says the writer has something belonging to you.' Richard frowned and shook his head. 'What could it mean?'

'Oh, Richard.' Camille's trembling hands flew to her face. 'Do you think it's Honoré?'

Richard's face cleared and he nodded. 'We can hope, Camille. We can hope.' He glanced at the note again. 'It says just you and your friend must go. The one in the red hat.' He chuckled. 'What?'

'It means Elsie. She wore a red hat when we went to Le Chabanais.'

'So it's someone from Le Chabanais?'

Camille nodded. 'I'm sure of it.'

'Does she know?'

'Yes, she's gone to get ready. Cecily will stay here with Ottilie and Rose.'

'I should go with you.'

'No, Richard. I can't put Honoré's life in danger if it is Honoré they plan to return to us.'

'Don't give them money, Camille.'

'I won't, I promise.'

Richard wasn't happy. 'I'll be behind you, Camille. Somewhere in the crowd. It's not safe for you and Mrs West to be totally alone.' Camille acquiesced, sighing, knowing Richard would not agree to anything less.

As expected the crowds were heavy at the foot of the Eiffel Tower. The chatter from the milling throng was overwhelming, and Camille wondered how they could possibly find Honoré amongst them all, if it was indeed Honoré they were to find.

'Blimey,' said Elsie. 'It's even busier than before. It's like the 'ole world is 'ere.'

'Do you think it's Honoré, Elsie?'

'Who else could it be?'

'But surely she wasn't held at Le Chabanais?'

'Well, we'll soon find out, ducks. If it's not 'er who else could it be. The writer of the note knows she's important to you. 'Ow they'd know that I've no idea.' She pursed her lips. 'Paris is a strange place I must admit. I thought London was a den of thieves, vagabonds and murderers, but this is somethin' else altogether.'

Elsie looked around the crowds until she spotted someone she knew. Her mouth curled into a smile of delight and she inhaled a satisfied breath.

'I reckon today is goin' ter turn out just fine,' she breathed.

Camille stared at her. 'What are you talking about, Elsie? How can it be a good day when Honoré is still missing?'

'She ain't,' said Elsie, inclining her head to one of the enormous feet of the tower. 'She's over there, love.'

Camille turned. There was Honoré, her slight body looked so diminutive against the man she stood with. Camille began to run across the court, tears running down her face and dropping onto her dress.

'Honoré,' she cried. 'Honoré.' Camille and Honoré fell into each other's arms, both crying, both laughing at the same time. Elsie stood back, her eyes on someone else. Camille glanced over Honoré's shoulder and gasped. She gently pushed Honoré away from her and strode towards Michel Vachon, slapping his face with a gloved hand.

'How dare you?' she cried. 'You monster. How could you hold a woman like this,' she indicated Honoré, 'for so long, frightening her, frightening her friends?' Michel Vachon stepped back, his hand to his cheek, his eyes twinkling with amusement.

Elsie ran up to them her hands outstretched to Camille. 'Camille,' she cried, pulling her away from Vachon. 'I think you got it wrong.' Camille stared at Elsie, then Vachon. Honoré grabbed her hand.

'Monsieur Vachon brought me back to you, Camille. It was not Monsieur Vachon who abducted me or held me prisoner.'

Camille straightened her hat and adjusted her dress. 'Oh. Well.' She took a step back looking contrite. 'You can't blame me for thinking so.'

Michel Vachon smiled and bowed to Camille. 'Lady Divine I presume. Madame Tatou has told me all about you.'

Camille looked surprised. 'Has she?'

'And I am not her abductor I can assure you. I have a busy life, far too busy for kidnapping beautiful women.' Honoré giggled like a girl and flushed quite pink.

'I'm sorry, Monsieur,' said Camille, putting an arm around Honoré. 'I thought it was you who had taken her and kept her. Feelings are running high as you can imagine.'

'I sympathise, Lady Divine. The feelings in my family are also running high. My cousin, Lucas Vachon was found in the Seine this morning. He was attended to by Inspecteur Apollinaire and your...friend, I understand.'

'I don't know anything about it, Monsieur. I'm truly sorry for your loss. I expect Chief Inspector Owen will tell me about it when he returns to the hotel.'

Vachon frowned, smiling. 'But is that not him there?' He pointed through the crowd at where Richard was trying to look anonymous.

Elsie giggled. ''E didn't make a very good job of tailin' us did he, Camille?' She put her arms around Camille and gave her a hug. 'Why don't you take Honoré back to the hotel. 'Ave a nice cup a tea and a pastry. It'll settle your stomach.'

'So who was it?' Camille asked Michel Vachon. 'Who took Madame Tatou?'

Michel Vachon looked contrite. 'My cousin, Lucas. He thought he was a master criminal. He traded on his name. I am the first to admit my family run certain businesses, Lady Divine, but even if you do not agree with what I do I can assure you Le Chabanais is above board. I pay my taxes and I help the police if and when they ask, but Lucas was not the same. He behaved like a petty criminal which was always going to get him into trouble. And he crossed one of the other Parisienne families which was unwise. One does not cross the line or mess with the daughters of the Herouxs. I'm sure your Inspector will explain it to you.'

Camille nodded looking thoughtful. 'Very well, Monsieur Vachon.' She inhaled deeply and made a small smile. 'Thank you for returning Honoré to us. I apologise for slapping you. We were so very worried.'

Vachon bowed again. 'And I can understand why. I can only apologise for my cousin's behaviour. The Vachon's are more honourable I can assure you.' Camille raised her eyebrows thinking his idea of honour and hers were very different but was simply grateful to see Honoré again. 'Let's go to the hotel, Honoré.'

Honoré shook her head. 'I need my apartment, Camille. Albert will be waiting. It has been days since we have been together.'

Camille nodded. 'Elsie?' She glanced at Elsie who was speaking with Michel Vachon.

'Monsieur Vachon is taking me for a late lunch, Camille. I'll see you back at the 'otel for dinner.' She slipped her arm though his. 'Don't wait up,' she giggled.

Camille shook her head. Lunch, she thought, smiling. That's one name for it.

Honoré gave Camille the key so she could unlock the door to the apartment.

'Did you come here while I was away, Camille?' she asked as she stepped into the vestibule. She took a deep breath of satisfaction as she walked into the salon, closing her eyes momentarily with utter relief.

'I came here once,' answered Camille.

'To look for my notebook?' Camille nodded. 'And you found it?'

'I did.' Honoré looked sheepish. 'I'm sorry, Honoré. I had to find it because I knew you had the addresses and telephone numbers of some of your friends written in it, not that it did us any good. None of your friends could help us. They all said the same thing; it was out of character and someone else must have been involved.'

'They didn't mention Guillaume?'

'None of them.' They sat on the plush seats in the salon and Honoré breathed a sigh of relief.

'I expect you're wondering who he is?'

Camille shrugged. 'It's none of my business, Honoré.'

Honoré grabbed her hand. 'But I want you to know. Need you to know. I was never unfaithful to Albert. I adored him with all my heart.' She looked sad. 'I still do. There could never be anyone else for me.'

'The letter made it sound as though you and Guillaume were close.'

'We were, but just as friends. Or so I thought. Sometimes I went to the theatre or the ballet without Albert. He could not go, he was far too ill, but he didn't want to stop me from going. He gave me his blessing and told me to go out and enjoy myself.' Sorrow crossed her lined features. 'And I must confess it was a relief to get out of the apartment for a while. There were times when I didn't leave here for days because I was caring for him, and it became oppressive. I got quite depressed. My friends continued to invite me when they were planning an outing and sometimes I accepted. Guillaume was one of those friends.'

'Do you think he got the wrong idea?'

'I think he mistook my excitement at seeing them all as a personal delight. I hugged all of them of course when I saw them. It was sometimes months where I was not touched by another human being, only to roll Albert in the bed to stop bedsores or administer medication. I would do it all again because I loved him...but, it was so hard.'

'And Guillaume thought you were attracted to him.'

'I was, Camille, but not in that way. I realised what had happened when he suggested when Albert died we became a couple and maybe married. I was furious. He was waiting for Albert to die, the very thing I did not want to happen. How could I ever love such a man?'

'But you saw him at the theatre?'

'Yes. I was shocked. So utterly shocked. I had not seen him for many months after we had argued. I said some terrible things, so did he. I hoped I would never see him again. When I saw him with some friends at the theatre I decided to be polite and friendly, but then of course he misconstrued my friendliness as a sign I wanted to take it further. Stupid, stupid man. He wrote to me. Well,' she sighed with embarrassment, 'I know you saw the letter.'

'I never thought you were unfaithful to Albert, Honoré. I know how much you loved him. I could not ever imagine you doing such a thing. Were you frightened of him, darling? We, that is Cecily and I, saw the Bach remedies in your bathroom cabinet. They were for fear.'

'I bought them long ago. I know it is not an exact science but I needed a little help. I was frightened of Albert's leaving me, or being alone, of Guillaume in a way although he was not a threat. Once Albert had gone I knew I would be alright, that as long as I stayed here,' she lifted her hand to indicate the apartment, 'I would be alright.'

Honoré glanced up at Camille and squeezed her hand. 'I'm not lonely, Camille. I miss Albert of course, but I have my memories, my wonderful memories. Many would think it is not much to have for a lifetime of just being, but it is enough for me.'

Chapter 35

'Are we going home, Mama?' Ottilie asked Camille. 'Is it time do you think?'

Camille nodded. 'I suppose it is, darling. Your father will want to see you before you return to school.'

'Will we go away again?'

'Oh, yes...I have some plans for us. Have you enjoyed it here, your first visit to Paris?'

Ottilie frowned. 'But not my last.'

'Oh, no darling. Paris is so easy to get to now, and it is rather addictive isn't it. We'll return I promise.'

'And will Cecily come back with us?' She glanced grinning at Cecily who was folding clothes and placing them in the valises.'

'If Cecily want to come she is always welcome. What do you say, Cecily?'

'I say I 'ope it'll be a bit of a quieter visit than the one we've 'ad this time,' she chuckled. 'I've never known anything like it.'

'No,' Camille sighed. 'Nor me. It's been quite the adventure.'

'One I should think Madame Tatou could 'ave done without, I'm sure.'

'Is she alright now, Mama? Madame Tatou?'

'She is. Happy to be back in her apartment so she can live her life quietly and without incident. These past few days have been quite enough for her I should think.'

'What about the man who took her? And why did he take her do you think?'

'I'm afraid the man who took her is no longer with us, Ottilie. He made a big mistake he could not easily undo and it caused a lot of trouble. He was using Honoré to extort money from me because he thought I was wealthy. He knew about me visiting Honoré because Janine had told her family. Angelique was seeing Lucas Vachon and told him. They had planned to run away together and they needed the money to do it. At least it is what he told her.'

Ottilie looked quizzical. 'But don't they have their own money? Even I get a small allowance, and they're much older than me.'

'I don't think it works like that in some of these criminal families. Everything they earn, I use the word 'earn' loosely, goes into the central pot. They see it as family money. Even the money Janine earnt from working for Madame Tatou wasn't her own. They don't need their own money, not allowed it because they're not permitted to do anything without permission.'

'How awful for them.'

'Yes,' Camille nodded. 'Yes, I suppose it is.'

'Where was Madame Tatou all this time, Madam?'

'In an apartment on the Avenue Rapp. She said she didn't see daylight but was held in a small room with few facilities. They were not cruel to her and gave her meals from a restaurant, but she was terrified. She thought she would never be released.'

'They, Madam?'

'Angelique Heroux and Lucas Vachon. They planned it together to extort money from me. Madam Tatou thinks Janine may have confirmed my visit to Honoré to her sister, and they came up with the idea between them.' She sighed. 'Look at them now. One has died and one about to be charged for their criminal activities. So young, so misguided.'

'Is Mrs West coming back with us, Madam,' asked Cecily. 'We 'aven't seen much of 'er these past couple of days.'

Camille laughed. 'She's been busy, Cecily.' She raised her eyebrows and Cecily nodded and chucked. 'I rather think she's fallen in love.'

'She'll be back then, and it won't be long I shouldn't think, Madam. She looked a bit dreamy when I saw her this mornin'.'

'What about Lord Fortesque-Wallsey though,' Ottilie asked. 'I thought she was in love with him.'

'Mm, so did we.'

There was a knock on the door and Cecily went to open it. Richard stood in the corridor.

'Chief Inspector,' said Cecily, bobbing him a quick curtsey. 'Come in, sir.'

'Thanks, Cecily, and you don't need to curtsey to me. As I've mentioned before, we're both in service.'

'Oh, yes, sir,' said Cecily. 'I'd forgotten. We *are* aren't we?'

'And you did an excellent job. It was brave of you to go into the lion's den as it were. Weren't you frightened?'

'I was a bit, but, well I just 'ad this feeling. Women what are pregnant walk different, and I was almost sure Angelique Heroux was walkin' in the same way as them women what I'd seen in the rookeries what 'ad been pregnant, but I 'ad to go and see for meself. And I was right. There she was, looking dead miserable and keeping away from everyone.'

'What will happen to her, Richard?' asked Camille as he removed his hat and took a seat.

'I don't know. It's different here than in England. She'll serve a term, perhaps manslaughter. I believe her when she says she did not intend for Janine Heroux to be murdered although she was insanely jealous of her relationship with Lucas Vachon.'

'Will she not give up who actually did it?'

Richard shook his head. 'No, under instruction from her father I should imagine. They won't give away the names of their associates. They're too valuable to them...and also they know far too much about the family. Who knows what they would tell the police.'

'And Pierre Baptiste? Do you know if anything happened there?'

'I understand from Inspecteur Apollinaire that the boy hated his father's new wife after his mother had died; that he never took to Sophie Guillard and was jealous of Amandine and her closeness to both her mother and her father. He told Apollinaire he thought she would be safe with Fabrice Ozanne, and just wanted to frighten her.'

'Do you believe it?'

Richard shook his head. 'No, and neither does Inspecteur Apollinaire.'

Camille tutted. 'And Amandine went through so much simply because of jealousy.' She shook her head. 'It's so very sad.'

'It is. And not a good move for him either. He will never be allowed within the walls of the Elysée Palace.'

'What are your plans, Richard. Will you return to London with us?'

'Perhaps not. I thought as I'm technically not working I would go to the south and visit with Helen's relatives. I haven't seen them for years and they said I should always visit if I could. It would be good to see them again.'

'And beautiful at this time of year.' Richard suddenly look uncomfortable. 'Something on your mind, Richard? Is everything alright? You have seemed out of sorts somewhat since we've been in Paris.'

'I wondered, could we have lunch together, before you go to the airport. There's something I need to talk with you about.'

'Of course. I'd love to. I hope it's nothing serious.'

'Er, well... He was interrupted by the suite telephone ringing and it startled him..

'I'll get it, Madam,' cried Cecily. She lifted the receiver from the candlestick. 'It's the concierge, Madam. He has an important call for you from London.'

Camille rose from her seat and took the receiver from Cecily, her relaxed expression changing to one of fear as she conversed with whoever had made the telephone call.

'Yes, yes, don't worry, we're coming home today. We'll be home soon. Tell her will you. Tell her we're on our way.' Camille replaced the receiver, a frown crossing her face.

'Who was it, Mama?' asked Ottilie, looking concerned, frightened by her mother's expression.

'It was Phillips. Knolly's been taken ill. He called the doctor because he was so worried, but she may have to be admitted to hospital.'

Cecily's eyes filled with tears. 'Oh, no. Poor Knolly. How long will it take for us to get home, Madam? Is it serious?'

'I'm not sure, Cecily, but I will move heaven and earth to arrange an earlier aeroplane. Let's pack up quickly and go to the airport.' She shook her head, swallowing back tears. 'I wish we were there. I wish we were there to be with her. We've stayed too long.'

'You had to, Camille,' said Richard calmly. 'For Honoré.'

Camille glanced at him and smiled. 'Yes, yes I know you're right.' She put out her hand and rested it on his forearm. 'I'm sorry, Richard, I'm afraid lunch will have to wait until we're back in London. How long will you be in France?'

'Just a week. I'm sorry to hear about Knolly. Give her my best wishes won't you?'

'Could you tell, Elsie, please? She won't be happy but there's nothing I can do.'

Richard made a wry smile. 'I think she has other things on her mind at present.'

Richard waited until they were packed and ready, then watched them leave the suite, saying their goodbyes. The suite door slammed after them and he was left alone with his thoughts.

Camille had gone. He'd planned to tell her everything but yet again he was thwarted. He went to the window and watched Camille, Ottilie, and Cecily climb into a taxicab which then drove off and turned the corner out of sight.

The salon seemed so utterly quiet and devoid of life without her. Her beauty and mellow voice were no longer there and he had never felt more alone.

'This is how it would be,' he said aloud. 'Without her my life is meaningless. I will tell her when I return to London, and hope she can find it within her heart to accept me for who I am.'

A Note from the Author

Hello,

I wanted to thank you for reading MURDER IN PARIS, the fifth story in the Camille Divine Murder Mysteries. I hope you enjoyed it. It felt very much like a roller-coaster ride when I wrote it, and the characters, who seem to simply present themselves to me from out of the blue, really enriched the story. I particularly fell for Inspecteur Apollinaire and his rather dry wit.

Have you visited Paris? I have a few times and I always find something new to see each time I go. I'm planning another trip soon because as Camille says to Ottilie, 'It's so easy to get to from London'. I'm lucky to live so close.

I hope you will continue to follow The Camille Divine Murder Mysteries, and Camille, Cecily, and Richard on their next adventure. There are many new adventures in Camille's diary which are set to take us all over the world. You'll be so welcome to join us. We look forward to seeing you there.

Warmest regards,

Andrea

www.andreahicks-writer.com

The next in the series...

MURDER AT THE CAFÉ BONBON
AUTUMN 1923

Chief Inspector Richard Owen dresses carefully at his house in Chiswick. He is due to see Lady Camille Divine at Café Bonbon, a well-known nightclub, after a six-week separation when he decided to visit his late wife's relatives in the South of France. He is due to go back to work at Scotland Yard after a two-month sabbatical, but he and Camille have some unfinished business.

When they last saw each other in Paris they were parted before Richard had an opportunity to tell Camille what was on his mind. Camille's cook, Knolly, had been taken ill at Camille's house in Duke Street in London. Camille had been desperate to return to England to see Knolly, her cook and one of her dearest friends, to ensure she got the best treatment. Richard knew how much she cared about her staff and reluctantly said goodbye.

Six weeks later and they're both back in London. It's the perfect time to tell her what he'd so wanted to tell her in Paris, but an incident at the Café Bonbon where a cigarette girl is murdered seems as though it will thwart his intentions yet again. Will Richard get the chance to tell Camille about his past, or will their involvement in another murder mean he won't get the chance to discover if Camille, the woman he has fallen in love with, is the women he hopes she is. Will she accept his past life, or will she walk away?

Books in the Camille Divine Murder Mysteries Series

THE CHRISTMAS TREE MURDERS

MURDER ON THE DANCEFLOOR

THE BRIGHTON MURDERS

MURDER AT THE CHRISTMAS GROTTO

MURDER IN PARIS

MURDER AT THE CAFÉ BONBON

MURDER IN MANHATTAN

THE WESTMINSTER MURDERS

THE SICILIAN MURDERS

THE EDINBURGH MURDERS

MURDER IN CAIRO

99 NIGHTINGALE LANE

The complete series Books 1 - 8
London, Christmas 1914

Eighteen-year-old Carrie Dobbs has a secret. When her parents discover her condition, Carrie's mother, Florrie takes matters into her own hands and arranges a marriage with Arnold Bateman to get Carrie out of Whitechapel and away from the gossips. He is a man Carrie could never love, the opposite of Johan, the young man she adores. Arnold has been posted to India and expects her to go with him and be the wife he needs to further his promotion and position in the army. India is a country she only knows from an atlas and she is terrified she will never see her family and her beloved best friend, Pearl again. Feeling she has no choice, she travels to India with a heavy heart, wondering if she will ever return to the place she calls home? India is a mystery to her, but this strange and vibrant country gets under her skin, and when someone she admires from afar is kind to her, Carrie wonders if she will find love again.

Join Carrie in her spell-binding journey into love and independence, and discover the consequences when she makes a decision that will change all their lives!

Books in the 99 Nightingale Lane Series
MRS COYLE'S COOKBOOK

INSPIRED BY STORIES FROM 99 NIGHTINGALE LANE and to accompany the popular series.

Stories and recipes from 99 Nightingale Lane from Ida Coyle

'I do believe I was born thinking about food, which didn't do me much good seeing as we didn't have much of it. I know I'm lucky compared to many who had it harder than me…I've worked at 99 Nightingale Lane for most of my life, taken in by the family who lived there before the Sterns when my Ma was killed by The Ripper. They were an old London family, not that I would have taken any notice then. I was just a smidgen of a girl, one of many who worked here, nearly as many as the fleas on a dog's tail. And…this is one of the things I learned from Mrs Brimble, the cook who taught me everything I know.

'When I think about where I was born, where we lived over the tanners shop, and what my Ma had to do to put food on the table,' I shook my head, 'she wouldn't believe that I stood there in that grand room, amongst all those beautiful things. And now I'm here in this kitchen with you, cooking the Hamilton's luncheon. I so wish she could see me now.' Mrs Brimble put a hand on my arm. 'She is watching, Ida, and I know she'd be proud of how well you've done and how hardworking you are, but not because of who you work for. She'd be proud because of who you are, the type of person you've become. That's what's important, ducky, not money and things what can be bought. Not tables of silverware and fruits from the continents or gowns from the salons of Bond Street. You're just a little'un really, still young, but you will learn about what's important, and there will be more laughter and smiles and happiness below stairs around our simple table when we have our Christmas dinner than there will be in that beautiful room, you mark my words.' She lowered her voice. 'Y'see, Ida, they haven't learned how to count their blessings. This is just another day to them. They see rooms like that all the time so they've forgotten how to be swept away by it. Do you think Lady Davinia will go into

that room and widen her eyes in wonder like you did? Do you think Mr and Mrs Hamilton will take much notice of the table that the upstairs maids and the footman worked so hard to make look lovely? They'll give it a glance only to find an imperfection. It's how they are. They have plenty, they definitely do, but none of them appreciate it.' She stared at me. *'And that's for your ears only,'* she whispered.

You see. I had the best teacher. This is my story, of when I was a girl starting work at the age of thirteen and how I fought my way through the ranks below stairs to become cook at 99 Nightingale Lane. And I've brought my favourite recipes with me, documented in MRS COYLE'S COOKBOOK for you to make yourself for you and your family to enjoy.

I hope you love my story and my recipes. It means so much to me that I've been given the opportunity to share them with you.

Warmest wishes from your friend, Ida Coyle, Cook at 99 Nightingale Lane'

Books in the Lily Pond Victorian Murder Mysteries Series
THE CURIOUS LIFE OF LILY POND

THE DORSET STREET MURDERS

THE DANDELION CLOCK

Sixteen-year-old Kate McGuire has a secret. Her father, Joe has disappeared, and Kate, her mother, Stella and sister, Emma are left to fend for themselves with little income and no one to turn to. For two years they are heartbroken, wondering why he left, or whether he is still alive. Kate decides she must take on a role she never wanted; as carer for her abusive alcoholic mother, and guardian of her sister who seems intent on finding the solace she needs her own way, a decision that leaves Kate almost unable to continue because of the hurt she causes. Kate is devastated because in her heart she is almost certain she will never see her father again, and wishes for his return on the dandelion clock he gave her years before, the seed heads of a flower she wrapped in a piece of pink fabric and placed in her memory box as a lucky charm. Kate wonders if she will ever find the love and affection she craves and whether her dad loves her enough to return to them and the place they call home.

Romantic Comedies

CHRISTMAS AT MISTLETOE ABBEY

A charming-to-read Christmas romance novella to snuggle up with under a tartan blanket, sipping a glass of spicy mulled wine. Enjoy! 'An enjoyable read that was entertaining from start to finish. It was simply delightful, and I highly recommend Christmas at Mistletoe Abbey.'
'From the first page to the last, this fun romance novel kept me hooked. A real page-turner I couldn't put down!'

THE CHOCOLATE SHOP ON CHRISTMAS STREET

The sweetest Christmas Romance to cuddle up with!

THE GIRL WITH THE RED SCARF

Tom Alexander has no memory of his life at House in the Hills orphanage on the outskirts of Sarajevo, or of his birth parents, the ones whose faces he wants to see, but doesn't remember. When he receives a letter from ChildAbroad, the agency that arranged his adoption in 1994, he is offered the opportunity to search for the boy he once was, Andreij Kurik—if he returns to Sarajevo. With Sulio Divjak, the driver and interpreter Tom befriends, he searches the derelict orphanage and discovers he has two siblings, one who was also at House in the Hills. Sulio uncovers a faded photograph in Andreij's file of a girl wearing a red scarf. She looks like Ellie; the girl Tom fell in love with at first sight in a café in Regent's Park. Devastated when he realises what it could mean, Tom goes back to the UK to get some answers. Accompanied by Ellie he returns to Sarajevo to find his birth parents, only to receive news that destroys everything he thought he knew about Tom Alexander—and Andreij Kurik.

A young love forged at the height of war, a chance meeting, and a collision of faded memories and half-truths, The Girl with the Red Scarf will appeal to fans of historical, women's and romantic fiction.

From the author of The Other Boy, shortlisted for the Richard & Judy Search for a Bestseller

THE OTHER BOY

A RICHARD AND JUDY BESTSELLER FINALIST

Their new home promises so much, an idyllic life in the countryside, a peaceful existence outside the busyness of London. She'd dreamt of it. A forever home. But something happened there, a heart-breaking tragedy infused in its walls. The history of the old house returns to haunt her, and when the memories she had buried return she isn't the only one who fears them.

Before you hide the truth, make sure the dead can't give up your secrets. If you love gripping, ghostly psychological thrillers that you can't forget, make a big pot of coffee - THE OTHER BOY won't let you go.

Find out why Amazon reviewers are saying, "Unputdownable and heart-breaking. Not just a psychological thriller, not just a ghost story, but so much more"…*Birdie Advanced Copy Reviewer*

"The Other Boy is beautifully written, as always. I expect nothing less from the author. This story is a revelation. By blending stunning writing with a heart-breaking ghost story and a psychological twist she had me captured from the very first moment." *MW Advanced Copy Reviewer*

'It's the other boy in the basement,' said Tobias. 'The other boy telled me.'

Political Science Fiction

DESTRUCTION OF BEES

The Year 2030

Embark on a gripping journey into the unknown with DESTRUCTION OF BEES – a heart-pounding thriller that will have you on the edge of your seat until the very last page.

When Nina Gourriel is rushed to hospital after a terrifying collapse, little does she know it's just the beginning of a harrowing ordeal. Instead of receiving medical care, she finds herself ensnared in a web of conspiracy and intrigue, whisked away to a clandestine government facility.

As Nina grapples with the mysterious tests forced upon her, she crosses paths with Cain, an enigmatic scientist who reveals the startling truth: she's being hunted for something she doesn't even know she possesses. With each passing moment Nina's world unravels further, plunging her into a deadly game of cat and mouse with multiple adversaries closing in on her. She doesn't know who to trust.

Is she a beacon of hope or the harbinger of destruction?

If you crave a pulse-pounding narrative that will haunt your thoughts long after you turn the final page, DESTRUCTION OF BEES is a must-read. Join Nina as she navigates a treacherous landscape where danger lurks at every corner, and the fate of humanity hangs in the balance.

Printed in Great Britain
by Amazon